DOOMFLOWER

A NOVEL BY
JENDIA GAMMON

Encyclopocalypse Publications
www.encyclopocalypse.com

For my children and for Gareth

DOOMFLOWER

DOOMFLOWER

Chapter 1

Dream Teen Queen

Camellia Dume was the richest girl in Killian High, and also the meanest. It wasn't easy being loved and hated at the same time, she knew. Camellia didn't care: it was all about image. She was the moment, aloof but zeitgeist. Nobody could succeed in opposing her, but nobody could work well with her, either. She didn't care about that. But she didn't realize it was the last normal day on Earth as she'd known it... the last normal day *anyone* had known.

She looked in one of her several mirrors and smoothed her auburn hair, sweeping it behind her pale ears. She had just finished her eye makeup and penciled in her brows with *Deep Mahogany* liner from the Marian Hillsworth line, a real bargain at seventy-five dollars, she thought. She applied primer to her cheeks, forehead, nose, and chin, and blended it all in. Next, she applied concealer; then foundation. She spritzed setting spray over everything. After perfecting her pale, matte-finish face and hiding all visible freckles, she slicked *Devil's Temptress* across her lips (this one by *Enchante*—and as she would say, a real bargain at sixty-two dollars). She leaned forward, just in front of her mirror, and formed a kiss with her mouth.

"I'm the baddest bitch there is," she said confidently. And she would have kissed her own image, but a knock on the door interrupted her.

"Time for school!" a muffled voice called.

She scowled.

Today was Monday, September 14th. Camellia would be given an air kiss and dropped off in her father's Lotus at Killian High. She had it all mapped in her mind, the same as every Monday. And this being so early in the new school year, sophomore Camellia, already the most popular girl in the entire school, had a lineup of "fresh meat" (or new recruits) in the Dream Teens' sorority. She could anticipate the boys' jeers of "Scream Queens" and other, more sordid monikers. She could even pre-roll her eyes at the pathetic girls vying for positions in the Dream Teens. If she were lucky, there might be two non-terrible recruits. The others would be suitably shoved off as unworthy and second tier to the richest, most beautiful girl at Killian High: Camellia herself, if anyone dared to doubt it. She warped reality around her, inheriting her father's particular gift of the con. Nobody could see the cracks beneath the veneer, because she wore enough lip gloss to cover them.

She texted her erstwhile gal pal, Selah: "Ready for the meat grinder? LOL," and anticipated receiving the usual "Yes honaaaay" back. But the text never came.

Camellia thought of six pithy things to text back, and began to type each one but deleted them and flushed with anger at herself and Selah. She clucked her tongue.

"Meems," called her father, "we need to get going. I have a ten o'clock."

In a huff, she snatched her purse, pulled on her vintage silver combat boots, adjusted her black lace Alexander McQueen skirt over a black, iridescent bodysuit with a DREAM TEEN QUEEN enamel pin attached above her right breast, and walked out of the mansion. Her father had pulled the Lotus out of the garage; the "store run Porsche" remained inside, along with the covered Bugatti and the vintage Aston Martin. Her father had another offsite garage as well. The gardeners were already parked in a pickup by the street, pulling out trimmers and rakes and a leaf blower, so she lowered her sunglasses to avoid eye contact with them.

The passenger door of the vivid orange Lotus stood open and Camellia sat in it petulantly while her father bellowed and lambasted on his phone. The AC was already on, so she shut her door and pulled the visor down to check her makeup. Finally, he entered the car and, with an irritated sigh, chucked his phone on the dashboard.

She glared at him.

"Why don't you put it in the holder?" she asked coldly. "It's just going to slide over and fall on me, like it always does."

He glanced at her, his lips downturned, and said, "You sound like Tanya."

Camellia took her sunglasses off, folded them carefully in her lap, and turned the full blast of her ire on her father, her green eyes blazing, her cheeks flushed beyond the confines of her SPF 75 foundation.

"Don't you *dare* compare me to that woman ever again," she hissed.

He flinched, for more reasons than she knew. For one thing, Tanya was now his ex-girlfriend after she had found him cozied up to a young starlet at a speakeasy in Hollywood. And also, at that moment, Camellia looked uncannily like her mother, who had died ten years prior in an accident. The accusing green eyes burrowed into him, and he coughed.

"S'all right, Meems, no offense," he simpered.

But she fixed him with that stare, and he shuddered.

"Apologize," she said, voice level but deadly.

"All right, all right," he said irritably. "I *apologize*."

She sniffed.

"What was that about, anyway?" she asked him as he spun around the steep Malibu curves on the way to her school.

Her dad made a disgusted sound. "Guy thinks he can bully his way onto the production," he muttered. "*I'm* the one with the investors. I have three from Malta lined up, ready to go, and not counting the Aussie contingent. I don't need that guy."

"So, axe him," Camellia suggested, touching up her mascara expertly while her father zoomed at high speed on the twisty roads.

"Yeah," said her father. "I might."

He glanced at his daughter and dared to ask, "So, what's got you extra riled today? Too much hate mail? Thought you lived for that sort of thing."

She rolled her eyes. "Oh, I do. They're so tragique, you know?"

"Wannabes," agreed her father.

"It's not that," she said, and her jaw went taut.

"What is it, then?"

"Selah's not texting back," said Camellia, pouting, her brow stern.

"So why don't you call her?" her dad suggested.

Camellia rounded on him, screeching, "Nobody fucking calls anybody, Dad! Except you bunch of *olds*."

He seemed visibly to shrink down into his seat, and he shrugged. The car rounded a curve, and his phone launched itself right onto Camellia's lap. She took it and briefly saw a news alert on the screen: "*Monster plants run amok! Vampire vines suck the life from their victims! Killer weeds wreak havoc on mountain town!*"

She snorted. "Everything you follow is full of shit," she sneered at her father. She flung the phone over her shoulder, where it fell out of reach behind her seat.

"Hey!" he yelled.

The car came to a squealing stop just outside her school, and before her father could put on the brakes, she'd already opened the door and slammed it shut.

"Listen, young lady," he barked at her through the open window, "you need to watch it with that attitude!"

A chorus of "Oooo" met Camellia as she turned away from the Lotus. A group of teens leered at her from the steps up to the front door of the school.

"You're just like your mother!" yelled her dad.

"Not yet, I'm not," she spat back. "Are you gonna drive me off a cliff next, too, Dad?"

"CAMELLIA!" he roared.

She swiveled away from him, her arm held up, middle finger pointed at the sky, and waltzed past her haters.

"Good morning, bitches," she said with a smile and sashayed onward, a cadre of obsessed high schoolers following in her wake.

CHAPTER 2

NEWBIE

Riding high on rage and style, Camellia strutted into school, with freaks and posers muttering, cheerleaders giving her plastic faux-smiles, jocks checking her out and grinning, and everyone else blending into the background like non-player characters to her. They simply didn't matter.

She walked past the front office where the usual line of Problematics stood outside, waiting for their daily detention schedules.

Some of them hissed together like coiled rattlers around a phone blaring news. One crowed, "Oh shit, look at that! The vine sliced him in *three places*."

"Gross," another made gagging sounds, but kept watching the phone.

"Awesome," laughed another.

"Dude, look how hard it squeezed him—"

"Oh, fuck, his eyes popped out!"

A chorus of "Damn!"

Classless shits, she thought. She sneered down her perfect nose, its freckles blotted out completely, and veered away from them. In so doing, her shoulder caught someone else's, and she swung a bit, sending her purse flying off her other shoulder.

"Fucking watch it, will you?" she snapped.

The offender stammered, "Sorry," and avoided eye contact.

Camellia halted in the middle of the hall, and everyone went silent, as though caught in a snow globe.

Not so fast, she thought.

"Oh shit," someone whispered, and various snickers flickered around as everyone got out their phones, set to record.

Camellia faced the stranger.

"No, no," she said in her low voice, "sorry's not going to cut it, little one."

The "little one" was at least as tall as Camellia, but as far as she was concerned, that meant small. She cast her eyes up and down the figure: slouching gray hoodie, its strings uneven, indiscriminate gray-green, baggy pants, steel-toe boots, hands in pockets, taut-jawed oval face with dark gray eyes, a mop of shaggy blue and blonde hair with dark roots.

"I don't know you," said Camellia in a low voice.

Someone gasped. That was the kiss of death.

The other teen backed up to leave the scene, but everyone had pressed in to watch the drama.

"I said I was sorry!" they said.

Camellia stood firmly, arms crossed. "What's your name?"

The teen looked ready to bolt, eyes darting to and fro, finding no escape.

Like a chick before a fox, mused Camellia, a smile curling at the corner of her mouth.

The teen's shoulders sagged, and they brushed their hair out of their eyes and muttered something.

"Say it louder," Camellia commanded, raising her own voice.

Cackles and whistles undulated in the hall, and finally two teachers approached from opposite ends.

The jangle of keys broke the still and ominous quiet, as if the air were charged with ozone.

"What's going on?"

It was Miss Ruthie, and she looked pissed, her mouth scowling, her salt and pepper bob waving.

The new student saw her and lifted their chin up, turning back to face Camellia.

"Wray," answered the teen.

"Wray *what*?" hissed Camellia.

"Wray of sunshine, Nosferatu witch queen."

The crowd went berserk.

Camellia's eyes glowed nearly acid green, accentuated by her flush of fury at being disrespected before the entire school.

"Okay, that's enough," tutted Miss Ruthie.

The other teacher, Mr. Levin, watched carefully over the rims of his glasses, but it was clear he was not going to step into the drama.

"Everyone," bellowed Miss Ruthie, "you need to get to your classes, or I'm writing *all* of you up. This is a *fire. Hazard.* And I've got the time. Don't test me; it's too early."

The crowd began to disperse, but Camellia and Wray stood still.

Wray did not flinch or look away. Instead, they stared defiantly back, in a way no one had ever looked at Camellia before.

How fucking dare you! she thought, feeling a strange surge of something within her.

"Nice try," murmured Camellia quietly, "but this isn't over."

"Are you gonna hold it against me as the new kid that I accidentally bumped into you?" said Wray angrily.

"You'll be lucky if I don't come for your wig," snapped Camellia.

"Miss Dume," said Mr. Levin, "I believe you're due for botany? Now, please."

"*Doom*?" Wray hooted and laughed.

The few lingering onlookers broke into hisses like a coil of snakes with a mouse.

"*Your* doom," said Camellia, and she turned on *The Look*.

Not only did Wray have the gall not to flinch this time, but they walked backward, making eye contact the whole way.

"Welcome to Killian High, Wraith," sneered Camellia, turning heel with a flounce to follow Mr. Levin to class, as everyone snickered ruthlessly.

CHAPTER 3

INVASIVE SPECIES

Mr. Levin droned on about plant ecology, and Camellia felt it was a bit much for a Monday morning. She wanted to nitpick his tweed jacket and blue jeans, because to her, they were giving thrift store vibes. Certainly the man never wore much in the way of designer clothing, although his tweeds were distinctive, and his afro was immaculate. She could not fault him for those but wished he would wear more vibrant hues… and of a proper label.

She passively absorbed Mr. Levin's words:

"…invasive species, which in their native habitat fill an ecological niche. That's where they evolved and had natural predators in the environment to keep them in check. But *removed* from that space, and put somewhere they don't belong, they may take over."

She could not sit comfortably, and was bored. She was listless, stifling yawns, feeling the brunt of a weekend of unwrapping influencer gift packages, turning down party invitations, and being generally irritated at her father, which took a lot out of her. She looked out the window and saw another student walking; they dropped something and leaned over to pick it up. Shortly after that, the door to the classroom opened, and in walked the new student, Wray.

She sat up sharply as if stung, eyebrows raised, teeth gritted.

"What are *you* doing here?" she blurted out, loudly enough that someone dropped their phone with a great clatter.

Wray stared back at her and raised their own eyebrows. Their lips twitched, and Camellia could not tell if they might become a smile or a frown.

Mr. Levin shot Camellia a look over his glasses; then he smiled at Wray.

"Hello, can I help you with something?" he asked in his melodious voice.

"My schedule was changed," said Wray. "You're Mr. Levin, right? This is Botany?"

Mr. Levin dipped his head. "It is! Welcome..." He gestured for Wray to say something.

"Wray," said the teen. They glanced at Camellia, who was breathing quickly.

"Wraith, you mean," she said acidly.

Mr. Levin cleared his throat and pierced Camellia with a glare.

"Do you have a last name, Wray?" he asked the newcomer kindly.

"Blythe," they answered, sweeping back their hair over their right ear, and slyly glancing at Camellia.

"Wraith Blight!" crowed Camellia brightly, setting the class ablaze with laughter.

Mr. Levin sighed and turned to her. "Save the turn of phrase for Literature, Miss Dume." He swiveled back to Wray, whose jaw clenched, and said, "Welcome to Killian High, Wray! Take a seat."

There were two empty desks in front of Camellia, so she

promptly stuck her legs onto the chair closer to her to block Wray from sitting there.

Someone whistled and she leaned back to see Vince Vasquez wink at her.

"Nice stems on that flower," he whispered loudly enough for everyone to hear. "For once the plant class pays off!" Camellia blew him a kiss and his surrounding friends howled, slapped him on the back, and offered high-fives.

Wray looked at Camellia's insolent expression and briefly at her legs, before they sighed quietly, and sat at the available desk.

"Ahem!" Mr. Levin clapped his hands together. "Back to the lesson, folks. Now. Invasive species."

"So," Camellia called out archly, "an invasive species enters an ecosystem and disrupts the routine."

Mr. Levin nodded and said, "For once, you paid attention, Camellia! I'm *impressed*. Now tell me what's missing from that ecosystem, allowing for the invader to take hold."

"Apex predator," Wray said quickly, before Camellia could respond.

She gaped in rage.

"Very good!" Mr. Levin nodded. "And what is an apex predator, if you don't mind, Wray?"

Wray straightened in their chair, turned just enough for Camellia to see the corners of their eyes, and cleared their throat. "An apex predator is the ultimate predator, the topmost point of a food web. Without an apex predator, everything falls apart."

"Yes!" said Mr. Levin, grinning. "Maybe *you* should teach the class."

Camellia loudly clucked her tongue.

Ignoring her, Mr. Levin asked, "Can anyone give me an example of an apex predator?"

Two hands shot up, one of them Camellia's, but Mr. Levin called upon the other student, Iris Sterling.

"I can show you one right now!" she chirped, blonde bimbo cheerleader that she was, and she pointed at Camellia.

The students guffawed.

Camellia nodded and grinned, and then withdrew her legs from the seat in front of her.

"Hear that, you shit kernels?" she cried. "Without me, everything falls apart."

Every student hooted except for Iris, who scowled, and Wray, who said nothing.

Mr. Levin pursed his mouth together and clapped his hands.

"Back to the less fascinating world of plant ecology," he said tersely, "which while nowhere *near* as scintillating as some of you seem to think yourselves," and he sent barbed looks to Camellia, Iris, Vince, and a few other completely checked-out teens in the back of the class, "is necessary to understand how we all fit together. Since this is a class about *plants*, let's talk about how their roles fit in, as Wray mentioned, the food web."

Must we? thought Camellia grimly, resting her head on her hands.

"A lot of plants," Mr. Levin went on, "are considered producers, and they take up most of the food web. Can't live without plants. Everything above them is a consumer, and the top predator, or apex predator, is the top consumer. You have grasses, zebras consume them, and the top predator of a zebra, a lion, consumes the zebra."

Shuffling and yawning and chuckling over memes undulated through the class.

Mr. Levin sighed. "Okay. So. We've established—thank you for the example—that taking away the apex predator leads to an ecosystem collapse. Is there any way it can be restored?"

"Yes," said Wray, raising their hand. "That happened in Yellowstone."

Mr. Levin lifted his eyebrows and nodded. "Correct! Enlighten us, Wray."

Wray cleared their throat. "Well, in Yellowstone, wolves were hunted to the point there weren't any left in the park. So that meant an overpopulation of their prey, which then ate too many of the plants."

"Go on," Mr. Levin encouraged.

Wray had a captive audience, and Camellia did not like that at all. But she listened. Resentfully.

"So, wolves were eventually reintroduced to the park by conservationists. And then very quickly, the ecosystem was restored. Even the waterways did better."

"Excellent!" exclaimed Mr. Levin. He pointed at Wray. "This one's going to be a scientist one day, folks."

Camellia stuck her tongue out.

"So!" Mr. Levin continued, "We see that the ecosystem *needed* that apex predator to function properly. For everything else to be in balance."

"Guess you're stuck with me," Camellia said, shimmying her hair over her shoulders. Wray turned to look at her, so she rolled her eyes at them.

Then she said, "And we've established that an invasive species doesn't belong in the ecosystem. An outsider comes in and disrupts everything." She stared at Wray, and Wray blinked. "Sounds like the best course of action is to remove it."

She felt hot under Wray's stare, but triumphant.

"Oh," Mr. Levin said, "sure. But that's not all that easy. You can't just get rid of an invasive species overnight. Look at Pampas grass. Ice plants. Kudzu!"

"So how do you get rid of it?" Camellia asked a little too loudly. Wray's brow furrowed.

"Persistence," answered Mr. Levin, "and making sure the apex predator survives, and the plant producers that feed its prey thrive too."

"And if that doesn't work?" Camellia asked.

"Then you adapt," Wray answered bluntly, making eye contact with her, and then they turned abruptly away from her.

Mr. Levin nodded. "Exactly. Anything that doesn't adapt is doomed. Next, let's talk about *plants* that are actually predators..."

Camellia's heart thumped fast in her chest, and she felt that if she could throw darts with her eyes, Wray would be the bullseye.

She made it through to lunch with no incidents, having two more classes, none with Wray in them. In the cafeteria, she sat adjacent to the Cadre table in her own special alcove, holding court as various hangers-on drifted toward her like bees to a flower. Wray was not one of them. She kept her eye on them, though, in the far corner of the lunchroom, sitting alone, hunched over a bagged lunch.

After sending various volleys of insults or thinly veiled, judgmental compliments at other students, Camellia walked out of the lunchroom and back into the thrumming halls of learning, approving of the parting of the seas of students before her as she did so. She felt breezy and in control. Then she entered Literature class and ran directly into Wray.

"What the *fuck*!" she cried loudly. "What are you doing here?"

"I *go* here," said Wray emphatically, and Camellia could see they were gritting their teeth. She ground hers as well.

"How are you *everywhere*?" she hissed, low enough so everyone couldn't hear.

Wray shrugged. "Maybe it's my job to make sure the... *apex predator* stays in balance."

She opened her mouth to hurl an insult, but Wray moved

aside so other students could pass, streaming around the rock that was Camellia. Riled, she made sure to see where Wray sat first, and then proceeded to a desk on the opposite side of the room, far away from them.

"Love your skirt," whispered Soleil Barton, next to her, and Camellia batted her eyes and did her best complimentary wink, while examining the girl's mismatched shirt and pants.

"Hmm, well, that's... interesting," she said, gesturing to Soleil's outfit.

Soleil beamed. "Thanks!"

Camellia rolled her eyes and focused on the teacher, Ms. Cooke.

"Today, you choose your favorite poem. Extra credit to whomever recites theirs before the class."

Wray's hand shot up, and Camellia seethed.

"Yes? I'm sorry, I don't know your name?" Ms. Cooke consulted her class list.

"Wray Blythe. I'm new."

Someone made a slow golf-clap.

Wray dipped their head.

"Welcome, Wray. Do you have a favorite poem?"

"I do," said Wray.

Of course you do, thought Camellia, sniffing.

"Well, grand!" Ms. Cooke looked elated. Camellia could have rolled her eyes so hard they'd have shot through the back of her skull and through the next two buildings. "I'll let you take over, then."

Camellia snorted. "Take over?" she murmured loudly.

Wray stood, facing the class, and turned their gaze to Camellia. They held a phone and said, "I don't have it completely memorized, and it's long, so I'll only read part of it. My favorite part. 'Ode to the West Wind' by Percy Bysshe Shelley."

Camellia closed her eyes but could feel Wray still watching her.

Wray recited in a clear, measured voice:

> *If I were a dead leaf thou mightest bear;*
> *If I were a swift cloud to fly with thee;*
> *A wave to pant beneath thy power, and share*

Camellia opened her eyes.

> *The impulse of thy strength, only less free*
> *Than thou, O uncontrollable! If even*
> *I were as in my boyhood, and could be*

Camellia bit her lower lip.

> *The comrade of thy wanderings over Heaven,*
> *As then, when to outstrip thy skiey speed*
> *Scarce seem'd a vision; I would ne'er have*
> *striven*

Camellia twisted her fingers together in her lap, out of sight.

> *As thus with thee in prayer in my sore need.*
> *Oh, lift me as a wave, a leaf, a cloud!*
> *I fall upon the thorns of life! I bleed!*

Camellia didn't realize it, but her mouth fell open just a touch, as she and Wray stared at each other, the rest of the room fallen away, forgotten.

Wray continued, swallowing first:

> *A heavy weight of hours has chain'd and*
> *bow'd*
> *One too like thee: tameless, and swift, and*
> *proud.*

Then, Wray bowed their head and the crowd whooped. Ms. Cooke clapped wildly.

"That was hot," someone muttered.

Wray took a last, lingering look at Camellia, whose face burned and whose green eyes shone like lamps over a dark ocean. Wray walked back to their seat and did not look at her again for the rest of the class.

CHAPTER 4

4-H CLUB

She slid her backpack off her shoulder and gave the driver a little wave with her pointy red fingernails. The door camera chimed and said, "Welcome home, Camellia!"

"Oh, fuck off," she replied, as the door clicked open at the command.

She sent the backpack skidding on the shiny floor of the long hallway, its arched ceiling reflecting the highly polished tiles in pale, stretched, geometric forms of light and shadow. She considered this, but barely. She stared down the hall and at the gardens beyond. She could see the fountain spraying and the thick palms waving at her. One of their swimming pools stretched beyond the fountain in a kidney bean shape, shimmering in turquoise blue, surrounded by chaise lounges and umbrellas that automatically tilted with the sun angle.

She never used the pool.

She never used the other one, either.

And she also didn't use the third slot pool outside her bedroom. Or the hot tub.

She also didn't use the pools at any of her father's other properties, and she didn't tend to use the chaise lounges...

not during the day, anyway. Her fair skin would freckle from the sun even through sunscreen, and she hated freckles.

Pool cleaning staff arrived on the dot every Tuesday morning, 8:30 sharp, which was when her high school classes began, so she never saw them. She only saw evidence of them in the pristine pools. Today was Monday and so the pools looked the worst they possibly could... which is to say, not at all bad. But she could see dead leaves floating on parts of it, and ominous little cloud-balls of midges bobbing above the surface; perhaps they were mosquitos. She didn't know, and she wouldn't be finding out.

She also avoided the walled garden.

It was an exquisite place, full of treasured ornamental plants, some of them quite rare, and with some sculptured, wee bonsai displayed among them. Each quadrant of the garden held different themes, and they were tended to lovingly by Clifton, the gardener, who was quite stooped and gnarled, very like some of the oldest trees themselves. If he caught sight of her, he would wave his warped, arthritic hands, and usually she would only royal wave back, since he was British, continuing about her business as if he'd been a dog on a sidewalk.

For that matter, she might have paid a dog more attention.

Not to pet one; never that. Perhaps a perfunctory glance, and then a wide berth.

She had no pets.

That was something that had changed after her mother died. That and the garden thing.

It had been her mother's pride garden, that and the attached greenhouse.

As a young girl, Camellia had viewed those as wonderlands, full of whimsy and magic among the fecund growing things, full of nooks and crannies and secret little oases that only she was small enough to find. Now they were castles of the past, crumbled in her eyes like ruins on hills nearly out of sight. And yet they were part of her home.

She blinked and shook her dark red tresses, picked a small leaf out of them, and walked toward the kitchen. The backpack would remain on the floor until one of the staff found it and sorted things for her. She couldn't be bothered.

She strode into the kitchen. This was the downstairs main kitchen, not the one with the bar attached, and not the upper-level kitchenette, and not the kitchen off the garden; this was the path-of-least-resistance kitchen closest to the front door, and therefore closest to her when she came home from school. The downstairs *main* kitchen held three islands, an elaborate coffee bar with the finest Italian espresso machines (four of them in this kitchen alone), an elaborate tea service (she never understood why; she suspected it was a nod to Clifton, some-how, though she'd never seen the man use it, much less anything else in the kitchen; he had a rear entry and rarely set foot in the main house). One of the islands held a great copper cover shipped from Europe. The other was a butcher block made of an ancient German castle door. The third was hooded with gleaming bronze and bore one of the ranges of the kitchen. Everything top of the line, even if neither Camellia nor her father ever touched a single knob on any of it.

The only things Camellia did touch were the microwaves, one of the sinks, and one of the refrigerators, and only those particular three.

Her mother had been an accomplished cook, and back in the day the kitchens had echoed with merriment whenever she'd held soirees, which was at least once a month, and always with a different theme. She was generous with food and money alike, and always held a smile for anyone, no matter their station, and would give anyone a plate who showed up, even if they had nowhere else to go. *Especially* if they had nowhere else to go.

Now the kitchens were maws of emptiness to feed only the hungry inhabitants of the house itself, and their number had dwindled over the years. Once her mother had died, Camellia noticed that more people began to leave. Not just because of her mother's passing; her father would have kept them on, maybe, as a favor. But really it was because both he and his daughter grew to become insufferable at best, and malicious at worst. Which was often.

She pulled open her favored fridge's door and stared at the bottles of Perrier and Fever Tree lined up like bowling pins, ready for her to crash through them. And she was tempted to; she was tempted to smash them all, throw them on the floor, only because it was so very quiet in there. So quiet she could hear the pulse in her ears and the incessant yipping of a dog up the street, which made her grind her teeth. Her temples hurt and the glare from outside reflected in on the polished copper and chrome and bronze and gleaming marble surfaces, making her head hurt worse. She pulled a bottle out, snatched the lid off, and slammed the door of the fridge, only of course it wouldn't slam, because it was a gentle closing door.

"Shall I order more, Camellia?" the fridge asked.

Sucking on the fizzy water and scowling, she snapped, "I truly don't give a shit."

"I will order a dozen more, then," the fridge responded right on cue.

Taking another sip, Camellia scowled as she combed through her social feeds. A viral video of twisting, giant vines and leaves like sabers slicing through fences and snapping at people running made her snort. One vine appeared to have caught the unfortunate onlooker filming, and threw the person high in the air, screaming until the feed ended abruptly.

She rolled her eyes. "Yeah, I saw that movie before. Nice try, you desperate, clout-chasing chud," she grumbled. Fridge said nothing. "They're not even trying with the effects," she sniffed.

It was an empty space, the shell of its former self; vacant and gleaming and sterile and boring and… dead. That was not only it, she knew, deep down. It was devoid of life in a way something dead couldn't be; it was worse than dead, it was *sapped*, drained, scoured out.

Just like she and her father were, and would always be, since her mother's car had plummeted off that curve on the Pacific Coast Highway ten years ago, at night, in the fog… a fog which would never lift from the hearts of the husband and daughter left behind.

She only thought sourly of the foggy memories since, bitterness crystallizing like a shard of broken glass in her soul. She never showed that side of herself to anyone: she was determined not to let them see she was weak or soft. She would hold onto that broken glass and cut herself on it, if that's what it took.

A litany of alerts chimed in rapid succession. She jerked out of her daze and listened with a scowl.

"Someone is approaching the front walk," droned one message from the house intercom.

For one wild split second, she wondered if it might be Wray, and a current of some new emotion jolted through her.

"Three individuals are approaching the front door," chimed another.

Ah.

"There are three individuals at the front—"

"Oh, shut *up*!" Camellia yelled.

The doorbell rang.

Huffing out a sigh, Camellia glanced at the fridge, which displayed who stood there: two young children and someone taller.

"Hi, Camellia," the person spoke into the door camera. "We've got a question for you, O queen on high."

She rolled her eyes.

"How'd they get in the gate?" murmured Camellia, and then she suspected perhaps the gardener, because she knew the taller person. It was Agatha Trenton, a vociferous, active student at Killian High.

She could easily have ignored them and waited for them to move on. But she felt the impulse to greet them.

I guess I'm just that bored, she thought.

She smoothed her copper hair in the grand foyer mirror, scrolled with silver and gold and intricate tiled vines around its border. Sighing again, chiefly from boredom, she approached the door and opened it.

There stood Agatha, a Black junior Camellia's age, with purple-tinged hair twists, staring at her with ebony eyes just slightly tilted in bemusement, smirking. Next to her, two children stood nervously, gazing up with large eyes: twins, by the look of them, and Camellia could see they looked like younger versions of Agatha. They each held cardboard boxes in their arms and bore enamel clover pins on little green vests. The pins read "4-H" and Camellia stared, fixated, at the pins.

A wave of memories flooded over her. Her mother, volunteering at her elementary school, giving her a similar pin.

"When you're older you can do all kinds of things with 4-H, like I did as a girl!"

And then, fast-forwarding, when late in her freshman year at KHS, Camellia was given the hissed nickname of 4-H. At the time she'd thought it a strange thing to nickname someone. After her mother had died, she never desired to have anything to do with the organization again. So why would anyone call her that? She later found out they'd called her 4-H because someone came up with the idea to christen her "Hot Haute Hunty Hoe." It was whispered urgently. "Here comes 4-H!" and students would scurry off before she verbally flayed them in front of everyone.

Agatha cleared her throat.

Camellia felt a brief flash of annoyance that she refused to name embarrassment.

"Hello, Agatha," she answered crisply. "What are you doing here?"

Agatha leveled her with an unwavering gaze, straightened her back, arched her eyebrows, and said, "I'll let my sisters tell you. Gertie, Casie, go ahead."

The two younger girls glanced at each other, and interrupted each other until Agatha said, "Ah! One at a time. Casie, you first."

Casie stared up at Camellia, who stood framed in her open doorway, her arms folded, one eyebrow lifted, cold green eyes blazing down. The little girl tried to speak but choked.

"Okay, Gertie?" Agatha suggested, but Gertie shook her head.

Agatha's jaw muscles worked, and she feigned a sweet smile at Camellia.

"Gertie and Casie are raising money for the 4-H Club Fall Festival," she told Camellia with an even voice. "I believe you're familiar with 4-H?"

She's pushing it, thought Camellia, fighting a blush.

"Quite, Agatha," responded Camellia, almost in a whisper.

The two girls shook their boxes, and now Camellia could see they contained chocolate bars.

"I only eat Belgian chocolate," she said acidly, and moved to close the door.

Agatha stuck her foot out to block the door from closing and looked straight into Camellia's eyes.

"I know you have the cash, Miss Scarlett," she murmured.

Camellia arched her eyebrow.

"So does every other house here," Camellia replied, holding her arms out, gesturing to the neighborhood. "Why don't you go shake them down?"

Agatha's shoulders raised and lowered, and she said sharply, "Maybe these aren't Belgian chocolate, but they're for a good cause. Wasn't your mother head of the 4-H back in the day? Her picture is framed in the clubhouse, and she had medals."

Camellia turned her full fury on Agatha with one tilt of her head and gleam of her flashing green eyes. Agatha stepped back as if she might fall.

"You," whispered Camellia out of earshot of the twins, "will *never* mention my mother again."

Agatha rose to the occasion, however, and said, "None of your other neighborhood creeps have given a dime. This is something they"—she nodded over her shoulder at her sisters—"have to do to get their next pin."

"I told you, I only eat—" Camellia began, but she heard sniffles.

The twins' eyes welled with tears.

Agatha turned back to Camellia and said, "Fine. We're leaving."

As she started back down the front steps, Camellia called, "Wait."

The three sisters turned to look at her. She stepped out and the wind caught her hair and flung it into her face. Agatha smirked at that. Camellia swept it back away from her cheeks and over her shoulders and held out her wrist, with its rose gold watch catching the sun.

"I don't have cash," she told them. The girls looked uncertain. "But if you can take this, I'll buy them all."

"All of them?" the twins asked in unison.

"All," agreed Camellia. Agatha stared at her coldly. "Plus a thousand dollars."

Agatha blinked at her. "That's too much," she murmured.

"It'll never be enough," said Camellia in a deep, quiet voice. Agatha looked startled. "Give me the boxes and get out of my sight before I change my mind, and don't come back, Agatha."

Agatha set her mouth and nodded.

"You don't ever have to worry about that," she agreed in a firm tone.

Her sisters bounced up and down, ecstatic, and took the chocolate boxes to Camellia.

"Thank you!" they chorused.

"Here," Gertie squeaked, and she handed Camellia an enamel pin from her pocket, just like the one she wore.

"We want you to have it," Casie told her.

"You can be an honorary 4-H member now!" Gertie agreed.

They looked at each other, giggled, and looked up at Agatha.

Agatha gave Camellia a long, unspoken look, blinked slowly, nodded, and turned herself and her sisters away.

Camellia watched them go, the two boxes in her arms, and she furrowed her brow.

She entered her house and walked to the kitchen again and set the boxes on the counter.

"Hmmph," she said to the air.

She opened one of the boxes and pulled out a chocolate bar.

"Caramel nougat crunch," she read aloud.

Caramel was *another* one of the pet names she was given. She smirked over that one. The grantor of that name was given a special pass for special reasons. She tore open the bar, took a bite, and then slid down to the floor, her back against Fridge, her legs splayed outward, and she chewed absently. She held the chocolate in her left hand and turned the little enamel pin over and over in her right hand. Then, she squeezed it until it pressed into her hand sharply, leaving little dents. Her throat hurt; her eyes stung. But she only sat and chewed in silence.

CHAPTER 5

COWL'S MOUNTAIN

Tuesday dawned and Camellia jerked awake, annoyed to find herself creased from a deep slumber.

She scuffed in her $900 slippers down to the kitchen, where the fridge greeted her in melodious tones.

"Happy Tuesday, Camellia!"

Yawning, she returned: "Fuuuck off."

Her father hadn't come home the night before, nor this morning, so she angrily gnawed on a Kate Switch raw chocolate chip power bar and chugged a turquoise algae-banana smoothie (wincing) while her morning eye mask soaked into her porcelain skin.

"Out with another fucking junkie ass bitch," she growled, wondering vaguely—but briefly—who her dad's latest conquest was. She had seen many come and go and assumed there were many more she'd never meet. For which she was glad.

Something flickered in the corner of her eye, and she turned. The morning sun slanting into the shadowed garden looked strange to her. A muted gold, as though it were foggy outside. But when she looked out of the front windows of house, the sky looked clear, all the way to the horizon, where the cobalt Pacific met the azure morning sky. It was rare not to see the marine layer. No clouds anywhere. But the light shone as if scattered.

"Some hillside on fire again," she muttered aloud.

"I can look for you!" chirped Fridge immediately.

"Oh, really?" she droned, rolling her eyes.

"There are no wildfires in Los Angeles County currently. There is a fire in Enyo Coun—"

"Shut *up*! I don't care!"

And she stalked back up the stairs to shower.

After that, she dressed in one outfit, scowled in her five-way mirror dais, and then switched into another. Three more outfits later and her calendar chimed, "You'll need to call a ride soon or you'll be late for school."

"I'm glad you care more than Dad!" she shouted. "Call him, will you?"

"Calling now."

She pulled on black knee-high socks and a pleated, dark green tartan skirt, hand woven from Scotland. Then she yanked a black, cap-sleeved cashmere top over her still-damp head, deciding to let her natural waves dry in the warming morning. Donning her phone watch, earrings of jet and diamond and emerald, and a black choker with a dangling green emerald, she approached her boot closet.

"There is no answer," the soft, contralto voice of her house intercom told her.

She clucked her tongue.

"Call a ride then."

Clattering step by marble step down the sweeping front staircase, her footfalls echoed throughout the empty house. It was unusually so: the gardener hadn't arrived, and none of the pool cleaners or housekeepers had either. A little crease formed between her arched, dark ginger eyebrows. She stopped by the ornate foyer mirror.

"Check yourself before you wreck yourself," she

muttered, pulling a lipstick, this time in *Enchante No. 72: Carnelian Savagery*, out of a small, hidden pocket in the skirt.

Her wristwatch alerted her to the ride.

It was a gleaming, black hydrogen Lotus SUV, and the driver was a middle-aged woman with deep magenta hair cropped at the chin. She wore purple aviator sunglasses, a smart, black pantsuit, and white gloves. She opened the rear passenger door for Camellia and reached for her backpack.

"No thanks," said Camellia.

She paid the driver no further attention; they were separated by a tinted barrier window. She twisted the top off a bottle of Topo Chico that sat in a cupholder next to her and sipped at it while she went through her watch messages.

She spoke into it: "Dad, where the fuck are you this time? Thanks a lot for taking me to school, by the way!"

This was the fifth message she'd left that morning, and with no response, she grew angrier. She could feel heat rising up her neck into her cheeks, and knew there was a fine line between attractive angry-blushing and breaking into a rash, for someone with sensitive, fair skin like hers. So, she made a lame attempt to control her breathing.

It was Tuesday: it was *Terror Tuesday* at Killian High, according to the plebes she went to school with. Because on Tuesdays, Camellia wore green, and she demanded everyone else do as well, and if you didn't, you went on her Shit List; not a place anyone chose to go willingly. Hence the terror.

Already in a hideous mood, she tersely credited the driver with a large tip and said nothing to her as she left the vehicle, her tall, black, chunky heels striking the curb of the school like a warning. Heads whipped around as she shouldered her backpack. Raising her Ferrari shades to form a headband over her long, flaming waves, she put her hands on her hips and assessed.

"All right, you shits!" she called out loudly, smirking at the shaking heads of staff outside. "You know what today is.

Terror Tuesday! I'm your Leprechaun of Lashings. Show me your green or be destroyed."

A current of caws and coos arose like an excited group of crows as all the students turned to her and flashed their bits of green. All except one. The new student, Wray. They wore enormously baggy, faded jeans, torn in places that meant they weren't fashionable. Their top was a curious, familiar-looking blue material, and tilting her head, Camellia felt the comfortable thrill of her Bitch Bubble rising, filling her mind, intoxicating her.

So:

"Is that an encampment tarp, Wraith?" she hollered.

Her eyes locked onto the other teen's like a cheetah's upon a gazelle.

And Wray flinched visibly.

Camellia's scarlet lips pulled back in a smile like a gash of blood.

"You know," Camellia called, walking slowly as the crowds parted before her, everyone's eyes wide, the air crackling with imminent chaos that no one could turn away from, "the problem with most of you shits in this school is you're trust fund babies, Old Hollywood blue-bloods, drip-dry inheritance cookies, or worse, new tech fundie chicks."

Each insult landed appropriately upon the correct crowds. But her magnetism still pulled them in even while it repulsed them.

"But some of you," and the scrape-click of her heels was the only sound in a sea of silent, dropped-jaw teens, and some staff members craning their necks, "some of you are charity cases. Some of you are someone's *idea* of a feel-good moment to absolve them of their own fuckery. Some of you are *invasive* species. Like you, Wraith." One word for each ring of a heel upon the concrete courtyard: "You." -*crack*- "Don't." -*crack*- "Belong." -*crack*- "Here." -*crack*-

Now she stood staring into Wray's sunglasses, watching their nose flaring, seeing the bounce of Wray's neck pulse.

Wray opened their mouth, trembling, when the first bell rang.

Mr. Levin stepped forward briskly, his brow stern, and he bellowed:

"Get inside, all of you! Camellia, with me."

Camellia smirked as the chorus of "Wooooo" rippled around her. As she walked past Wray, she plucked at their blue top with her perfectly manicured nails.

"It suits you," she whispered.

With that, she tossed her red mane over her shoulder and followed Mr. Levin.

She ignored half of what he said as she pointed and thumbs-upped everyone who instantly flashed their bits of green attire or accessories so as not incur her ire. As other students coursed around them like salmon struggling upstream, Mr. Levin clenched his jaw, bent his head down, and spoke to her in low tones.

"Miss Dume, I've just about had enough of your behavior."

She shimmied her hair a bit toward the onlooking kids streaming by, her wicked smirk deepening; she lowered her vivid green eyes to the halfway mark to stare up at Mr. Levin coldly.

"Which behavior would that be, Mr. Levin?" she asked, gazing down at her manicured hands. "The good grades? The excellent posture? The taste-making of all the nerds taking botany? Tell me this, Plant Man. How's my class compared to your others? How's the behavior? Do you have a silent and obedient class for each of those, other than the fawning of these idiots currying favor for *me*? Because word gets around!"

Another teacher, Ms. Hughes, stood outside the doorway of her class, pretending not to pay attention to the showdown, touching her hand to her lips at Camellia's last statement.

"Word gets around about *what*, exactly?" fumed Mr. Levin coldly. "You are a bully."

"Oh, *I'm* a bully?" she said loudly. "I'm not the one publicly picking on a teenager out where everyone can see, Mr. Levin."

Dead silence as everyone in that hallway, teachers, students, and janitor alike, stopped in their tracks. The squeak of sneakers on tile echoed as everyone crowded back to the doorways to peek out. The second bell rang.

"Do you know a little bit of trivia?" Camellia continued, knowing she had the audience, gazing innocently up at Mr. Levin. "My father makes sure you're funded every year. I can't imagine why. But *he's* the reason you have a job, Mr. Levin. Not your credentials, which are frankly beneath the hallowed halls of Killian High. We could've had a doctorate from *Oxford*. No: you have the job solely because of my father. Now you know, and now everyone else knows."

She nodded to all the tablets, phones, watches, and she counted three small, hovering drones filming everything, likely straight to social media, *TMZ*, and *The Hollywood Reporter*. She poised her Louboutin boots so the flash of their red soles could be seen and twitched her Alexander McQueen phone bag, so its label stood out on her hip. Brand recognition was essential.

And with that, she flounced like a runway model, stepping around Mr. Levin, who stood breathing quickly. She walked into his class as every other gaping student scurried to their seats. Wray watched her with a cold glare, but she ignored them. She sat perfectly poised in her desk, the same as yesterday's, and then said archly: "Mind your manners, school ghouls. Mother is here!"

Appreciative snickers from nerds or tuts of disdain from a rare set of cheerleaders (the kind who never voluntarily took science courses of any kind) ricocheted as Mr. Levin walked inside the class and shut his door with a little too much force.

The silence of those forty-five minutes seemed to unnerve everyone. For her part, Camellia chose to ignore the triggered tones of Mr. Levin's voice and glanced out the nearest window, past the vines of the plants he had placed on its sill. Again, despite the blue bowl of the late summer Malibu sky, something along the edges didn't look quite normal to her. Her wrist buzzed, and she hastily turned off its sound, meeting Mr. Levin's furious stare.

It was her dad.

"Hey Meems, sorry I missed your call."

My six fucking calls, you mean?

"I'll be there to pick you up after school."

She grimaced.

She sent back a thumbs-down.

Nothing.

The air hung with animosity between her and Mr. Levin, as well as with Wray... who mercifully never looked at her the entire class. When the bell rang for the next class, she deliberately waited to leave in order to be last. She had a feeling Mr. Levin had something more to say to her, and she was right.

After everyone poured out of the room, with Wray stealing a glance at her without making eye contact before leaving also, she walked regally up to the front by the door.

"A word, Miss Dume," Mr. Levin's voice came quietly, with a sinister undertone. He shut the door.

"I have class," she interjected, simpering.

"You? Have class? No, you don't," he returned. "You have classes. No class."

"How fuc-"

"I'm warning you." A crease formed between his eyebrows, making him look older than usual. "And also, your little bit of trivia? That little show you put on in the hallway?

You don't know what you're talking about. It wasn't your dad who brought me on."

"Of course it is," she replied, one eyebrow lifted. "Dad told me."

"Then he didn't tell you everything."

"Bullshit."

"Camellia," he growled. "Use your head."

She sniffed and turned on her heel and left.

After the next two classes rolled on, she caught sight of Wray before lunch; they saw her and rushed away and out of sight. She grinned to herself.

"Let the trash take itself out," she muttered.

She entered the cafeteria and walked right over to a spindly, wrinkled, older man in a white paper hat and chef's coat who winked at her. He held a bag in his shaking hands.

"Here ya go, Miss Camellia! Your favorite!"

She did her little neck shimmy, making her hair sparkle, distracting at least five people in her vicinity, and reached out to almost-boop the lunch worker on the nose.

She took her special bag, turned, and walked through the hungry masses.

As she did so, she heard a snatch of a phrase ending in "Cowl's Mountain."

She stopped in her tracks. A cold wave of something flickered all through her. Something unfamiliar to her. She didn't like it.

"What about Cowl's Mountain?" she asked the boy, pointing at him with her scarlet-manicured forefinger.

He wore a McLaren shirt and cargo pants, his brown hair slicked back, his hands in his pockets, a slack-jawed look of insolence and ego all about him.

A junior, she assessed.

"Who cares?" the guy replied. "Some inbred place in Tennessee swallowed whole."

She lowered her eyelids.

Someone else saw her expression and shouted, "Rome is burning!"

That was another one of their code words at school. It was an alarm system for when Camellia Dume was about to fly into a rage.

"Rome is burning!" echoed someone else.

"Oh, *shit*!"

"Fuck!"

"Rome is *burrrrniiiiing*!"

Looking down her nose at him she said, "Inbred, huh? Sounds like you know a lot about that. Is that so-called girl-friend you text bathroom dick pics to really your sister?"

Gales of laughter rang out.

He sat up straight and almost bounded to his feet, but another jock held him back.

"Later," advised the smarmy-looking blonde, a senior named Bale. He winked at his friend.

As she marched on through the cafeteria and to the outside tables; she heard along the way:

The sophomore Myx, saying, "Gross, it says the thing vomited up their bones."

The senior, Bale: "Darwin Award!"

She snatched his phone.

"Hey!" He tried grabbing it back.

"Console yourself," she snapped. "I'm breaking the wardrobe rule." She turned her back to the table so she could read the news about first one, then two, then more Appalachian towns consumed. Headlines screaming: "Killer kudzu on the run!"

Keeping her face unreadable, she air kissed the phone and handed it back. "There, material for your flesh-light fantasies between 3rd and 4th period."

Bale's face fell a tick.

"I don't need one of those," he boasted among peals of knowing laughter from the table. "I've got Ava."

Popular brunette Ava sashayed up in cheerleading gear just in time to hear Camellia say loudly while looking at her, "Then maybe Ava needs to know you're cheating on her with plastic and lube in between classes!"

"I'm not—" gasped Bale.

Camellia gave him *The Look*. "You might want to be careful with security cameras in the utility closets."

She waved at Ava, wiggling her pinky finger.

"Oh Ava, you deserve better! In size as well as foundation brands."

And on she walked, sowing awe, hate, admiration, and conflicted crushes with every booted step. Inwardly, she felt as if an abyss had opened beneath her feet.

Cowl's Mountain. Where her Mammaw had lived all her life.

Gone.

CHAPTER 6

HERE WE GO AGAIN

Her Mammaw had died five years prior, claimed by metastatic disease. Camellia suspected it resulted from runaway stress and grief from her mother's death. Camellia merely observed the *idea* of her grandmother's death, and never examined closely its effect on her.

Then again, she never did that for her own mother, either.

So, what she felt upon hearing that Mammaw's town— and presumably the graveyard where she had rested in peace —had collapsed in some sort of disaster, she chose to set in a little segment of her mind. She could look at that feeling if she wanted to... later. She had things to do. She had classmates to dominate and morons to humiliate, after all. Everything else could wait.

On her way to Literature class, her wrist chimed. Her dad's face shone up and she rolled her eyes.

It's probably about Mammaw, she thought.

But no: "Hey Meems, I'm running behind. There's another meeting, and I won't be home tonight. Tell Mirabella if you need anything. Oh, and tip the gardener, will you? I forgot last week."

"For fuck's sake," she hissed, and her watch began to construct that as her response until she stopped it.

Instead, she gave a thumbs-up response and shut the messages off.

Her face flushed and she curled her red-tipped fingernails into her palms, digging them in deep until it hurt. She knew her dad was probably not in any meeting at all: he was gambling, whoring, something like that... and anyway, it meant she had the house to herself again.

In Literature class, she let her eyes glaze over a bit and pursed her lips. Wray sat in the same place as yesterday but did not look at her. She huffed out a disgruntled sigh. She listened to the droning of the teacher and felt far more bored by today's class, than when Wray had recited the poem. Thinking about it again made her squirm.

"What's the matter, Miss Doom?" hissed Else. "Did you suck on a lemon, or some old guy's dick again?"

Camellia whipped her coppery head around, alert, a leopard staring at twitching prey, and she heard the quick intakes of breath in gasps as the room went still as a forest pond.

"Else Clendennon," Camellia intoned quietly and slowly. "Did you ever figure out whose grades you stole when you hacked into the school network last year?"

A squeal of scandalized laughter erupted from one corner of the room. Else's hands began to tremble, her eyes flickered wide. *Now* Wray looked back and caught her eye. She flushed and sat up straighter, a wry grin forming in the corner of her mouth.

Camellia, knowing she had the room, including the curious teacher, in her sway, turned her eyes to Ms. Cooke. She sat upright and poised and raised her hand. The teacher nodded. "May I be excused?" she asked.

"And why might that be, Camellia?" Ms. Cooke asked,

pushing her graying, dark blonde hair behind her ears and staring over red-rimmed glasses. Her large eyes cast an inter-rogating gaze.

"It's just," Camellia simpered, batting her eyes back at Else, "that I can't bear to sit in the same room as someone who behaves so *unconscionably* as Else. She also stole some of the donations from the middle school reading mentorship club." She waved her first finger back and forth at Else and clicked her tongue. She noticed, barely, that Wray's mouth had fallen open.

Ms. Cooke blinked twice, raised her eyebrows, and her lips began to curl downward.

Camellia knew that was the closest thing to a major reaction one could get from Ms. Cooke, and could tell the teacher believed her. The other incriminating evidence was the completely ashen face and full-on shaking of Else in her seat, where she gripped the edges of her desk, tears springing into her eyes.

"I applaud your use of 'unconscionably,' Camellia," said Ms. Cooke. "And while I know it must be quite a challenge to… endure the presence of others, we've still got a lesson, and you need to turn your assignment in just like everyone else."

Snorts of laughter circled the room, until:

"And as for Else," Ms. Cooke said suddenly—and the room sat frozen again, "I would like to speak with you after class."

"But I didn't—" Else choked in a higher-than-usual voice.

Ms. Cooke cleared her throat.

"Back to your essays. Bonus points for recounting *The Taming of the Shrew.*"

Camellia smirked impishly and settled into her seat. She caught sight of Wray and tensed ever so slightly. They stared at her coldly with their stormy gray sea eyes for a long moment over their shoulder before turning around to resume work. Camellia sat and struggled through her assignment, irritated by the look from Wray, and frustrated at her father.

She noticed an empty seat: Selah's. She checked her messages, and the last one from the girl was two days prior. They were friends... inasmuch as Camellia could bear to *have* friends. Really it was a mutually beneficial symbiosis kind of thing: gossip and notes traded, secrets bandied, grudges tallied. Occasionally it grew more parasitic, when one girl or the other would pull the dynamic over to their side. Camellia always won; and as long as Selah recognized that, they could tolerate each other's bullshit. A bit.

She only half-listened to the light droning of the noises of a classroom. The air conditioner blasted in a cold column of air just behind her, ruffling her copper hair, and she scowled. Still, she was glad not to be outside, with the late summer torpor lingering on, the humidity hanging like guilt in the air. She blinked for a moment, jerked, and sat up ramrod straight. Her phone had vibrated. Whoever it was, it hadn't gone to her watch. Furtively, she slipped her hand down to her backpack to retrieve the phone, and saw a message:

"Hi Camellia. Please call."

It was from Selah's number, but that was not something Selah would ever write.

Then, swiftly the words glowed: "This is Selah's dad."

She blinked and, catching Ms. Cooke's eye, let the phone fall back into the darkness of her book bag, out of sight. Staring ahead, uncertain what to think, she began to chew at the corner of her mouth, something she had not done in a long time (because it chapped her lips and ruined the job of the various high-end scrubs and creams and glosses she regularly bought, used only a few times, and discarded, resulting in many pitched battles with her father over the expense and frivolity of her purchases). And yet he eventually would relent, as she often pointed out to him that he was *gone* a great deal of the time and spending far more money gambling or whatever he was doing out of sight of her. Surely, a Parisian gloss was a small price to pay for being left alone. And of course, her father did not know about *him*.

He was in the Navy and stationed in San Diego. He was six years older, and so twenty-two, and far too comfortable with someone sixteen. He would text her when he was back from deployment, and rarely, when he was in L.A. Which was not often, as he handwaved the place disdainfully. In her phone, she had saved his number as Sydney Grohl. His real name was Syd Riemelt. They had met at a party, on the balcony of a mansion overlooking a deep cleft of Laurel Canyon. One of the parties of a starlet, Kate Switch (of the hit show *Kate and Switch*), and her greater and lesser Hollywood affiliates. Camellia had scored an invite after posing with her on the red carpet at the Emmys the year prior, and no one had guessed exactly why Camellia was there, because no one cared. The point was that Kate and Camellia were on camera together, and Camellia was sashayed in to sit at Kate's table. Her bodyguard was a compatriot of Syd's, and so Camellia, fizzing from an illicit Kir Royale while overlooking the mist-crowded canyon, smudging the lights of town over the horizon, had giggled into Syd's neck, not realizing how much older he was.

He was boyish and a bit of a smartass, but in a clever way that belied his true nature. Camellia had taken note of his poise and muscular physique, hidden by a simple T-shirt and khaki pants, and wondered about him.

Kate had grazed her rhinestone-tipped fingers around Camellia's face; the young woman bubbled from a dose of Molly and a shot of tequila, yanking Camellia's hand into the air and crowing, "THIS IS MY FRIEND!" before dissolving into giggles and rippling away in her halter-top gown, its long skirt fluttering like dove wings behind her.

Syd wanted to know all about her: what classes she took, who her best friend was. Camellia sensed his intelligence and, finding that a rare quality among her classmates, indulged his questions, rattling off minor details unconcernedly.

"You're telling me," Syd had said, his mouth wry, his dark blue eyes glinting but alert, one hand around the neck of a Corona beer, the other quite close to Camellia's pale arm with its few copper freckles, "you don't have a best friend?"

"Well," she'd sighed, "not really. I have a cadre of queens who adore my fashions and gossip with me. I have the usual jocks who try to grab my ass. I have the cheerleading squad who hate and love me at the same time."

He'd laughed at that.

"And I have Selah."

"Tell me all about Selah."

What had she said? "Oh, her mom knew my mom when we were kids"—Syd reacted not at all to that statement—"but her parents divorced, and she spends half the year with her mom, and half with her dad. Or something like that. Anyway she's here with her dad—I mean in Malibu—for school."

"But, like, are you BFFs? Do you watch movies together? Do you go to the mall? The beach?"

Camellia grinned at him. "You're so old-fashioned! No, we just text. Sometimes we'll visit each other and try on outfits."

Her eyes had glazed over and then she heard a sharp hiss: "*What?*"

She jerked her chin up, back to the present, and met Wray's eyes. She flounced her hair and stared piercingly back.

"What yourself!" she whispered back. "Stop staring at me, Wraith."

"You're the one staring at me, Camphor," blurted Wray.

Camellia's mouth fell open, ready to emit a scold, and the bell rang.

"The fuck is your problem," muttered Wray, shouldering their bag and quickly walking off with a scowl.

"You, if you keep fucking with me," snapped Camellia softly.

But inwardly she trembled. She seized the phone from her bag and ignored her usual target, Derf Dorset, a nerd with profound disregard for hygiene who she loved to call "Pigpen" like from the Charlie Brown cartoons. Derf looked expectantly at her, primed for his insult, and... nothing. His lower lip pushed out in surprise as Camellia advanced toward the door, clutching her phone, her designer book bag flung over one shoulder, snagging her hair without her noticing at first.

Outside, she skimmed through Selah's texts again. Was it really her dad? There was only one way to find out.

She walked over to a bench under a tree and spread her things out so that no one could sit next to her. She held the phone uncertainly, staring at the messages, trying to absorb them. She, like most teens, hated calling anyone. She was hesitant now. But something pulled at her.

She dialed.

In the soporific, sultry air she waited, listening to the dial tone. Three rings in, someone answered.

"Hello?"

A man's voice, dull, exhausted.

She cleared her throat. "Mr. Fassett?"

A pause. "Camellia?"

"This is she," proper, alert, *mature*.

"Camellia!" he exclaimed, and he puffed out a great sigh. "I'm so glad you called. I... this is going to sound strange, but have you seen Selah?"

Camellia twisted her lips and furrowed her brow.

"No, I... assumed she was with you. Sick or taking the day off or something."

"No."

A long pause this time.

A tingle of something swept down Camellia's neck. Unease, maybe... a sensation she was not very familiar with, and so had trouble deciding what it was.

Mr. Fassett coughed, away from the phone, and then returned.

"I've not heard from her or her mother. They were... visiting family back East. And supposed to be back yesterday. I called the airline, and they hadn't boarded the flight. I kept calling family and—"

His voice began to break.

Ah, there. Faltering. Camellia knew what to do. It left a space for her to step in.

"Got it," she replied. "Look, it's probably bad weather, phone reception, something like that. I'm sure they're fine. I'll let you know the *very second* I hear from Selah. Promise."

The relief in his voice was thin, but it was there.

"Thank you."

Another cough.

"I just... the news is weird, you know?"

Well. She knew a little... but now she began to wonder.

"I just hope it's... not like... another pandemic or something."

Camellia swallowed, feeling uncomfortable.

"I'm sure it's no big deal." She oozed breezy reassurance. "I'll be in touch. Take care, Mr. Fassett."

"Okay. You too, Camellia. Give your dad my best."

"Mmkay. Bye now."

She ignored the torrent of sensory overload that passing time between classes brought. Normally she would filter through the many conversations for gossip; she was innately, uniquely talented when it came to picking it up and using it as she saw fit. But today, she was focused on something else.

Selah and her mother missing? A strange situation where her Mammaw had lived...

"Both back East," she muttered. "He didn't say where."

She shuddered, and then glanced around quickly to make sure no one saw, and just to be safe, tossed her hair and applied lip gloss. She glanced into her mirror compact and could see a little furrow between her ginger eyebrows, so she took a deep breath and relaxed her expression back into its normal imperiousness.

She murmured to her reflection, "Another fucking pandemic. Here we go again."

CHAPTER 7

PCH

Her irritation made her itch all over. Or perhaps it was the air pollution. The afternoon had taken on a honeyed hue, a Maxfield Parrish light, the clouds building up to the north and east in the mountains, coral and gold over bases of purple-gray. The mountains cloaked in amorphous, indigo cloud shadows. She regarded them with her brow creasing again; she didn't realize she was doing that...

"Who pissed in your granola?" someone snarked.

She sailed around like a gun turret and set her fierce, green eyes upon the Problematic named Landon.

"You would know about piss!" she cried. "Didn't you wet your pants the first semester of freshman year? Or was that a result of you fapping while watching the pep rally?"

Coils of guffaws and screeches of catty, raucous comments shot through the air like fireworks.

Landon stood and faced her, a full half-head taller. His perfectly faded, light brown hair struck her as vaguely fascist, and his crisp, high-end button-up shirt looked try-hard even in this setting.

The air between them crackled, or seemed to. Class was

now out, but the crowd gathered round, everyone ignoring the bell, the intercom, their rides.

Camellia caught sight of Wray over by the flagpole and she bristled.

"Look here, *Cuntmellia*," Landon began, and the crowd completely lost it. Phones, watches, handheld cameras flicked out from everywhere, catching sparks of sunlight. The band teacher leaned fully out of door to his classroom and gaped. "We all know you're a fucking fraud. You and your shitstain of a dad. Complete con; that's what my dad says."

The cheerleader Candace Ritter, Landon's erstwhile girl-friend, sidled up to him, short cheerleading skirt revealing spray-tanned legs, her perfectly coiffed, thousand-dollar hair foils gleaming in gold, bronze, and platinum... much like the jewelry circling her wrists and peeking out on her toes.

"Aw, Camellia!" cooed Candace, her vapid, thousand-yard-stare rich-bitch hazel eyes round and insipid. "Hurts to get it dished back to you, doesn't it, bestie?"

Camellia lowered her eyes just a tick, and arched her right eyebrow, tilting her fiery head to catch the strange afternoon light so that she appeared to have a halo of fire.

"Ohhh, *Candace*." Camellia extended the final syllable in a long hiss.

Dead silence all around. They could all hear a distant heli-copter *thwap-thwap-thwap* in the Malibu hills, up around the recreation area. The pause held everyone and everything else still, it seemed.

"Candace and Landon, *Candon! Landiss!*" and Camellia giggled. "You know, it's funny," she said more loudly. "Every *single day* I hear rumors about how my family's a fraud, how my father *lied* about our heritage." She sighed. "It's so unorig-inal, no? Kind of like the two of you. And as for fakes, you might want to keep your own sides of the street clean, you two. Human trafficking... tsk, tsk, Candon! Don't think some of us don't know where your families' money goes. All in the guise of mission work and charitable foundations." She clicked her tongue.

Landon clenched his fists. "That's defamation! I'll see you in court, bitch!"

"No," snapped Camellia, "I'll see your congressional daddy before Congress, if you don't fuck off. And Candace, everyone knows you're blowing his dad on the side."

Sharp gasps rang out, and Landon pivoted uncertainly on his feet, before turning to Candace... but that didn't matter to Camellia anymore. She saw the flash of a chiseled grin that she knew. Her face turned rosy, the light still gleaming on her hair, and she smiled a true smile and bounded away from everyone else toward the drop-off zone.

It was Syd, standing next to his Corvette, hands in pockets, muscular forearms shining in the sun. Wray, meanwhile, watched with cold curiosity as Camellia zeroed in on the young man. Wray then shuffled in their baggy pants over to a beat-up old blue Ford pickup truck, creaked the door open, climbed in, and slammed the door with a sharp metallic *bang*. Camellia blinked, noting the truck, before turning back to Syd.

"Hey," he said softly as she walked up to him, beaming. "Save that look for me, won't you?"

Camellia shook her head a bit and grinned at him. "What look?"

Without realizing it, her eyes darted to the now quite loud old pickup Wray had started and was now driving slowly. Wray pulled alongside Syd's vehicle and into Camellia's line of sight. They made eye contact. Camellia felt a surge of anger and blinked.

"That one," Syd answered.

He reached forward while she blinked, watching Wray slowly drive forward, and he traced her chin with his forefinger. He caught a stray lock of her vivid hair and swept it gently aside her long neck. Wray then left, out of her sight, and Camellia returned her focus fully back to Syd. She lowered her eyelids for a moment, then opened her eyes widely, locking her green gaze with his indigo blue one.

He was hard to read, but his pupils dilated when she did that. She laughed softly.

"What are you doing up here?" she asked, adjusting herself, posing, coquettish. She bit on her lower lip and then pushed it out again.

Syd sighed and with a lopsided grin said, "Well, I was in the area. Thought I might stop by. Want me to take you home?"

"Sure!" she chirped, and instantly chucked her backpack through the open passenger window.

Syd laughed. He opened the door for her, and she arranged her high-heeled, pale legs inside. He shut the door and walked around to the other side. As he sat down, Camellia leaned forward to check her phone, and her hair spilled away from her neck.

"I never noticed that before," Syd remarked.

She leaned back and secured her seatbelt.

"What?" she asked, confused.

"Your tattoo. On the back of your neck."

Her left hand shot to her neck and then back to her lap to join her other hand. She shrugged and grinned at him.

"Oh, that's nothing. Old tattoo." She draped her hair so that he could no longer see it.

"What's it of? Was it a flower?"

Something made her pause, and she felt her mouth go dry.

"Mmhmm," she answered. She pushed a bubble of some archaic emotion down into her little container in her mind.

"Which flower?"

She shrugged. "A camellia."

Syd gave a short laugh. "Of course!" As he pulled the Corvette away, Camellia spied Landon practically spitting in

Candace's face, and the girl wheeled, running off, Landon in pursuit.

Camellia felt a knot of cold dread seize her stomach.

The fuck is he going to do to her?

And she felt... something. She refused to admit to herself what it was.

"Hey, you okay, gorgeous?" Syd asked her.

She beamed back at him. Down into the box with that emotion.

"Fine! Weird day, huh?"

An odd flicker passed over Syd's face and his cut-glass jaw muscle twitched as he stared at the road ahead. His dark blue eyes went cold for a second like agate marbles. Camellia wondered.

"Pretty weird, all right," he murmured.

Then, "Hey, before we head back to your place, what say we take a drive out past Zuma?"

Camellia let out a relieved sigh. "Yes, please."

Syd lowered the top on the car and watched the red-gold current of Camellia's long hair arc out like a living torch. Her sunglasses on, her lips scarlet, she looked every bit the part of a movie star, and she knew it. And she knew *he* knew it, and grinned at him.

So off they raced, westward along the Pacific Coast Highway, Syd flooring the car when he could get away with it on the straighter sections, Camellia laughing at his daring as he took the curves sharply. The blue bowl of the Pacific beckoned, the sun blazed, the sparkles danced upon the wavetops like flecks of mica.

She felt *alive*. For a moment she forgot her irritation with her father, the chaotic duty of being the Top Bitch at school, the strange tension with Wray, Selah missing, the weird shit with her Mammaw's old home... it was all wind and waves and fluid air surging around her. The immense power and calm and beauty of the Pacific, the air currents that attempted to tame or rile it by turns; this sea was timeless to Camellia, immutable even as it shifted constantly. In many ways, the Pacific Ocean was the mother she craved. And as Syd whisked her around the slim and scenic necklace of shifting land that made the highway famous, she did not realize how much of that sensation was tied to the fact that her mother likely drew her last breath not of air, but of that very ocean, before she had died.

CHAPTER 8

STORM WARNING

Her dad's message pinged her.

"Where are you?"

She twisted her mouth, thinking of something pithy, but kept it short.

"Getting Vitamin D. You'd be proud."

"No. Where are you? Am I seeing this right? Are you out near Zuma?"

She rolled her eyes back and forth, skyward, and shook her head.

"Yeah, why?"

"Get back to the house this instant."

Snorting, she clicked her tongue. She tossed aside an errant coil of red hair that had fallen onto her wrist and caught on the watch. That hair fluttered out into the wind as the car sped along. Syd glanced over at her and continued on.

"WTF?" Her fingernails clicked the reply on the surface of the watch.

"Camellia."

He never called her by her full name. She felt a jagged bolt of both anger and surprise.

"Whoever the driver is, tell them to turn around and take

you home. Right now. We'll talk when you get there. I'll be watching."

She sent an eye roll emoji back and a wrote, "Fine."

Then she flicked the phone down into her purse and chucked that in the floorboard at her feet.

"Problems?" Syd asked, as they sat at a stoplight. She could hear the surf foaming nearby.

"Dad," she grumbled. "Wants me to come home."

"Oh, is he there?"

She didn't catch the strange change in pitch to his voice at first, although she wondered about it later.

"No, but he told me to call him as soon as I get there."

"Did he say why?"

"No, he's just being a twat. Why don't we walk the beach?"

Syd caught her eye before the light turned green and then he surged forward. "We'll drive out, but I'll turn around."

"The fuck for? I thought you were taking me to the beach."

"I need to get you back."

His wrist buzzed; he glanced down, and he scowled. Shrugging, he said, "Work. I'll do a quick drive by."

Cold disappointment washed over her, colder than the deep blue waves offshore.

"So now both of you want to wreck my afternoon," she sulked.

"Sorry, Caramel." Syd's tone sounded apologetic. "Duty calls for us both."

Another message pinged her wrist, and, prepared to unleash a stream of epithets at her father, she instead drew in a delicate gasp.

"What is it?" Syd asked, eyeing her for a few seconds and whipping around a curve.

"Fucking *fuck*. The masquerade. I was supposed to—fuck it, I'll take care of it later."

"Did you say *masquerade*?" Bemusement in Syd's voice then.

She blinked at him coquettishly.

"You could come."

He laughed.

"What, is this at your school?"

"Yes, unfortunately. In that tasteless basketball stadium slash auditorium, can you imagine?"

"Not really, no."

"Well, it is. As bland as a barn house. It's giving *Stepford Wives* vibes. I'm transforming it into something worth a shit. Glamming it up."

"Sounds like you're the right person for the job."

"Well, along with the Cadre."

Syd slowed and turned his car around close to Zuma Beach, without entering the road up to the Point. The water rippled: cobalt farther out, turquoise closer to shore, and flecked with diamond sun shimmer. The arc of beach curving like a sliver of abalone shell. The mountains ochre and mauve. She loved this view, but not as much as the one from Point Dume above it. It gave her a strange ache, like she was missing something.

"Did you say the *Cadre*?"

"Mmhmm."

"What is that, a band?"

She shrieked with laughter. "No!" She shoved her manicured hand into his shoulder gently and drew her fingernails away slowly, feeling the muscles. She met his gaze then and felt herself grow hot.

"The Cadre," she told him, lowering her sunglasses to meet his gold-flecked, dark blue eyes with her bright green ones, "is the pack of queens who kick ass in design. Second only to me in bitchiness."

Syd laughed out loud at that. "As long as they know who's boss!"

JENDIA GAMMON

"They *doooo*," she cooed, grinning.

Syd reached across and held her face in his palm for a moment.

"They don't know what they've got, with you," he murmured.

She blushed. And she shimmied a bit in her seat.

"I hope you do."

"Oh, I do," he smirked. They were off again, sailing up and over the hills along the coast highway, and heading east, her hair a brilliant rampart fluttering in the wind.

He drove up to the curb of her house.

She tried catching his eye again.

He was looking at his watch, which was glowing soft green. He grimaced, a brief shadow passing over his face before he returned to his amiable, handsome, mature jock-looking self.

"Problem?" she questioned.

"Ah, just some shit going down somewhere," he said in a level voice.

She bit her lower lip.

"It's a pandemic again, isn't it?"

His lip twitched.

"Don't you worry about it; I know you well enough. Whatever happens, you'll figure it out."

She went cold at that.

So it IS another goddamn pandemic.

"We… we're equipped."

She tossed her hair.

"No doubt," he answered without looking at her.

He kept looking at his watch, keeping it turned away from her so she couldn't see.

"Aren't you going to say 'bye'?" she prodded him.

"Oh, sorry, Caramel," Syd said. He was the only person she allowed to call her that; she loved it. He dipped his head. "'Til next time."

She looked at him expectantly, but he simply winked at her.

She heaved a big sigh.

"Guess so," she said, and shut the passenger door a little forcefully.

He was off in a flash, and she scowled to herself.

Her watch chimed.

It was her dad again.

Huffing an irritated sigh, she walked up toward the front door. A distant flash caught her eye, and she looked up toward the hills. The light looked even stranger now than it had earlier, and something... (was it fog?) shimmered there. Another time, she might not have noticed such a thing, but today, it struck her as odd. Smoke? But she didn't see the telltale string of it wafting above and smudging the air. Also, it was more humid. Not the usual nightly, cool, marine layer humidity. Something far soupier. She flicked through her phone's apps and looked at the weather.

"Wait, what the fuck?" she murmured.

"Tropical storm warning. Unusual, rare tropical cyclone in the eastern Pacific threatens Southern California."

She sniffed. "Fun." That explained the moisture surge ahead of the thing, now off the coast of the Baja peninsula. So far, the wave action had not reached Malibu's shores. The Pacific Ocean lived up to its name today, but that would not last.

And Camellia knew—although she would never admit publicly to such knowledge—that the water temperatures of L.A.'s coast were too cold to sustain a tropical system, unlike East Coast counterparts in warmer waters. The thing would likely fall apart in a number of ways: hit the cold water and dissipate, hit the combination of complex topography like L.A.'s mountains and fall apart, but maybe not before the orographic lift dumped rain on the windward side of the area... and so forth. It had happened before.

"I swear to God, if this fucks with the masquerade," she gritted her teeth bitterly.

She cast her eyes again up at the strange cloud-like glimmer in the hills.

Maybe just some storm-related thing, she pondered.

But something about it wasn't right. She'd never seen anything quite like that before, in any tropical area; and she'd had to bail on a few yacht parties in her young life in tropical regions, thanks to hurricanes and the occasional intrusive sky-finger of a waterspout, down in the Florida Keys. Nothing ended a party faster than a burst of gale-force wind sending the drinks into the sea.

Blinking, she entered the house and shut the door. There sat a stack of packages, one gaudily emblazoned "Kate Mates." That was Kate Switch's subscription program, an exorbitant monthly (or bi-monthly, for those feeling toothsome for more overpriced and essentially worthless swag) box that Kate comped for Camellia in exchange for occasional influencer posts. Even though Camellia had insisted upon paying, despite the price tag that could have singed even *her* already fiery eyebrows, Kate had waved it off with a giggle.

"I need someone to show off my shit! Work, my Scarlet Bitch!"

Camellia had cackled at that, and they had indulged in a little shoulder-nudging, bitchy jiggle-and-giggle fest before Kate floated off to some other starlet, breezy and diaphanous, much like the depth of her thought processes.

Camellia sighed a little and called her dad.

Surprisingly, he answered immediately.

"I'm home," she said abruptly.

"Good. I tracked you."

His voice sounded tense to her.

"What's up?" she asked casually, but her heart rate betrayed her.

"Look, I... I'll be out of town a few more days."

She let out a sharp sigh. "Again? Where, Vegas?"

"Doesn't matter," he rumbled.

"Oh, so it doesn't matter where *you* are but you're keeping tabs on *me*?"

"Meems," he said, voice escalating. "What were you doing out by Zuma?"

"The fuck is it to you?" she barked back.

"I don't want you out there. Do you understand?"

The look on his face set her blinking, troubled. She shook her head.

"Why?"

He closed his eyes for a second, and when he opened them, they looked red. He said in a breaking voice, "Just, please. Promise me you won't go out there again. I can't... Promise me, Camellia."

Her pulse hammering in her ears, she snapped, "Fine, Jesus! You're being weird."

"Look," he said, running his hands through his thinning hair. "Things *are* weird."

"Then why don't you come home?"

The question hung there in the air like an obstructive bit of cloud, and a long pause unnerved her.

"I will soon. Okay? Just. Just take care of yourself. I may ask Darla to drop in."

"Darla!" she cried with a caustic laugh. Darla was her dad's cousin; older, judgmental, and, crucially, not rich.

"She can stay in the mother-in-law," her dad pleaded, referring to the guest cottage in the back of the house.

"The hell she *will*," whispered Camellia, enraged at the idea of such a thing.

"Meems, don't be mean," her father pleaded, but even his face reflected the absurdity of such a statement. He rolled his eyes. "Whatever. You've got plenty of food, water, all the stuff you need. I'll be back soon. Love you."

"Mm," she answered, and was about to hit the end button, but then, "Love you."

The call severed them.

Plunking her phone down on the marble foyer table, she eyed the packages from Kate.

"I hope there's some good masks in there," she grumbled. "Gonna be one helluva masquerade this year."

CHAPTER 9

MASKED

She loathed pep rallies. *Loathed*. And yet some part of her loved the spotlight, on the rare occasions in which she was MC. She could dispense with the cartwheels of the insipid cheerleaders and the jocks snickering at their exposed crotches in mid-spin. The drumbeats of the school band made her grind her teeth, as if they prepared the school for war. But she knew how to hold a room, and the school administrators knew that as well. While she would never be universally loved by any of them, they could count on her to electrify an audience for the milliseconds of attention any teenagers could possibly latch onto anything.

And so, she found herself in the heaving, undulating mass of teens, the pale-gold, uber-waxed floor of the basketball court gleaming from the bright overhead lights, the bleachers creaking and popping in all the din as everyone clambered over them or stomped on them. She could smell the body odor of the jocks, the overpriced hair products of the cheerleaders, the stench of desperation from anyone not already in a clique, and the putrefaction of all the others jockeying for one spark of attention in a vacuous part of their lives. The light was ghastly upon her pale skin, making her freckles look orange, her hair a strange orange-brown-purple mix, the deeper garnet hues masked. She *hated* this. But she'd mixed her lip color accordingly and wore a low-cut, fitted-bodice teal gown with broad shoulders, wildly and outrageously out of place, rather like something a 1940s movie star would have worn. She looked more mature than anyone there, as a result. She could have taken the mic and crooned into it, and she imagined a jazz trio blooming from behind her; the lights going low, the thrumming of a bass and the hoots of a clarinet as a haze snaked through the dark club...

God, I fucking WISH.

But no. Just hideous lighting, ungrateful Malibu teens, barely controlled by the clueless teachers and administrators jangling keys upon wrist cords, walkie-talkies at their hips squawking, hissing for everyone to be quiet. She rolled her vivid green eyes at them all.

A whistle screeched out, and Coach Russell bellowed, "Quiet please!"

The din diminished slightly, and Camellia's mic pierced them all with brief feedback, which set her head raging. Clenching her jaw, she smiled, bristling, tossing her mane of hair, her bleached teeth vivid between raspberry-hued lips (a mixture of *Enchante Emollient Stain Number 45: Deep Berry*, with UV protection, and *Spill It Number 107*). Really, she was baring her teeth at them all.

"May I have your attention, please?" her clear, contralto voice echoed through the auditorium.

"No you may not, bitch!" someone called out through cupped hands. She squinted but could not discern who it was, and the ripple of cackles and snickers made her cheeks turn red under her blush (*Enchante Enchanted Crème Blush*).

She smirked in defiance. Shimmying enough to set the deep teal satin suit reflecting splendidly even in that nauseating light, she caught everyone in her sway finally. She cleared her throat.

"Darlings. Beloveds. Puling chits." She grinned, knowing most of them didn't understand the final insult. "We have forty-eight hours to transform this circa 1987 particle-board pavilion into the toniest place in L.A. We're talking Oscars, Emmys… let's call it an EGOT."

Whoops of approval from the audience.

She lowered her head and gave them all a Lauren Bacall fuck-you stare.

"I want to see every single one of you contributing in some way. Send your dollars, support the causes we've chosen this year. Or maybe I'll let slip some unfortunate facts on *Kate and Switch*. And y'all *know* I know more than the *Reporter*."

She wagged her finger and snickered as the crowd undulated with laughter and hisses and boos. Landon caught her eye, then, and stared at her coldly. Next to him, Candace sat prim and stiff, wearing a white mock turtleneck pulled up to her chin despite the heat.

Camellia's false smile flickered momentarily at that.

Now, why would she need to be so covered up?

She met Landon's gaze again, and bored hatred into him.

You hit her, didn't you?

His gaze faltered and fell away, and she knew she was right. She didn't like Candace. But she knew that girl had to get away from Landon.

Camellia tossed her hair back and pulled forth something shimmering on a stick: a sparkling chartreuse masquerade mask. She brought it up to her face and called out to the crowd, "The game is afoot!"

And then she curtsied… mostly to wild applause.

Flouncing off the podium, she swept forth, a field marshal before the Cadre, and one of their members, Dewayne, bowed to her.

"Oh my *goddess*."

"Mother!"

"Slay."

"Fab."

"Killed it."

The Cadre sprinkled praise upon her with every step as she walked away from the podium. Two long tables stood off to the left of her, from which banners hung with glittery mask illustrations. Students began lining up to get tickets. Many would pay via app, but they would miss out on the special swag of goody bags donated by Kate Switch. (Camellia suspected that these were leftovers from Kate's Malta party the year before.) The trick worked, and Camellia sighed in satisfaction as the sales-meter on a propped-up tablet zoomed skyward.

"Oh my God, who are you going as?" Dewayne whispered loudly to Mel Venegas.

"My favorite exótico, do you even have to ask, bitch?" Mel rolled his eyes.

"What was their name?" another of the Cadre (and also a Pinstripe) asked. That was Michel.

"Cassandro!" cried Mel. "You heretic!" He crossed himself.

"Seriously!" hissed Dewayne.

"What about you, Queen?" Michel asked Camellia. The Cadre curled around her like a comma.

She flounced, and they gushed again, seeing now her full, Postwar glamorous outfit. "It's a surprise," she teased them, blowing each a kiss. She drew out little, special velvet bags from her purse, and winked at them as she doled them out.

"*Ohmyfuckinggod*, what are these?" squealed Dewayne.

"For the party, beloved," Camellia answered breathily.

They screeched in delight.

Her mischievous grin faded when Wray walked up to her and said, "Do we have to dress up for this thing?"

Camellia stood ramrod straight, leaned forward with her hands on teal-silk hips, and murmured, "Oh, don't worry. I don't expect you to have anything *remotely* resembling proper attire. Just show up in your usual, I dunno... hayseed persona," she gestured, "or whatever this is."

The Cadre guffawed and Wray blanched.

"Forget I asked."

Wray turned aside and the odd light of the stadium struck their face.

Camellia blinked.

Something wasn't right.

Discoloration.

Thinking quickly, she said crisply, "Fine. I'll do you a solid. I'll loan you somethi—"

"Like I'd *ever* take charity from you!" said Wray forcefully.

"Would you shut up?" snapped Camellia. "I—I need your help."

She cringed inwardly.

Wray blew a raspberry. Camellia couldn't fault them for *that*.

"I very much doubt it."

Oh, goddammit.

"Fucking wear what you want, but I could *actually* use your help. You have a truck, right?"

Wray blinked.

"I'm surprised you noticed."

"Well, you sort of made it a *point* by slowing down and staring at me like a fucking freak the other day."

Wray blushed.

Michel leaned in for a second and, glancing between Wray and Camellia (both of them with cheeks aflame) and suggested, "We've got this. Truly."

"No," Camellia said firmly; and that was that. "Wray is new here and needs to know the ropes." She smirked. "Who better to teach them than me?"

The looks on the Cadre's faces mirrored her own inner unease.

She did her best to ignore this.

"Walk and talk," she said to Wray. It was a command.

Among all the bustle and gossip, Camellia spoke in serious tones.

"First off, I need to get you up to speed."

"No, you do—"

"Yes. I do. Shut up! Listen to me. If you *must know*, and note! I'm doing this as a *favor*," she said acidly, while Wray huffed out a disgruntled breath and adjusted their sunglasses on the top of their head, "here's how it breaks down: the Cadre, whom you've met. The Problematics are detention types. The Bubbleheads: rich, dumb, Malibu blondes. The Jugs... the twins, I'm sure you've noticed"—Wray snorted— "The Glitches, aka tech bros and their ilk. The Vamps... goths, etc. The Ballsacks: jocks, in other words. The Monistat 7s: cheerleaders. The Pinstripes, the fashion gays—some overlap with the Cadre but not as much. Team Onyx: lesbians. The Bandages: band kids. The Ku Klux Kunts: my little pet name for the white supremacist bitches. The Holy Rollers: Christian autumn-type girls, about to level up with boots, lattes, cowboy hats, and leaves in about a month or so. The Chuds: right-wing assholes, incels, that sort. And there's some bleed-through between some of these groups, natch."

"Why are you telling me all this?" Wray demanded, halting.

Camellia shrugged. "I have the best understanding of this place." *Except for you.*

"It's all bullshit though!"

"Yeah, just like every single high school there ever was."

Wray snickered.

"For once, you're right."

Camellia lifted her chin high and threw her shoulders back. Wray's eyes darted over her furtively, but she noticed, and she almost squirmed.

"I'm always right."

"I'm gonna regret this *helping*," Wray grumbled. "I already do."

Camellia fairly growled, "Oh, I do too."

Their eyes locked, and Camellia tried to suppress a tingling sensation making its way through her. Wray's stormy-hued eyes were deep and clear. Camellia's thoughts slipped through several adjectives trying to capture their hue; she was masterful with color matching. But she had never seen this color in anything but storms. It was indefinable. As was the feeling that looking into them gave her.

But she could see Wray continually pulling the side of their hair down, held in place by the sunglasses on their head.

The hair was an attempt to hide bruises.

It wasn't working.

Camellia had a duty of care now, and she very much disliked it. But she knew, deep down, she had to do something. Even if she hated it, even if she and Wray hated each other.

This will be my greatest experiment of all, she thought grimly, leading Wray away from the massive crowd and out into the afternoon sun, which, once again looked filtered in an odd way.

CHAPTER 10

DANSE MACABRE

"Be still!" snapped Camellia, taking her blending blush delicately to Wray's cheeks. She barked past the teen's head: "Straighten up!" toward Dewayne, Mel, and the rest of the Cadre.

They guffawed.

"You're asking *gays* to straighten up, Queen?" hollered Mel.

Ok, they got me this time. Her lips twitched as she stifled a smile, but Wray caught sight of it and smirked back at her. She pretended not to notice.

"Do the moves again!" she shouted back. "Don't make me embarrass you all tonight. I'll do it."

Mel and Dewayne nodded to each other, and Mel muttered, "It's true."

Wray watched her with their deep, gray-blue-green eyes, which Camellia did not stay in contact with for long. She was focused solely on covering their face with makeup. But she kept glancing back at Wray's eyes, and Wray caught her gaze every time. She turned aside to swallow, so that Wray could not see her face for a moment.

She beheld the entire group dressed in Revolutionary

outfits of varying elaboration, Camellia's the most extraordinary.

She commanded into her phone, "Play 'Stand and Deliver' again," and the song blared. The Cadre shifted in unison to the song. She shimmied her own hips and conducted the group with her left hand while placing dark eyeshadow on Wray's lids with her right hand.

"A real multi-tasker," Wray noted wryly.

"I can do a lot of things at once, it's true," Camellia grinned, eyes half-lidded.

Finally, the two of them *did* make full eye contact. Camellia was glad for the white matte makeup on her cheeks. She looked away quickly, feeling heat rising up her neck.

"That should do it," she said crisply.

"Thanks," Wray said, offering a hand to shake.

Camellia gave it a shake and found Wray's hand both strong and tender. She turned away from them and coiled her hair, pinned it with bobby pins, and looked into the lighted mirror she'd brought with her from home. She adjusted the powdered wig and pinned it appropriately. She dusted herself and turned to preen.

"Nice ass in that outfit," catcalled a junior.

"Even nicer out of it!" she called back, and a chorus of hoots and one "Yeow!" rose around them.

Wray snorted.

"You sure know how to turn a phrase."

"I know how to turn a lot of things," murmured Camellia.

"Oh?"

The room seemed very hot to her suddenly, and she fanned herself. Wray stood solid next to her.

"So... now what?" they asked.

Camellia crinkled her brow.

"Now you can fuck off!" she answered simply. "Go on then. Bye."

And she waved her fingers at Wray. Wray rolled her eyes and shook her head.

"So long, ice queen."

"Like I've not heard that one before," muttered Camellia.

"Oh, I've got more choice words for you than that," Wray returned bitterly.

"I'll just bet you do, hayseed!" Camellia smiled sweetly at them. "Off you pop, now. I've got places to see and people to do. Oh, whoops."

She grinned and turned away from Wray, but fought a visible shiver. She didn't exactly like their exchange, and she wasn't sure why. She blinked several times and adjusted her wig as though it were a highly fragile crown. She felt, indeed, rather royal, despite the irony of her outfit.

She moved among the Cadre to direct their dance moves, and finally satisfied—or as much as she could ever be, about anything—she gave them a curt nod. That was enough for them all to relax, joke, and prep their outfits.

It was all a haze to Camellia after that. She felt strangely distracted.

Just what sort *of choice words, Wray?* She caught herself thinking. That angered her. Why was she thinking about them at all? And why did it matter how Wray had stared up at her, so intently, while she added makeup to their face? She remembered Wray's cinnamon-scented breath upon her neck —that's how close they stood together.

She tossed back a sparkling water with a glug of mango juice and grenadine, its stir stick a handled mask, and she greeted costumed teens and some teachers as they flooded the glittery ball court. Her "helpers" had indeed done the best they could. Balloons and disco balls shivered everywhere, hiding the bleachers. Camera drones hovered at the ready for formal pictures. Tables were laden with punch and soda and water, catered hors d'oeuvres, extra masks, and raffle tickets. She was the head organizer, and each helper had done their part. She could relax now and enjoy herself. Inasmuch as she ever did, anyway.

When everyone was properly fed and hydrated and raucous, the dance sets began.

She winked at the DJ—really just one of the freshmen—and they began playing Adam and the Ants. The Cadre spun artfully out of the shadows, and she joined them at their head. The trumpets of the song rang out and the group began their routine, which she had helped them rehearse over a period of weeks. Every movement had the audience in rapturous shouts and applause, thumping and bumping. When it ended, she swept off her troubadour hat as she and the Cadre bowed. She threw the hat into the air like a great Frisbee, and someone caught it with a whoop.

She sauntered off in her outfit to retrieve water. The music thundered on. She felt her wristwatch vibrate, rolled her eyes, and paid it no mind. She held court as everyone complimented her, or outright hit on her. She took it in stride, and felt empowered in her costume, as though she were impervious to anything. This went on, and she danced from time to time inside rings of hooting partiers, back-to-back with some of them, vamping it up.

Then, quite abruptly, the mode of the crowd changed. And it wasn't even halfway through the masquerade.

She swept her eyes over spotlit teens, covered in special effects holographic lighting projected from above or from drones. There was a dynamic shift happening. There were… to her horror… *distractions*.

"What's going on? Are you all seriously looking at your phones tonight? *Tonight*?"

The music warbled a moment and Camellia's sharp eyes took in contortions on the faces of the other teens, clamoring around someone's tablet, or looking at their phones or watches.

She raised her voice. "What. The fuck. Is going. On!" and

her clarion shout made them all whip their heads around to look at her before turning back.

One of the Jugs bounced past, wearing a vivid red cape; she halted, turned, and twisted her mask a bit off her eyes to squawk, "Didn't Selah say she went to Atlanta?"

Camellia felt a cold spike of dread shoot through her, but she pushed it down, just as she pushed down so many other things.

"Yeah, why?" she snapped, gritting her teeth at the chaos unfolding around her.

"It's—uh, it's under attack or something," the girl said, biting her lower lip. "You might want to check on her."

Camellia stared. "*Excuse* me?"

She marched, regal in her jacket and powdered wig, up to the group huddled around phones and shouted, "Somebody better tell me what's going on *fast* or I'm spilling all your shitty details on the mic in five minutes."

They all went silent, chiefly because they knew she was serious; and she knew that they knew.

Mel swept over to her, followed by Dewayne; she could also see Agatha off to one side, in a dazzling green outfit covered in leaves, twisting her hands together, her eyes large and bright and... worried.

"Camellia, honey," Mel simpered, and that set her on edge. She flushed.

"What?" she spat. She was losing control of this party now. She could see Mr. Levin speaking urgently to someone over near the speakers, then the two of them walking quickly away from the sound and out into the hall. She did not catch who he was speaking with.

"It's just—" Dewayne began, as he, Mel, and Michel glanced at each other through their masks. By the widening of their eyes, Camellia detected fear. "We don't want to upset you..."

"But *maaaaybe*," Mel drew out the word almost musically, "we should… cancel the rest of the evening?"

"Cancel!" she cried, and she threw her shoulders back like the master and commander she was. "Get a hold of yourselves. What, there's some terrorist attack on Atlanta? What is it?"

"Uhhh…" Wray murmured, and Camellia spun around to glare at them. "It's not just Atlanta. It's… like… most of the upper South."

Camellia tilted her head, scrunched up her eyes and said, "Say *what* now?"

The throng of students stared at her, with her hands on her hips; she dashed forward into the cluster, seized a tablet and held it up. She flicked off a few ads to reveal the headline beneath. Overhead, "Mr. Brightside" began to play. It angered her to be distracted by the song's fast beat and clever words, while she read in huge font, "BIO-ATTACK ON ATLANTA."

She stared at the image and ignored the other kids swarming around her like bees, clamoring to see her reaction.

"The fuck is this?" she growled, expanding the image. "What am I even looking at?"

Agatha stepped forward, her leafy outfit glittering green, and said, "Vines. It's vines."

Camellia hissed, "What? *Vines*? A bio attack by… *vines*?"

"Watch the video!" cried Agatha. "I have family there."

Camellia noted how the girl jutted her hands, and how her jaw ground.

She played the video of the article and did not understand what she was seeing.

A deep green, pulsating mass roared across a highway, thrusting through cars, twisting around them, crushing them like cans; the video skipped with warnings of graphic images… Chance Freeling grabbed the pad and shouted, "Watch *this*. Nobody's filtered out this stuff," and brought up an uncensored video.

By now no one was dancing; the disco balls whirred overhead, and the musical choices grew ever more ridiculous in light of what Camellia and the others watched. Someone screamed. Another person vomited. Camellia simply stared, taking it in.

Her wrist chimed.

She ignored it.

She watched the screen.

Green tendrils whipped all around anything in their path, surging and snapping, sending buses plunging off overpasses, tearing along sidewalks, and finally... squeezing people to death, their intestines rupturing, blood squirming, eyeballs popping, screams undulating.

And then... the helicopters. Two hovering over the scene trying to get footage for the news, recorded by a small drone... incredibly fast bolts of green shot into the air in all directions, and several wound around the helicopters...

And brought them crashing down.

Camellia heard snatches of bizarre words: "National guard..."

"The military..."

"The President..."

"Stay indoors..."

"Stay away from windows..."

"Avoid plants..."

A bubble of something between a gasp and a laugh shot out of her mouth and for the first time, she covered it in shock.

"Thank *fuck* it's not here!" someone shouted.

"It's all through the South though."

"Someone said it's in Chicago."

"Bull-fucking-shit. This is fake news."

"Oh fuck, it's sucking up the water along the Great Lakes."

"Fuck off, you're overreacting."

Camellia scowled at her wrist, until she saw two things: Her dad's texts, and... Syd's.

She ignored her father's and focused on Syd's.

"Hey, can you call me? Soon. It's urgent."

She turned away from them all, adjusted her wig, and stepped up to the mic. A sickly blue-purple stage light shone down on her silver wig and dark lips, giving her a ghostly hue. She said loudly, "It appears there's a situation happening in the news. I'll leave it to the administrators to decide what to do. But maybe for now, let's give one last hurrah to our seniors for the Masquerade! Let's fucking *dance* like there's no tomorrow!"

Shouts of approval rang out, and the music pumped again; she smiled her perfunctory, model-perfect smile. Then she bolted.

She walked quickly, her heels clacking, and slipped out one end of the hallway opposite of Mr. Levin. She heard his voice ("Camellia!") and pretended she hadn't. She kept walking and returned the corner out of earshot. She slipped her phone out of her jacket and dialed Syd.

He answered quickly, to her surprise. Her cheeks tingled.

"You okay?" he asked, his voice sounding urgent.

"Yeah, I'm fine," she replied, trying to believe it.

"Sweet Caramel, I'm in town. Can I stop by your place?"

Now her cheeks burned even more.

"Oh really?" She attempted to act casual, but her heart began behaving strangely. She felt a little dizzy.

"Yeah, I... might be away for a little while. It's important stuff. I'd love to see you before I go."

"Okay, sure," she replied, heart in her mouth.

"Cool, I'll see you in a bit."

"Wait!" she gasped.

"Yeah?"

"I'm—I'm at the school party."

"When's it over?"

"Now, I think," and she knew when she said it that she was probably right; no matter what sort of denial the other teens cloaked about themselves, the vibe was chilled.

"I'll pick you up."

"Oh. Okay. Um. I look a little funky," and she giggled, touching her wig.

"You never look funky. I'll see you in ten."

"Oh, you're that close?"

"I'm that fast."

She turned on her heels and walked back toward the auditorium. She grimaced. Mr. Levin stood there. The look on his face made her furrow her brow.

What's he up to?

"Camellia, can I speak to you for a minute?"

She tapped her phone with her gloved hand.

"Actually, I've got to go," she told him with an innocent shake of the head. "My... father needs me."

"Okay, but just for one second."

She would've bitten out an insulting response, but his tone confused her. His dark eyes, blinking through his glasses, looked disturbed.

"Yes, Mr. Levin?" she asked, in almost a singsong voice.

"Do you... are you in touch with your mother's former colleagues, by chance?"

She twisted her head back and forth and stared him in the eyes while saying, "What on God's green earth makes you ask that? I don't know who any of them *are*."

"Well, not true," Mr. Levin shook his head. "You know *me*."

She blinked at him.

"*You*?" she said sternly. "My mom never knew you."

"Actually, she did. Look, I... did she leave any of her office work behind, did your dad keep any of it?"

"Mr. Levin, you're sounding like a creeper," she snapped, hands on her hips.

He held his hands up and then swept them through his afro. "It sounds weird, yes. But... it could be important. Maybe I could speak to your dad?"

"He's busy," came her curt and fast reply.

"But you said you're going to him—"

She sighed and glared at him. "You can call him if you want, but don't count on a response."

Mr. Levin sighed and steepled his fingers under his chin. He looked at her through his round glasses, which winked like soap bubbles in the light.

"Camellia, look, I knew your mom. We worked together. What's happening right now... she'd have known about it. We *talked* about it."

"What do you mean?"

She was completely confused. The noise of revelers and gossipers spilled out of the party and into the hall, along with the bumping bass from the music, and all the glitter from many masks spinning into the air. It was all dazzling and beautiful and terrible at once; and overwhelming and nauseating besides. She held her fingers to her temples.

"I mean the disaster. In the South. It's—it's something she predicted."

A wave of vertigo overcame Camellia, and she threw her gloved hands out. Mr. Levin caught them and held them still.

"I don't know anything about this shit," she said thickly. She pulled her hands away from his and yanked off her wig. She began unpinning her red hair with her right hand while holding onto the wig with her left.

Bedlam and partying and gruesome words "...did you fucking *see that thing*? Ripped his head right off!"

"...gross as hell, right up through the toilets too."

"...really goddamn glad we live where there's like no plants."

"...you dumbass, we have plants everywhere."

"...yeah, but it's a desert."

"...yeah, but we have a fucking hurricane coming."

The storm. She'd forgotten about the storm churning west of the Baja. No wonder her head ached. The barometric pressure throughout the L.A. basin had plummeted, and the air now felt syrupy and smelled fetid.

She blinked through her mask, her copper hair now all down her shoulders, tousled but free from its former protection. She said in a low voice, "I truly wish I could help you, Mr. Levin."

"Just… if she had anything in her office… it could help…" and his voice trailed off as she waved at him and walked away. "If you do find something, let me know."

Wray caught sight of Camellia and approached her as she distractingly paced down the flickering hallway toward the front door of the school.

"Hey," Wray called.

Camellia paused for a second, not processing at first who had spoken to her. She frowned when she realized.

"Hey, so," Wray continued, "thanks."

Camellia lifted her chin in regal fashion. "For?"

"You know, the makeu—oh, forget it."

"I already had," she said, giving Wray a withering look.

"Good party," stammered Wray.

"Well, it *was*," she replied acidly, and their eyes met for several seconds.

"So, you're leaving?" Wray asked.

"Mmhmm." Camellia broke eye contact.

The guttural sound of a Corvette rang through the hall.

Wray's mouth fell open.

"Him again?"

Camellia shook her head. "What's it to you, Wraith?" she hissed.

"What's so great about him?"

"Well, for starters, he's an actual *adult*. So few of those around, no matter the age. Kind of a refreshing change."

Wray puffed out a sigh. "I don't get it. You insult everybody, but there's a big red circle around someone you don't insult at all. Don't you see it? Who is that guy? What's he want with a teenager?"

Agatha then stepped up next to Wray, nodding in agreement: "There's a word for men like that. Groomer."

Camellia rolled her eyes. "Oh, you too, is it? Ganging up on me?" Her words were bitter, clipped. "Please. He's got better things to do than be a predator. He's legit *saving the country*."

"By hanging out with a rich teen girl in Malibu?" Wray barbed.

"Maybe he actually appreciates me!" said Camellia archly. "Anyway, time for me to go."

"Maybe you're being conned," Agatha suggested.

"Maybe he seems nice now, but he'll hurt you later," Wray pointed out, and then they pulled their sleeves down further over their hands.

But Camellia saw. More bruises.

I can't deal with this right now.

"Well. Goodnight, children. Don't stay up. And stay away from *plants*. Or something."

She snorted, shook her head, and marched out of the school, dropping the costume wig in the trashcan as she did.

She had better places to be. *And a hotter person to be with*, she thought.

For there stood Syd, leaning against his car, arms folded, grinning at the red-headed girl with the chalk-white makeup, dressed as a Revolutionary, ready for anything.

He was ready for her.

Chapter 11

In Bloom

Syd grinned at her, lowering his eyelids just a tick, as Camellia settled into the passenger's seat and adjusted her stockings. The epaulets on her costume jacket caught her hair, but she kept it on, for the air had chilled, feeling sluggish and damp. Still, the storm to the south hadn't quite reached the California bight. The weather app on her watch kept pinging her with watches that morphed into warnings. She ignored each one. She also ignored her father's texts, because she much preferred looking at Syd. His muscles bulged as he gripped the steering wheel, tossing an occasional smirk at her, and her face tingled each time. There was an unspoken crackling of the air, both outside and inside that car. An expectant moment, like just before a lightning strike. Everything felt heavy to Camellia, weighted with importance, with *something*. Something was about to happen. She felt the thrill of it course through her and rubbed her hands on her thighs.

"Cold?" asked Syd.

She shivered but shook her head.

"No, not really."

Still, she felt her seat grow warmer, for he'd turned on the seat controls.

"You know, it always feels like I've pissed myself when the seat warmers start," she said with a laugh.

He laughed too, and reached over to turn it off, but she touched his right hand with her left one, and so he kept it on, and took her fingers into his. He then brought both their hands down to the gear shift, and she could feel his power shifting the car.

Control.

She beamed in admiration at him in the dim light of the car. Every part of her coursed with energy, feeling his hand in hers. Her heart began steadily hammering a bit faster, the closer Syd took her to her house.

As they turned onto her street, Camellia caught sight of an old pickup truck, and she gasped.

Is that Wray?

A coil of fury welled inside her.

But then she saw that the pickup was a rusted, faded gray, and a Chevy at that. Not a blue Ford.

Syd watched her and squinted.

"What's up?"

She giggled, took her hand off his, and adjusted her epaulets. "Oh, nothing. I thought it was maybe one of the... the... gardeners working late. They shouldn't be."

Syd grinned as he parked the car. The air inside the vehicle felt sultry, and the windows began to fog. The humidity had increased everywhere.

"You're so sensitive to your staff's needs," Syd told her, turning toward her, the street light reflection bouncing off the hood of the car, outlining his face in yellowish light on one side, while it remained in blue shadow on the other.

Camellia gave a short laugh. "Sure," she said, shrugging.

"So..." said Syd.

For a long moment, that was the only word said, as they sat awkwardly in the car.

Finally, Camellia shrugged, again snagging her hair on epaulets, and she deftly unhooked the hair and her seatbelt.

"Let's go in," her voice cracked a bit.

"You sure? I can go... I can't stay long anyway."

Her heart sank.

I wish you'd stay just long enough.

She bit her lower lip, which trembled.

"No, no, come in. I'll get you something to drink."

She climbed out of the car, and the lights of her walkway came on. The house was lit from garden lights, shining upward, illuminating hedges and topiary trees, and some camellias as well.

"That's some outfit," Syd remarked, as Camellia's heels rang on the stone walk.

She laughed out loud.

"Silly, I know. But I figured almost nobody would get it."

"Goody two-shoes," teased Syd, and she whipped around.

"How'd you guess?"

"I love 80s music!" exclaimed Syd. They were at her door now, and he looked down at her.

She blushed, although through the white makeup, he would not be able to see. For which she was relieved. Then she turned to the door panel.

"Let me in, house," she said tersely.

"Welcome, Camellia," came the house's voice, recognizing her speech pattern immediately.

The door clicked open, and she pushed it wider. Once inside, she shut the door behind Syd. They stared at each other.

She cleared her throat. Then she took off her boots, setting them on a boot tray in the foyer. Syd nodded and then took off his shoes, which relieved her, for she noticed they had been caked with dried, pale gray mud. She wondered briefly where he could have been in any mud, but pushed the thought aside.

In her stockings, Camellia scooted across the marble floor as though she were skating.

"Kitchen's this way," she called, noting that Syd was taking in everything, his eyes darting all around the foyer, the ceiling, the stairway. She cocked her head at him.

"There's water, beer, wine… I think Dad's bar is well-stocked, since he's never here."

The last phrase came out with a barb of anger. She twisted her downturned mouth back into a flashy, bright smile toward Syd.

He smirked back at her and followed her into the kitchen.

"Jesus," he said, laughing lightly. "Your kitchen is huge!"

Camellia's laughter rang through the sterility of that space. She spun around on the floor, twirled herself over to Syd, and murmured, "So, what do you want?"

He blinked a couple of times, grinned, and said, "Water's good. Long drive later."

"Aw," she crooned in a tone of regret.

She retrieved two bottled waters from the fridge. She watched its display arrange itself into a bouquet of red camellias. She stared at it.

"Huh," she murmured.

"Everything all right?" Syd asked her, taking her offered bottle.

"I've never seen Fridge do *that* before," she noted.

"A rose bouquet?" Syd questioned, staring at the image. "I think your fridge likes you."

Camellia burst out laughing. "First of all, those are *camellias*! And you know, it is just a fridge!"

"Ah," said Syd with a soft laugh. "I'm not as up on my plants as some people. Sweet that it's responded to your name."

"I'm named after the flower," she told him.

Syd looked her up and down as she took a sip of her water. "You definitely are in bloom," he murmured.

Again she blushed, and wiped her brow. The white makeup was starting to come off.

"Oh!" she exclaimed. "I forgot I had this shit on my face." She laughed. "I'm going up to shower," she said, looking up into his eyes. His pupils dilated, and her own heart raced. "Help yourself to anything you want," she added. She winked at him.

He chuckled and winked back.

"Thanks," he said. "Maybe the fridge can give me a sandwich…"

"Make yourself at home. Watch a show, check out the art, play music… whatever you like. See you soon!" She flounced away and climbed carefully up the stairs. She stopped occasionally to glance back, to see if he might be below. But he was not; he remained in the kitchen. She felt a mixture of disappointed, intrigued, and a little uneasy at the same time. Sighing, she continued.

She entered her room and looked at her door from within. She thought of leaving it open, but ultimately decided to shut it. After doing so, she opened it again, just a few inches. She felt that she was roasting, her blood pumping. She took off her stockings and then her jacket, and stepped into her white, marbled bathroom. She wondered how big it was compared to Syd's. She retrieved white, gold-embroidered towels from the towel warming cabinet, and set them next to her shower. She considered starting the jacuzzi tub, but decided against that.

She opened a gold-handled drawer, pulled out a pack of makeup remover wipes, and set to work removing her face paint. The white makeup was easy to remove, whereas the dark eye makeup and fancy liner proved to be stubborn. She did the best she could, using four wipes in all, and realized soapy water would have to suffice. She piled her hair on top of her head and used her special, French facial cleaner with its light, high-end scent, to wash her face with.

Still, the dark mask-like eye makeup remained. Growing irritable, she said, "Fuck it," and started the tap on her shower. As she waited a few seconds, she peeked around to look at her bedroom door. It was still open at the same level.

She pushed the bathroom door so that it was also slightly open and turned on the bathroom vent. She heard music and realized Syd must have asked the house to play something. It wasn't her usual house soundtrack. She stepped into the shower and stared at the array of fine soap pumps, shampoos, conditioners, and essential oils. But she did not want to waste time, with Syd downstairs. So she made haste, cleaned herself, turned the tap off, and reached for her warm towels. Still, no movement of the doors.

I thought maybe he'd come in…

She had a thrill of fear, for the first time.

What if he *did* come in?

What would happen then?

She knew where her thoughts had gone.

But faced with him in her house, so close by, she felt a new emotion, and she didn't like it. Sighing irritably, she towel-dried her hair and put on clear lip gloss. The remnants of her eye makeup now made her look like she wore smoky eyeshadow.

It actually works, she thought with a shrug. She dressed in a bodycon, deep green dress, and put on thigh-high cable-knit, cream-colored stockings. The back of her neck itched, so she rubbed it, right where it was tattooed.

She walked out.

She heard a shuffling sound and turned her head.

"Syd?" she called.

There was no answer, but she heard the same sound again and looked down the stairs. He stood there looking up at her, holding a plate in his hands.

"I've got sandwiches," he said as she descended, holding

delicately to the curving, engraved railing, and pausing at the landing to pose.

"You look like a diva," he said with a little laugh.

"Good!" she cried. "I *am* a diva."

Soon, she then stood face to face with Syd.

"Yes, you are."

He offered her a plate. He'd made a hoagie sandwich, with what he could find in Fridge.

"Did you know that thing locks certain drawers?"

He followed her into the kitchen. She looked at the breakfast nook table, walked toward it, set the plate down, and patted the seat next to her. He sat there and watched her take the sandwich in her pale hands, their fingernails bright scarlet, her hair looking dark auburn-brown from being still wet.

"Yeah," she said, shrugging, between chews. "It doesn't let everyone have access, if you're not coded in."

"What's in the locked drawers?" he wondered, after swallowing a bite of sandwich. "They weren't clear, so I couldn't see."

"Who the fuck knows," she grumbled. "Dad's got them locked. Probably drugs or something, lol."

Syd laughed raucously at that.

"You sure don't think highly of your dad, do you?"

For a second, she nearly agreed. But then she felt a lance of something… a defensive prickling at the base of her neck.

"He's a mess," she answered carefully.

"He seems to leave you alone a lot," Syd noted.

And how would you know that? she wondered.

Blinking at him, she studied his face. In the light of the breakfast nook, he looked older for some reason, with more obvious crow's feet at the corners of his eyes. Still ruggedly handsome, though. He reached forward with his thumb toward her and touched the corner of her lower lip.

"Mustard," he told her, drawing his thumb back—but she caught it, and kissed it.

Then there was a moment of quick movement. She stood, he stood, and she pressed her lips into his, and he held her. She could smell onions on his breath, but still she kissed him anyway. He held her face and kissed her neck, and her bare shoulder. She gasped. She pulled him closer into an embrace. Then he pulled back.

He laughed, panting, and ran his hand through his hair.

"I should get going," he said.

"You don't have to," she answered. "No one is here but us."

"Camellia, I…"

She blushed and looked down.

"I know. You've got a long drive, or whatever."

"I—it's not that. It's just that…"

"Look, I know what I want, if that's what you're worried about," she said firmly.

Syd nodded at her, his lips twitching.

"Let the record show that the whole *world* knows that you know what you want, Camellia Dume. Sweet Caramel." He winked at her.

"Then why go?" she asked him, genuinely curious. "You came here knowing it was just us."

"Ah, if you were older," he murmured, taking her hands into his.

She could feel the blood draining from her face.

"And," he said slowly, taking her chin in his hands then, "if I were *available*."

She barely heard the word, as a surge of blood returned to her face, but she heard her own pulse in her ears.

"Maybe one day, when we both align…" he said, voice trailing off.

"What are you saying to me?" she demanded. "You have a *girlfriend*?"

Syd backed up.

"Actually, she's my fiancée…"

She breathed quickly.

"What. The. Fuck," she whispered, and she thought she could recognize actual fear in the man's eyes. It quickly vanished, and his eyes went cold and hard.

Fridge called out, "Camellia, the weather alert says we could lose power shortly. I am going into backup mode. Do you need me?"

She wheeled around and shrieked, "Are you fucking *kidding me* right now? Shut up!"

Syd took a deep breath and then quickly puffed it out.

"I should go."

She didn't know what to say.

She kept shaking her head and fighting the stinging sensation in her eyes.

"Why," she said coldly. "Why did you come here, then?"

Syd opened his eyes wide and held his hands out in a placating manner. "I wanted to make sure you were safe."

She laughed bitterly. "So, am I?"

He attempted to take her hands again but she backed away from him, and stood rigid, as tall as she could.

"I'm safe. You can go."

He didn't hesitate. He turned and walked out of the kitchen, and then stopped. She considered not following, but she couldn't help herself, and followed him into the foyer.

"Take care of yourself, Caramel," he murmured, reaching down swiftly to hug her.

She hugged him back, hating herself for doing so, and felt tears begin to well, so she quickly wiped her face on his shoulder.

"I always do," she said, voice muffled.

He put his shoes on and gave her a sheepish nod before leaving her house. She did not watch him go.

She listened.

The roar of his engine flared, and he peeled away. After

she was certain he was gone, she exhaled. She inhaled, and then she let out a scream.

She ran back into the kitchen, put her back against the fridge, and sank to the floor. She sobbed, tears spilling, snot dripping, and hugged her knees, shaking.

A rumble of thunder echoed outside then.

"Camellia," called Fridge softly. "You are safe now."

She wept in earnest. Long, shaking sobs intermixed with wails. She hadn't felt this hollow in a long time.

The music, which had been playing in the background, stopped abruptly. The house fell still and quiet.

Another crack of thunder, much closer.

The lights flickered, and the power went out.

Chapter 12

Squall

She reached for her watch and realized she hadn't put it back on after her shower.

"I must've left it up there," she muttered. She let another sob escape and gritted her teeth.

"That *fucker*!"

The tears runneled forth again.

"How could you, how could you?" she moaned, standing in the emergency-lit kitchen, considering her muted shadow on the floor.

She shook off her fresh tears and set her teeth together in a snap. She ground them and stomped off toward her father's office.

She found the door open, and for a tiny second, that struck her as odd. Usually, it was kept closed. She never understood why; there was nothing remarkable in there, she reasoned, much less to her taste. It was a gaudy man cave.

She pushed it fully open and breathed in.

What am I smelling?

Her thoughts tickled with some knowledge, deep down, that something wasn't quite right. But she could not pull it to the surface of her thoughts. Her rage and hurt encased her like a sticky web, and she did not know if she could escape it.

She did see her father's small bar, glinting in low light. The curtains to the room were open, and another flash of lightning was followed by a shuddering boom. The storm was over her now, or at least, its easternmost bands were. The lightning lit all the bottles of booze like a photographic flash, so she made her way to them. She closed her eyes and reached toward them, and her fingers found themselves on a knobby-topped bottle. She seized it, opened her eyes and pulled it from its place. She held it limply in her left hand, by her side. She trudged out of the room, but again the lightning blazed, and she noticed something: a foot depression in the carpet. Larger than her own.

She shivered and closed the office door behind her. She pushed on the door to make sure it stayed closed; it did. She walked slowly across the living room and out, hearing rain beating down all over the house in great swishes, like a car wash.

The great staircase was lit by emergency lights that glowed pale blue-green, and she followed those lights back upstairs. She entered her bedroom and set the bottle on her left nightstand, where her watch glowed. With a heavy sigh, she picked it up.

News reports blared; she scrolled through them, one after the other:

"...disaster declaration... Atlanta airport evacuated... Columbus state of emergency... Brooklyn Bridge closed... widespread panic at St. Louis arch... Des Moines on fire..."

And then the shouting of alert after alert from the weather: "FLASH FLOOD WARNING. THUNDERSTORM WARNING. TROPICAL STORM WARNING. MARINE WARNING: SANTA BARBARA CHANNEL WATERSPOUTS."

In a numb, enraged daze, she found her texts.

"Meems, text me back to say you're all right, I got a house alert."

Her dad.

"Queen, you left your purse at the bash! I'll hold it for you, bb."

Dewayne.

More alerts, this time Amber Alerts. She set the watch back down and turned, dull, toward the bottle. She realized she'd chosen a Barbados rum.

"Fuck it," she muttered, popping the knobby top off—which she now recognized as being a wooden, carved pineapple shape—and tilted the bottle against her lips and chugged.

She felt around in the drawers of her nightstands and found an old flashlight, and a box of matches. She took the latter and slinked toward her bathroom, bottle in one hand, matches in the other.

The candles that lined the ledges of the bathroom were solid in her hand, and she held each one for a few moments before striking a match. She lit one candle, then used that candle to light the others. The ring of candles flickering in the bathroom looked strangely ritualistic to her.

Despite herself, she laughed.

"Maybe I should call a séance," she muttered. "Mammaw, you out there?" Then, more quietly, "Mom?"

A mixture of silence, candles snapping softly, and more thunder met her ears. The rain pelted down outside. She shuddered despite herself.

She set the drain stopper on the jacuzzi, knowing she couldn't access its fancier features with limited power; but the water heater was gas-powered, so she turned on the tap full blast. She took a swig of the rum and fumbled around the inside of the bathroom cabinets. She found a bottle of bubble bath. She unscrewed the top, sniffed it, scowled at the lavender scent (normally appealing; not so when her senses were rum-marinated), and stood over the large, oval tub. She held the rum, glistening like bottled amber, in her left hand, and the bubble bath bottle, like an apothecary spirit, in her right hand. She poured most of the contents of the bubble bath into the tube and giggled, feeling the rum flooding her body, from her feet, up her legs, and she knew she must be quite flushed. She felt herself numbing a bit and smiled stupidly. Climbing out of her clothes, she slid into the froth, which was absurdly foamy from the excess bubble bath. She took three big swigs of rum, and set the bottle down outside the tub. And she sang.

She cried and she sang by turns.

She bellowed out blues songs at the top of her lungs, followed by Taylor Swift classics, and old Patsy Cline tunes, the ones her dad said her mother had loved. She swished around the tub like an olive sloshing in a martini glass.

The storm raged, and, finally, she could hear the snapping of tree branches.

She had some vague thought that they might be close by. Maybe there were even in her garden.

She didn't care.

She still howled, tears and snot flowing down her face as her words became ever more garbled. Another swig of rum.

Then a terrific crack, like a gunshot.

That silenced her.

She sat up, the soap bubbles hanging off her hair, giving her the same wigged appearance she'd had earlier at the masquerade bash.

"The fuck was that?" she whispered aloud.

Her head swam, and her stomach lurched.

The storm seemed to have lulled for a moment, in between bands of squalls. The candles flickered benignly, but other than that, the house was quite silent. Eerily so. Normally it hummed with appliances and devices, but not now, with the main power off.

She bit her lip and felt some of her rationality return. She pulled the tub stopper, and it began to drain. Finally, it gurgled toward emptiness, and made horrible sucking noises as the last of the water drained out, leaving a foot of fragrant foam in its wake. She extended one leg over the tub and reached for the towels she'd used earlier. She slid the rest of the way out, onto her bottom with a thud, and it hurt.

"Fuck!" she hissed.

She felt dizzy, so decided to dry herself off while she sat splayed out on the floor. She could see from the bathroom window, high up above the grounds, that the tops of the tallest palm trees were bent in wind, swirling around like upside-down mops in the tropical weather.

When she was dried off, she decided not to dress in her spicy bodycon again. In fact, she now looked at it and the stockings with disgust.

"Maybe I'll burn them," she mused. She laughed, and started hiccuping, which was not a good development. She felt very close to vomiting. She stilled her breathing as best she could and stumbled around the candlelit bathroom. She peed, flushed, washed her hands, seized the glass next to the sink and filled it from the filtered tap. It tasted sharply metallic, and, for a second, she gagged. But she craved water, so she gulped it down anyway. Another taste and smell emerged from it: Sulphur.

"Gross," she whispered.

Swaying like the palms outside, she padded across her room to the larger walk-in closet and stood facing its darkness. She didn't care; she opened one of the drawers and clawed her way through soft clothing until she found flannel, winter-print pajamas. She pulled them on and crawled on hands and knees over to her bed and pulled herself up.

She realized she'd left the rum bottle next to the tub, but she shrugged.

The old flashlight sat next to her watch, which occasionally gleamed from a message, but eventually stopped. Its charge ran down and she didn't care. She had chargers, but in many ways, right then, she wished the watch would die.

"Just fucking die."

She wished the world outside would disappear and stop bothering her.

She found the flashlight wanting in terms of bright light, but its feeble little wedge of photons reassured her somehow. She walked out of her room and stared down the hall. In one direction were a few rooms, and in the other, the hall ended in a closed door. That led to the spare room that used to be her mother's office. These days, it was used to cram old and unwanted or outgrown things into: Camellia's teddy bears, old clothes, boxes of supplies of all sorts, framed art stacked.

She approached the door and blinked.

This one was partially open as well.

It was quite subtle—as though the person who had closed it maybe thought they'd pulled it the whole way, but hadn't, and left it as it was.

She shivered and pushed the door slowly open.

"Hello?" she called quietly.

She felt so enormously alone that she thought the world might fall away. Like she teetered above an abyss.

Would the house alarms still work in the storm?

Could someone have got in?

She realized she should have kept her mouth shut, but it was too late.

She stared at the door, and covered her mouth for a moment. Her thoughts were muddied but her instincts were on high alert, sobering her quickly and unpleasantly as adrenaline surged.

What had been the loud sound she'd heard earlier? She

couldn't figure it out. The house was largely soundproof, although nothing could hide the storm's fury and the sound of close thunder. Still, during this lull, it had been a tremendous sound. And despite the noise insulation, she could hear, faintly, several sirens, in the distance. She did not know how far away.

What if it was a gun? What if one of the staff were here, and got shot?

Her mind then leapt full-bore into extreme anxiety, and she shook where she stood. She felt pinned to the spot.

"Fuck this," she hissed, and she surged forward, pushing the door open until it struck the interior wall of her mother's old office with a bang.

It was cold inside the room, and she realized the curtains were closed off, leaving it ominously dark. So dark that she could see nothing beyond the wedge of the flashlight.

"Oh, hell no," she murmured.

She walked as steadily as she could back to her room. She seized a makeup tray, dumped its lipsticks and compacts and brushes onto her bed, and loaded it with candles from the bathroom. She marched out into the hall, the little flames bending and winking from the breeze of her walking, and entered that office, invader be damned.

Her mother's desk provided a flat surface, so she set the tray of candles down. They lit the room warmly, like a little portable fireplace. She looked about, leaned down, looked under the desk, snooped behind a sofa, and pulled back the curtains. She was alone.

She didn't realize that these windows afforded such a wonderful view of the gardens below. The best view of them, in fact, in the whole house. That had been for her mother, the plant lover; a gift from her father. The dark rectangle of green life below glistened in its baptism of tropical rain. Impulsively, she unlocked the window and threw it open.

A blast of warm, petrichor-scented, heady air hit her face.

It almost made her sick. She heard the lashing of wind and rain, but something else unnerved her. Popping.

Popping and more popping, coming from below.

She looked down into that dark mass of biota and watched the trees and shrubs swaying, bending to the rhythm of the tropical wind, so aberrant here... yet they responded. By making popping sounds.

She didn't like that.

Shuddering, she slammed the window shut, locked it, stared back down, and closed the curtains. She hugged herself and turned her attention back to the room. On the desk, only the tray of candles and a few sets of pictures rested on its dark mahogany surface, nearly the color of Camellia's hair. It was pristine. There was no dust. She realized that the staff must occasionally come in here and clean everything.

She picked up one of the frames, and, holding it up to candlelight, felt a jolt.

It was her mother, sitting on the beach, holding Camellia around the waist, and she with her little pale arms clinging to her mother's arm and smiling up, presumably at her father taking the picture. Her mother was only looking at her daughter, her dark blonde hair falling forward over tanned shoulders, the wide white hat on her head falling back. And there was only one expression on her mother's face: pure, distilled love.

Camellia's face grew wet from tears. She held the picture to her chest and pressed it into her skin, almost nicking her exposed neck. Slowly she set it back down. She sat in her mother's old chair and twirled around, realizing how fully grown she actually was. The last time she'd done this was many years before, while her mother was still alive, and she could not touch the floor without reaching her toes down to push herself around.

That was how long it had been since she sat in that chair.

Or even entered that room.

She opened the drawers and leaned down to smell them, for anything—any scent. She found the ghosts of old, familiar scents. This room had been a joyful, busy place, off limits for much of the time, but still inviting, as the candles now reminded her.

Inside the middle drawer on the right, she found a beautiful little case, shaped like a white camellia. Its lid was off kilter, which surprised her. She opened it easily and tilted it into the candlelight to examine its contents. It contained a little molded enclosure, like for earbuds or jewelry. Whatever had been inside of it was gone now.

"Headphones?" she wondered aloud.

She placed the gorgeous case upon the desktop.

She blinked at it, not understanding what it was. She rubbed the back of her neck.

She stood and walked to the closets of the room. There she could see the faint glinting of her mother's gowns, now essentially vintage. She remembered that her mother had once attended many tony events in the past, before she was born, and a few after. Camellia had been delighted by these sparkling confections of fabric and rhinestones and sequins, because it made her mother seem like she'd been a mysterious woman with a double life; always in jeans and casual blouses at home, but there were those gowns in her closet. Like, she would transform into someone glamorous and secretive, a double agent movie star by night, a mom and a scientist by day.

A small stack of boxes were shoved back behind them, she realized, and pulled the top one out. Opening it, she found her own smile shining back at her from a picture of her mother, her father next to her. That was one of the few things she'd had in common with her mother: her smile. Only Camellia almost never smiled now. Her parents, in the picture, looked glamorous and impossibly young.

Under this, she found a group photo of her mother in a lab

jacket, with a group of scientists, including a young Mr. Levin. She blinked. So he'd been right; they had worked together. Someone else in the picture stood off to the left, older, with very dark eyebrows, pale eyes and long, dark lashes. She did not like the look of him. She shivered. There was something familiar about him, and unpleasant. An old, vestigial memory tickled her thoughts.

Setting the pictures back in their box, she pulled forth one of the dresses. This one was dark green with vines embroidered all through it; very high-end. On the dress sheath, "Oscars" shone on the cover label.

"Wonder which year?" she muttered out loud.

Impulsively, she shuffled out of her pajamas and pulled the green dress on. It was snug on her, and a little short, for her mother had been more petite, but it still fit well enough that she was comfortable. She felt clothed in her mother's hug.

She slid onto the floor in the dress and held her knees.

The winds and rain churned again as another squall came through. The power flickered, coming on briefly, and then went off again.

Reasonably sober now, and feeling a deep contentment, she stood.

She realized she forgot to answer her father's texts. She walked back to her room and checked the watch battery. It was low, but still held charge.

She rang his number.

There was no answer.

She wondered where he was and looked for his location.

The watch did not pick up his location.

She ran back to her mother's office, grabbed the camellia-shaped container, set it on the candle tray, and stared at it.

She knew this from somewhere.

She noticed something amiss. The carpet: impressions.

Again. And again, not her own. They were subtle, but they were there.

Outside, the popping sounds grew in crescendo, even through the closed window.

Another great *crack*.

Something was deeply wrong outside. And something was amiss inside.

CHAPTER 13

POTS

Feeling nauseous, uneasy, and befuddled, Camellia changed back into her pajamas. She took her tray of candles and held it on her lap. The warmth from the small flames made her realize she was cold. The rain outside had been warm, tropical, coming in bands. There would be breaks, and the bands would return.

Somewhere, but not very far away, another *crack*.

It startled her. She jerked the tray. A splash of candle wax flew on to her pajamas.

"Dammit. The *fuck* is that?" she whispered.

The power flickered back on, and a surge of air blew onto her head: the air conditioner kicked in. The house alarm squawked five times before silencing, and the intercom's mellifluous female voice said, "System online."

"Well *that's* good news, I guess."

She looked fondly at the candles, then blew them all out, holding her copper curtain of hair back. She charged her phone, chucked her dirty clothes and bathroom towels down the laundry chute, and tried to scrape off the wax stain on her pajamas. The pattern on them was of snowflakes and lipsticks of all hues. Looking down at them, she remembered her actual lipsticks—at least, the ones she'd chucked off the tray to make way for the candles. She replaced the candles in the bathroom and grimaced at the lingering foam.

"Thank *God* nobody heard me singing," she muttered.

The hum of electricity met her ears, and she shivered.

She was alone, but felt... watched.

She had no idea why she felt so uneasy alone; she'd been alone many times over the years, particularly the past three, since she'd become a teenager. The staff would check in on her occasionally, but in the last year, she'd worn more of them down with her acerbic tongue. The few who remained tried to get their work done during her school hours, when it was in session; during the summer, if she were in, she would bark at them about the pool or how well Fridge was stocked. (The fridge could place orders without help, but someone still needed to stock grocery deliveries; and this was not Camellia's job. That wasn't even up for debate.)

Tonight, however, she'd have welcomed any of the staff. She thought about calling the gardener, but that disturbed her more; it was now after 11 PM. Theoretically, she had school the next day. And she felt like shit.

She was sober enough to feel a series of waves crash over her in the tsunami of strangeness from that day: exhaustion, nausea, rage at Syd for leading her on and revealing his engagement, irritation and worry about her father, fear about the news unfolding, helplessness to do anything about it, and finally, shame.

Her anger at Syd intermixed with that shame, and she began polishing the rage within her, working it and tooling it into something she could use. He had struck her confidence with a knockout blow. But she would not be defeated by him.

Still, the scene played on loop for her: the chaotic, passionate kiss, his odd behavior... and, as she stepped onto the chilly kitchen floor, seeing and smelling the remains of their sandwiches on the breakfast nook table, she thought of something else.

She walked back out into the foyer and knelt to look at the floor. With the lights on, she could see the tracks from Syd's shoes. Some of the dried, gray mud had come off, leaving a shoe print before he'd removed them. She held her hands over the print and measured. Walking in a wobbly gait, she first traversed the living room to her dad's office. She got down on her knees and held her hands over the impressions in the carpet. The tracks had been slightly larger; but not by much. So they'd allow for his having walked in sock feet in the house.

She knew, then.

He'd gone exploring throughout the house. He'd gone into her mother's office.

She sucked in her breath.

"You bastard," she whispered. "You freak and you creep!"

Then: "House, did you see a man walk around in here earlier?"

The small globe button on the wall by the living room entry glowed.

"The only person on the grounds is you, Camellia," answered the house chat.

"No, I mean *earlier*," she snapped. "When I got home, even."

"The only person on the grounds since the gardener left at 2:36 PM was you, Camellia."

"Bullshit!" she shouted. "You've got it recorded, right? The entry, the inside of the house?"

"Your presence is recorded, yes. Would you like to see?"

Camellia frowned and put her hands to her temples: her head pounded with the worst headache she'd ever had.

"You'd better show it to me, you bitch!"

Then she marched into the kitchen.

"Fridge," she said urgently, facing the appliance.

"Welcome, Camellia. The storms are ongoing, by the way. We may lose power again."

"I don't care," she hissed, although the thought unnerved her. She did not want to be in the dark again. "Look, you saw I had a guest earlier, yeah?"

She blushed deeply. The thought then occurred to her that if anything in that house had recorded Syd, it would have recorded her *with* him. She hadn't even considered it at the time.

"The fucking power of hormones," she rage-muttered.

Fridge answered gently, "Camellia, you are safe now."

"You didn't answer my question."

"I answered the only question that matters."

"Oho! What fuckery is this, Fridge!" she howled. "Did you or did you not realize there was a man in here with me?"

"Camellia, there is no man in here," answered Fridge. The panel displayed an adorable red panda face at her.

Her jaw dropped.

"Don't you try and sweet talk me, Fridge. What the hell is going on?"

"Camellia, as you know, we lost power, and I lost connection with the main relay. I've rerouted everything. You are safe now."

"H-how much danger was I in earlier, then?" she asked hesitantly, pushing her vibrant hair behind her ears and crossing her arms.

"I have secured the perimeter of the house and adjusted for gaps. I do recommend, however, that you consider placing all houseplants outside."

Camellia stared at the little orange mammalian avatar face.

"I'm sorry... what?"

"Everything is safe." Pause. "For now."

She blinked in confusion.

"What do you mean, for *now*?"

"As I said, I recommend you place the houseplants outside. Probably the sooner the better. I recommend now."

Chills shot up and down Camellia's spine.

"Okay, I don't know what in the hillbilly blue hell is going on, but you're freaking me out. Did you get struck by lightning or something during the storm?"

"I recommend… now."

And the red panda avatar crinkled its little brow at her.

"Shit," she murmured. She glanced around her. There was a pot of herbs on the cutting board. With shaking hands, she picked it up, stared at it, and gingerly sniffed it.

She carried it into the foyer, where she stared at a huge container of out-of-season tulips, red, yellow, and rose.

"Um, these too?" she wondered aloud.

"Those are cut flowers. Theoretically, they should be fine."

"The-theoretically? I… you're freaking me out."

"There probably are some potted plants in the living room over by the far corner. A Ficus, I believe? And in your father's office. Perhaps a few upstairs, but my readings aren't picking them up. The downstairs always had more plants."

"Did you actually just have an entire conversation with me… about *potted plants*?" cried Camellia. "What the shit is in that rum of Dad's…" she muttered.

This is a really goddamn weird as fuck day. But I'm not taking any chances.

She swept into the living room, saw the Ficus, plopped the potted herbs into the Ficus pot, and dragged it across the floor, where it spilled out some dirt.

"Fuckshit," she hissed, but the robot vacuum hummed into high gear and scooted over quickly.

She then hoisted the two pots and opened the front door.

Someone stood there.

She screamed.

CHAPTER 14

THE FLORTIDS

The person screamed back, and she screamed again and threw the pot of herbs at them.

"What the *fuck*, Camellia!" yelled the person.

Camellia gasped.

"*Dewayne*! Godfuckingdammit, Dewayne!"

She reached out and seized him and held onto his collar as the sky opened and dumped torrential rain on them.

"Gaaaaack!" shrieked Dewayne. "Jesus! What's got into you?"

"What are you doing here, you absolute shitting *turnip*?" screamed Camellia. "At eleven at night? Couldn't you have texted?"

"I *did*!" shouted Dewayne. "Holy shit, like ten times!" His eyes were wild. He held a bag up in front of his face. "Please don't throw another pot at me, Queen!" His voice quavered. "I brought your purse."

Camellia groaned and seized it.

"Christ!" she hissed. "Get inside."

"Wait, what are you doing with that tree?" Dewayne pointed at the Ficus on the porch.

Camellia then kicked the pot of herbs she'd launched at

him before until it rolled into the wet yard. She seized the Ficus around the slim trunk and tipped it over so that it fell off to the side.

Dewayne gaped at her.

"Mother of God, what did the rosemary and Ficus do to you? Did you think they were Flortids or something?"

She pointed at the open door. Dewayne sprang inside out of the rain.

"Flor-what-ids?"

Dewayne slipped his shoes off and she realized then they were Ralph Lauren Wellingtons. She could not fault Dewayne his taste. He unwrapped a matching trench coat and patted his black pompadour.

"Flortids," he repeated, rolling his eyes and shrugging. "You know, those plant monsters taking over half the country. They're like cryptids but they're like, flowers and plants?"

"Flortids," she repeated with a snort. "Did you come up with that yourself?"

Dewayne gesticulated wildly with his hands and said, "Look, I'm sorry, you didn't text back. I was worried."

"Awww," Camellia cooed and laughed. "You were worried about me?"

Dewayne glared at her, flinging the raindrops from his dripping hair.

She sighed. "Sorry, come and I'll get you cocoa or something."

"Oh, thank God, I'm freezing."

"You total Angeleno. It's fucking tropical rain."

"I don't care! I hate rain," confessed Dewayne.

"You seem on edge," she noted, reaching for two mugs.

"Well, *maybe*," hissed Dewayne, "because you fucking threw a *plant* at me." He composed himself as he watched her eyes narrow. "Sorry, Queen, but today's been *a lot*."

He heaved a great sigh, then grimaced.

"Ew, what's that smell?"

"I don't know, what does it smell *like*?"

Dewayne waved his hands around. "Like really shitty cologne and... and *onions*."

Camellia turned away from him, blushing furiously.

"And do I smell..."

She groaned.

"Have you been *drinking*?"

She spun around and glared at him.

"Dewayne. Really? You come to my house at eleven at night and scare the bejesus out of me, and now you're judging the way my house smells?"

"Well?" he shot back. "You threw a fucking *rosemary bomb* at my head! You could have given me a concussion!"

"It was a *plastic pot*, you complete troglodyte!" she shouted.

Huffing, Dewayne put his hands on his hips. "Okay. You're *welcome*. I'll get a ride home now."

"What about the cocoa?" she asked, holding out the mug.

Dewayne dithered, clearly put out, but the cocoa smell overpowered everything else, and he took it gingerly in his hands. He took a careful sip and his eyebrows perked up.

"Hey, this is really good!" he exclaimed, almost despite himself.

She gritted her teeth.

"Of course it is. I don't serve swill in my house," she sniffed.

"But ew, really... I still smell the onions," and Dewayne made a gagging gesture.

Camellia stomped over to the sink, grabbed paper towels and cleaning spray from the cabinet beneath it, and cleaned the breakfast nook of the remaining sandwiches, chucking everything in the trash. She wished she could throw Syd in with them. But he was miles away. In more ways than one.

How could I have been so wrong about him?

"Sit," she commanded, and Dewayne clicked his tongue and sat at the table grandly.

They held their cocoa mugs and stared at each other.

"What... happened?" he dared. "You look"—Camellia burrowed her bloodshot green eyes into him—"ahem, like you've had a-a *long day*," he finished uneasily.

She could almost see the phrase "Rome is burning!" flickering in his eyes. No doubt everyone at school would say the same, if they could see her right now.

"You'd better not tell anyone."

"Okay, Queen Launcher of Plant Missiles," snorted Dewayne. "Spill the tea. Er. Cocoa. Actually, don't spill it. It's too good. You know what I mean!"

She grinned despite the headache, the heartache, and the deep turmoil.

"I had... something happen—"

Dewayne gasped.

"Did you fuck that Navy guy?"

"GodDAMMIT, Dewayne!" yelled Camellia. She slammed the cocoa mug down on the table. "No. I did not fuck the Navy guy."

"Okay, because that was weird," Dewayne sighed, looking relieved.

She wanted to sink into the floor, melt right into it like caulk between the elaborate, $500 apiece tiles.

How could I have been so stupid?

"Look, it's been a *day*. I just... it was a bad night, okay? He stopped by for a sandwich, then took off."

"You blew him, didn't you?" Dewayne tsked and shook his head. "Girl, at least charge for that. Have some self-respect! Though he *is* hot. Hell, I'd have done that for free!" he cackled.

"Dewayne, let me find another plant to throw at your head, I sweartagod."

Her lips went into a thin line and her raccoon-stained eyes looked like cigar burns in bread dough.

"Jesus! Fine, what happened?"

"Oh, like I said… sandwiches. And he led me on."

Her voice rose a pitch, and she held her neck. Dewayne's eyes flitted from her eyes, to her neck, to her hands. She swallowed.

"I thought we were on a date."

"Go on," murmured Dewayne, licking his lips after taking another swig of cocoa.

"We'd had a… a thing, for lack of a better word. For some time."

"A thing. Okay. Then what?"

She took a deep breath, and, for a second, she wondered, if she let it out, if it might come out as a jet of flame and set the house on fire.

Dewayne physically leaned back away from her, as if reading her mind.

"He's fucking ENGAGED!" she bellowed.

Sharp came the gasp from Dewayne's mouth.

"Girl, *what*? You're his side piece? Oh honey, no!"

She jumped to her feet, nearly spilling the cocoa, balled her fists, and looked down at him with eyes blazing.

"If you say one word. One word. You're ruined, you hear me?"

Dewayne shuddered.

"Mmhmm. Yes, Queen. I hear you loud and clear."

They locked eyes.

He tentatively reached out to touch her hand, as if it were the head of a cobra he was trying to tame.

"Not one word," he agreed. "Come on, let's drink cocoa and plot revenge."

She let her shoulders fall then, and she half-laughed. She unfurled her clenched fists and sat heavily down in the chair and shook her head.

"I don't know what came over me," she confessed. "I thought... I thought it was going somewhere."

"Well, to jail, for him," snorted Dewayne. "If, you know, anything *had* happened." He sighed. "Queen, I know you're better than anyone your age, we all know that. But you can't go after guys like that. I'm glad nothing *really* bad happened, you know?"

She trembled. The alcohol was working its way out, and she felt a little sick.

"Oh, God," she groaned. "Tomorrow's school. We'd better get to bed. Thanks for bringing my purse. Did you get a ride over? I'll hail one for you. I know a great guy who's up late on the Malibu circuit."

"You would!" Dewayne grinned gratefully. "But seriously, was there something else that happened? Not that—not that anything should, you had enough."

"Well, I—" and she leaned back to look at the fridge. "We had a power outage. Did you guys?"

He shook his head. "No, but I'm not surprised. I hear the storm's coming back around. It's sitting and spinning out there, just riding that beachline like a whore! Not going anywhere."

She belly laughed.

"You should charge for your weather forecasts," she teased.

"Yeah, well, we either have fire, pilot, awards, or earthquake weather most of the time! I hate this climate change bullshit. I don't want real weather! That's for my grandma in Florida. My constitution deserves a Mediterranean climate, honey."

He ran his fingers through his perfect pompadour and checked his fingernails. She could not fault Dewayne for his immaculate grooming.

"Don't we all," she agreed ruefully. A bolt of lightning

streaked outside, followed a few seconds later by thunder. Not terribly close but signaling another squall line.

"Seriously, what happened?"

Dewayne looked into her tired, hungover face.

I must look like slapped shit to him right now.

"I think… I think he snooped while I showered," she confessed in a low voice, almost a whisper.

Dewayne's eyes went wide.

"For real? Did he steal something? Did the cameras show it?"

"That's the weirdest part," she said slowly. *Well, aside from the fucking weird noises outside.* "The house said it had no record of anyone but me here."

Dewayne sat bolt upright, rubbed his arms, and shivered.

"Okay, this is really creepy. You want to come over to my house? Not as fab as this one, never will be, but… girl, this is scary shit."

"I—I can't prove that he did anything wrong," she stammered.

"I don't like it."

They stared at each other.

"Neither do I."

"I don't like anything right now," confessed Dewayne. "What is all the Flortid shit, do you think?"

"Another pandemic, I think."

But really, she did not know what to think.

"Look, I'll be fine. Power's on. House is on alert."

"Where's your dad? Wait, let me guess. Vegas again."

"He was, yeah. No idea now."

"Well, that's nothing new."

"No shit."

She called out, "House, send for Mickey, please."

The intercom AI responded, "Requesting a ride from Mickey."

The two teens stood, and she took Dewayne's mug.

"Thank you," he said, warmly.

"Thank you, and I'm sorry about the plant." She felt disturbed by her own politeness. "Maybe don't show up late on people's doors. Could have been worse, you know!"

Dewayne shivered.

"I guess a lot of things could be worse, to hear the news."

Their exchange of glances was grim.

"Wow," Dewayne said in a quiet voice.

"What?" She lifted an eyebrow at him.

"This is the longest conversation we've ever had!"

She sniffed.

"Well, don't get used to it," she said, fighting a smirk.

Still, they changed the subject. She dug out her lipsticks and fixed her face, he complimented the art in the foyer, and Mickey the chauffeur arrived shortly after that. Dewayne dashed out into the heavier rain. It was after midnight. Camellia was sorry to see him go, she admitted to herself.

She turned, locked herself in the great, empty house, and ascended the stairs to her room. When she got there, she locked her door, retrieved a working movie prop sword from under her bed, and opened her curtains. She watched the lightning forking across the sky and the palms swaying, and she held onto the sword. She did not hear more of the popping from earlier, maybe because the wind had turned so ferocious. The power flickered but stayed stable.

"What did he call them?" she murmured to herself. "Flortids?"

She couldn't think straight anymore. Fatigue coiled itself around her body and mind. She staggered over to her bed with her sheathed sword, curled herself around it, and fell asleep.

CHAPTER 15

GREEN

"Camellia."

A voice entering her dreams.

In those dreams, she walked along the waves of Zuma Beach, and stood still, ankle-deep in the cold Pacific. She stared at the blue horizon, over which a shimmering, golden haze had settled. She could not see the sun, but she knew in the dream that it must be behind her, for she could see a short shadow below her. She wore a maxi skirt, gold with green embroidered leaves. Its hem was soaked about a foot from the bottom, where it sank into the water. She pulled the skirt up and watched the sea pull back away from her feet, where her toes were painted emerald green. As the water receded, the sand sucked away and buried her feet for a moment. She felt a nudge at her calves from behind, and watched as something dark green oozed around her. A seepage of something that looked like a slurry of matcha tea. Ground up leaves among it. She could see something red and stringy. All of this flooded from behind her from the sea. She turned, and met a wall of dark green in all directions, full of ground green bits, and speckled with sinew, blood, bones, intestines spilling shit. She opened her mouth to scream, and could not, for the green-blood-filth rose all around her, lifting her skirt, enveloping her body, and flooded her mouth until she began to choke...

"Camellia!"

She jolted awake, yelled, and struck the back of her head on the headboard. This made her bite her tongue, hard, and she tasted blood. She screamed again, out of fear and shock.

"Camellia!"

It was her house alarm, alerting her. She held a tissue onto her bleeding tongue and listened. In her other hand, she held the hilt of the prop sword.

Finally, she called through her bloody tissue, "Yeth?"

The voice rose in pitch and dialed back its musical qualities.

"Good morning, Camellia," it intoned. Now it was using Fridge's voice. "I ordered a smoothie for you, and it is sitting at the front step. I have checked the perimeter, and it is safe. Also, I received a proximity alert for Gardener. He will be here soon. Two of the staff have called in sick. It might just be Gardener today. You have two hours until school starts."

"Thank you," she answered thickly.

Good thing there will be a smoothie. She winced, looking at the bloody tissue.

Lifting herself up and using the sword for a cane, she wobbled toward her bathroom, her head pounding horribly. The room spun a bit, so she leaned on the sword.

"Ooooohhh fuck *me* on a tightrope," she groaned.

Swearing a blue streak, she cleaned herself up, then showered. She tried to shake off the dream. As her comfort level rose from being clean, and she combed her tangled, long hair, she watched her face turn pink as she thought of the night before.

"Fuck you, Syd," she whispered.

She set the broad comb down, ran *Enchante Exquisite Hair Polish* through her hair (it smelled like honeysuckle), and set about dressing. She felt subdued. The sky still drizzled, and she did not know what the weather forecast was (aside from various warnings on her watch). Still no new texts from her father, either. She could see the palms outside still swaying, and she creased her brow into a frown. She looked at her bed and sighed. If the staff weren't coming, the bed wouldn't get made. She tugged at the sheets, plumped up the pillows, adjusted the duvet and shams. She tipped her dirty laundry down the chute. She wondered how much laundry was in the basement.

"Am I going to have to do fucking *laundry*?" she muttered.

The house comm came on again.

"Would you like to order a laundry pickup today?" it asked.

She rolled her eyes.

"I'd like you to order a spa pickup today, to be honest."

"Dialing—"

"No!" she cried. "Stop dialing. I'm kidding. Sort of."

She pulled on jeans and a deep gold sweater. She blinked at its color. It reminded her of something.

The dream. The skirt in the dream was the same color as her sweater today.

That dream was fading. She assumed she'd dreamed it because of all the bootleg footage the other Killian High teens had been looking at, the night before. She shuddered, looking at her sweater. She considered taking it off and wearing something else.

The skirt in the dream. It had seemed familiar.

She walked out into the hall and stared at the closed door of her mother's office. A surge of disturbed fury coursed through her as she noticed the padded impressions of footsteps in the plush carpet. She clenched her fists and marched forward, opened the door to the office, and sucked in her breath.

Dread consumed her as she walked to her mother's closet. It pulled her: she did not feel she walked of her own volition.

She felt still trapped in the frothing green nightmare. She opened the door. Her mother's gowns sparkled there, revealed in the soft light of morning. She pushed and pulled them around, and found, off to the left, a hanger with a long, gold skirt, embroidered with green leaves. The same skirt as in the dream.

She blinked back hot tears.

"Camellia."

She jumped.

It was House again, specifically Fridge.

"Just a gentle reminder that your smoothie is here."

She pulled the skirt out of the closet and draped it over her mother's desk chair. She ran her fingers over the bumpy surface of the green leaves. It was indeed a good match for her sweater. Her face leaking, she took off her jeans, and pulled on the skirt. It was elastic. It was not a fancy brand. It was bohemian and cozy, much as her mother had been. It many ways it did not suit Camellia at all, and yet… it still fit her.

She walked back to her room, stuffed her jeans haphazardly back into the closet drawer, and stepped over to her shoe closet. There she found some soft, dark brown ankle boots that she never wore. In fact, she couldn't remember even buying them, and considered that she probably never *had*. They were probably an influencer promotional gift from some company. She bemusedly realized she'd probably worn them exactly once: for a social media ad campaign just for the boot makers. They were comfortable, however, and they complemented the skirt and sweater.

She looked at herself in one of her several body-length mirrors and hummed.

"It works. I guess."

She descended the stairs and halted at the foyer, noticing the cut flowers had wilted overnight.

"Relatable," she muttered.

She walked to the front door and opened it, finding a little travel box with a large silk flower tied on top; a fake camellia blossom.

"Nice touch," she sniffed, taking the box and shutting the door behind her.

Once in the kitchen, she removed the white faux camellia bloom and opened the box, finding a clear cup with a sealed top, a punching straw, and two wrapped raw chocolate chip grain bars. She pulled the cup out... and dropped it, stunned.

It was filled with thick, green liquid... with a red swirl in it.

Breathing fast, she gasped, "Fridge, what the fuck is this!"

Fridge chimed and answered, "This is the Breakfast Combo Number 4, on special. You requested more greens last time."

"Wha—what kind of—of greens are these?"

She stared at the cup, which had landed on its base, remarkably. She backed up from it, as if it were a landmine.

"Kale and supergreen mixtures, as well as their signature algal supplements, and a raspberry swirl."

She leaned against the countertop and put her hands on the temples, finding them shaking, and exhaled.

"Thank you," she breathed.

She glared at it, blinked several times, and then laughed at herself. "I'm being stupid."

She lifted the cup, punctured the lid, and took a tentative sip. She shrugged.

"Tastes like shit, but it's probably the best thing for a hangover right now."

Fridge displayed a sunrise over a cloud. The sun then put sunglasses on its face.

She snorted.

"Please follow the instructions they included," Fridge said.

"Instructions?" she echoed, giggling despite her headache.

She tugged at the packages and found nestled inside a little note:

"Please enjoy our Number 4, what we like to call 'The Day After', full of kale, supergreens, adaptogens, and a special fungal blend. Just right for nuking a hangover. Mushrooms, but no mushroom clouds."

Camellia rolled her eyes. "Grim. But effective."

She took painkillers and sucked down the smoothie, then set about her makeup routine in the downstairs bathroom off the kitchen. An arsenal of lipsticks, foundation, creams, contouring sticks and powders, and other implements unfolded from the wall. This was a much smaller collection than the one in her upstairs room and bathroom, but it contained enough of everything she needed for a school day. And she had, begrudgingly, decided she'd better go to school. The local high school system had chosen to say open, rather than follow the superintendent's lead of closing its own district due to the storms.

Once fully made up, she felt confident enough to hail a ride. Her headache subsided to a dull annoyance, a creature with a slow heartbeat, but manageable. She heard no more popping, and, for the moment had, forgotten many of the prior day's weird occurrences. But she did let her eyes fall on a picture in the foyer before she donned her raincoat and seized an umbrella from the coat closet. It was of camellias in a great pot. That made her turn and look out at the garden. It sat quiet... the trees and shrubs buffeted by occasional gusts, the plants glossy from the rain.

She shook her head. "What was in that rum, anyway?"

And she tried not to think of Syd's weird behavior and his having led her on. She pushed her hurt and rage down, down into a dark well, and pulled a lid over it like a manhole over a sewer.

Her ride arrived, and she chirped, "Okay, House, tell Gardener I said hello!"

"Will do, Camellia. Have a nice day at school."

She suddenly felt buoyant, despite the repressive rainfall and yesterday's events. She was feeling better. Better enough to feel increasingly bitchy, by the second. She was ready to tear into someone, anyone. Not the driver, per se: she needed to arrive in one piece. But the second she stepped out of their car at the entrance to Killian High, she found a target for her fury, for she could see the wet hems of baggy jeans and a slouching outfit under a faded black umbrella: Wray, walking toward the school, head out of sight.

A surge of discomfort swelled in her. She didn't like it. The very picture of Wray made her angry. What were they doing here, anyway, at *her* school? Where did they come from? What was their situation? An abusive home? It enraged her that she had to deal with Wray.

Wray stopped in their tracks just as Camellia stomped her way across the concrete in her brown boots, holding her smart umbrella in long, black-gloved hands. The foul weather was an excuse to wear her double breasted peacoat, but she fought the realization it was not quite cold enough to justify wearing it, as the heat made her want to rip the thing off and throw it aside. Wray stood like a dripping wall before her, blocking her entrance.

"The fuck is wrong with *you*, Wraith?" she hissed.

Wray rolled their eyes, and Camellia could see that some of the makeup was still covering the bruise. Her heart pounded and she felt a thousand epithets rise in her throat.

"Huh," Wray said, and they shook their head and snorted. "I see you're perfectly fine today after everything. Back to normal, doing your favorite exercise: bitch and bend."

Camellia took her open umbrella and slammed it against Wray's, sending water flying and Wray tripping backward a step. The wind seized Camellia's umbrella and yanked it high in the sky, whipping her hair about her as the rain drenched her. She heard hoots of rain-muffled laughter, but not from Wray.

Seething, she watched the umbrella bounce off the roof of Killian High and hurtle off somewhere out of sight; it could be the Land of Oz, she mused, for all the difference it made. She felt so consumed with rage that she wondered if the rain were turning to steam upon contact with her. She stepped forward and grabbed the stalk of Wray's umbrella, and the two faced each other, breathing heavily, two columns of fury more volatile than the storm above.

"You don't belong!" she shouted in Wray's face.

Wray blinked, with wide eyes, and swallowed, hands gripping their umbrella, but holding it over the two of them regardless. Camellia could see the shot took hold, and for a moment, she felt the rush of power.

The moment quivered as she met eyes with Wray and felt a flush, and opened her mouth, appalled to hear herself say,

"I'm sor—"

"Then that makes two of us," Wray snapped, jerking away from her, and stomping off toward the school.

Camellia stood for a moment, allowing herself to be soaked by the storm, as some of the students rushed up to her with umbrellas. She held her hands up.

"Fuck off," she said, voice cold.

She swept forward into the school, took off her gloves and her coat, dumped them into the arms of a freshman, smoothed her hair, and sashayed to first period. There would be plenty of time to deal with Wray's bullshit later, she reasoned. Now it was time to take back the narrative on the stormy day. Killian High needed Camellia's verve. In that way, and perhaps the only way, she *did* belong.

Or so she repeated to herself over and over, trying not to think about a moment under an umbrella, the cinnamon-scented breath of Wray in her face, their hands just touching hers.

CHAPTER 16

FLASH

Throughout Killian High, a current of disquiet worked its way through every grade level, every class. PE took place indoors due to the weather, which had actually calmed quite suddenly overhead. The storm had finally begun its barrel roll inward, dumping record-breaking rainfall in the mountains and deserts. In Malibu, everyone's phones and watches screeched constant flash flood warnings and other dire and relentless emergency messages. The teachers were beside themselves trying to keep a handle on the classes.

For her part, Camellia took the chaos as an opportunity to daydream. Her thoughts wavered from the fiery kiss with Syd, to his betrayal, to the electric tension she had with Wray. She shifted in her seat and bit her lip. She imagined lips of someone upon her neck, hands down her back, being pulled tight against the warmth of—

"What's today's look, Evil Stevie Nicks or something?" snarked Candace.

Camellia snapped her head around like a bullwhip, her reverie vaporized. She smoothed her mother's golden, embroidered skirt and tossed back her rain-and-wind-tousled dark ginger hair. Yes, she was more feral-looking than she'd ever been, but also, she felt alive, comfortable. She was wearing her mother's skirt. She had reclaimed some part of her she'd missed, or perhaps had never known. There was no time for fuckery from the clueless.

"Candace," she drew out the second syllable. She swept her keen eyes over the girl's outfit: largely beige, with artfully torn designer blue jeans and Italian shoes (likely ruined by the rain at this point). Then she took out her compact, and one of her lipsticks: *Enchante Ultra Riche No. 947: Stupefy*. A vivid, coral-red hue; commanding. She smoothed it over her lips, rubbed them together with a smack, and smiled. She turned the compact toward Candace. "What do you see?"

Candace scowled, which she was wont to do.

"What is this bullshit, Camel Toe?"

Camellia snickered while her classmates guffawed. "Nice try, Gourdess." *Not one of my stronger ones, but...* "Seriously, though, what do you see?"

Candace sniffed. "It's a fucking mirror, I don't know."

"Hmm, interesting." Camellia took the compact back and snapped it shut with a *clack*. "Because you should see yourself. You're *tragique*. From where *I'm* sitting you keep choosing to date an asshole who mistreats you."

Candace stood; her fists balled.

Camellia pushed her mouth into an "O" and raised her eyebrows. Then she whistled.

"You *ruined everything*!" Candace shouted.

"Miss Ritter, sit, please," the teacher, Ms. Fields, warned. "Miss Dume, that's enough."

Camellia shrugged, not caring. "Who's done the ruining for you, Candace? Really? You keep making terrible choices. Why is that? I'm just curious."

She saw, from the corner of her eye, some of the Cadre, especially Mel, turn away from her. She felt a tingle of something she didn't like creep into her.

"Bitch!" screamed Candace, and she drew back her hand

as though to strike Camellia, when the classroom phone rang. It startled everyone and broke the charged moment.

Ms. Fields shot dagger eyes at Candace and Camellia.

"Miss Ritter, sit now, or it's detention. Ms. Dume, I'm of a mind to send you home. Stop harassing other students."

That set the class into a frenzy, and an argument; students shouting on both sides for or against the two unpleasant girls.

Ms. Fields pounded on the table and screamed, "QUIET!" And with the room stunned and silent for a moment, all eyes on the teacher, who held the phone against her ear tightly, and spoke into it, "Come again? I'm sorry."

She locked eyes with Camellia.

Camellia went cold. She tapped her watch, and saw there were no messages. She checked her phone, and there was nothing there, either.

She did not hear, at first, what Ms. Fields was saying.

Then, "Camellia." She realized the teacher must have said it more than once, even as they stared at each other through the undulating mass of fractious sophomores and juniors.

Not Miss Dume. Camellia.

That was the only coherent thought she had.

"Could you please come with me outside? Bring your things."

She swallowed, her heart rate bouncing, and gathered her things.

"Fucking *finally*," crowed Candace. "Getting what you deserve!"

Ms. Fields stood ramrod straight and called out in a hard voice, "Candace Ritter. Detention. Office. GO!"

And there was such a hard edge to this normally benign, insipid teacher's tone that it frightened Camellia. By the looks of things, it had frightened Candace too, and the rest of the class, which sat momentarily still.

She did not even notice Candace leave. She simply tried to move out of the classroom without tripping over her skirt, adjusting her backpack, her purse, her hair, and wondering where the freshman she'd given her coat to had gone.

Once outside the classroom, with Candace darting hateful looks over her shoulder as she charged toward the office, Ms. Fields closed the door and turned to Camellia. Her ears were ringing. She rubbed the embroidered leaves on her mother's skirt.

"Camellia, dear," Ms. Fields began.

Well, that can't be good. Nobody calls me 'dear' who wants to live to the next day.

"Yes? What is it?" She tried inflecting an imperious tone. But her voice broke almost pre-teen high.

"Sweetie, I'm walking with you to the office," said Ms. Fields, and she locked the classroom door.

"Why, what's going on?" she blurted out.

"It's a private matter that the principal has been alerted to. I'll go with you."

The eye of the storm was overhead, and the air deadened, stilled; bright yet dull at the same time, voided of proper looking shadows. Everything reeked of petrichor and of something else, something putrid, sickly-sweet, but mixed with shit. And then the *popping*.

As Camellia walked along, an eternity to her, she heard popping all around her.

She shivered.

Ms. Fields turned to look at her and glanced all around the school grounds. They made eye contact.

"Do you hear that?" she asked.

Camellia gathered just enough of her verve to wear it like her own lipstick. "Hear what?" And she shrugged.

"No-nothing. Maybe it's... rainwater draining or something."

It's not fucking water *draining, for God's sake!*

But it followed Camellia as she walked. The popping: just

like she'd heard at her house. All along the colonnade, lined with trees and shrubs...

She was glad, at least, that there was a break in the rain. To the west, she could see a deep blue-violet sky, the western edge of the storm; the horizon smudged as though removed altogether, as though sea and sky were one great, dark boundary, beyond which something | cold and ancient and monstrous might dwell. She blinked, and glimpsed whitecaps through the little gap in the road opposite the school, out beyond the sea cliffs. They might be within the eye of the storm, but the ocean roiled still.

It was a long walk, full of popping, lit by ominous light. And once inside the office, she found Candace arguing on the front desk phone with someone. Flustered, she dropped the phone hard onto the receptionist's desk. An assistant came to guide her back and out of sight. Camellia felt her shoulders relax.

One less person to deal with.

She couldn't quite focus as Principal Marisol came forward, her fingers twisting together, her face full of concern. Because next to the principal stood a sheriff.

He was tall, dark-haired, with a bulbous belly but strangely slender arms. His nose was deep red, pocked with acne scars, and covered in rosacea. His eyes were a murky brown, and he smelled like drugstore aftershave. His sheriff's badge read "Lt. Eli."

"Are you Camellia Dume, daughter of Desmond Dume?"

"Yes," she answered simply, noticing the rounded tips of each point of the sheriff badge star on his chest.

"The Kern County sheriff's office reached out to us. We've located your father's vehicle in a mud flow from a flash flood, not far off the 15 freeway..."

Her ears rang so loudly, she barely heard him.

She did hear one thing.

"...missing."

CHAPTER 17

A MYRIAD-TWINING LIFE

The sheriff said other words, but Camellia did not let them in. She drew herself up, crossed her arms, tossed her hair, and cleared her throat.

"Will that be all?"

The principal and the sheriff exchanged glances. The room seemed to drop in temperature.

The sheriff put his hands on his hips and said, "We've tried contacting next of kin—"

"Why? I *am* the next of kin."

"There's record of a cousin."

"She wouldn't know where he is."

"Miss Dume," the sheriff began, as the principal's eyebrows sagged downward while tentatively reaching out a hand.

A surge of heat rose within Camellia, and she threw back her fiery hair. She stepped back from the pair, out of the reach of the principal.

"You have," Camellia said in a low voice, "nothing to go on. A car. One of Dad's several cars." She shrugged. "Could be someone else took it."

The Sheriff squinted at her. "Do you know anyone else who could have?"

Part of her tension released.

"So you don't have a body." She pressed her lacquered lips together, gave one nod, and said, "Right. Good luck with your little search. I'll wait for Dad's text. He's out there somewhere, and sooner or later he'll turn up. If there's one thing about Dad I know: he goes away for a while, and he comes back."

The principal, distracted by a text, jerked her head up.

"Camellia, do you have anyone staying with you currently? We should talk—"

All their phones and watches shrieked with storm warnings.

Sighing, the principal said, "I've got to give an alert, L.A. Unified just called for early dismissal, and we'll need to do the same. Camellia, if you'll—"

But she was already gone.

She threw the door to the school open. The wind struck her from the southwest and the dark horizon was upon them, bearing sheets of rain. The final bands of the storm had fully moved in, and the tropical storm's remaining power made the air unstable and volatile. Thunder echoed up the slopes of the Santa Monica Mountains and lightning seared the purpling sky. Yet even with this cacophony, her ears ringing from the blood pounding in her head, Camellia heard, again, the odd popping sound.

What the hell is that?

She stood next to a vivid, fuchsia bougainvillea and listened.

"Is it *you*?" she asked, blushing, embarrassed. She composed herself. "I'm talking to a fucking plant. Great day I'm having."

With school now dismissed, she watched the surge of students pouring out of Killian High. She imagined the frustrated parents or chauffeurs scrambling to reach them. She would not have such a problem. Her father would not be there.

She assumed he was not dead, that he had endured another bender; perhaps someone won blackjack and took his car for a spin and never came back. It would not surprise her at all. He talked the good talk, and made many business deals, but she began to understand that he'd built most of them on bullshit. He'd been lucky enough to have gotten away with that. Desmond Dume was crafty and cunning. She wondered, not for the first time, what her mother had seen in him.

All she felt for him at that moment was high-grade fury and disgust. Everything else was shoved down deep, out of sight. And as she remembered Syd picking her up from school so recently, she shoved that down too. No, it had to go deep down, out of sight of sunlight, out of reason. She did not need to feel this right now.

She did, however, need a ride.

Agatha approached her looking pensive, her left shoulder sagging from the weight of a full backpack.

"Hey, you okay?" she asked. "I saw you were called out. What happened?"

Camellia blinked at her. "I'm more than okay. I'm fabulous! Anyway, it was nothing. A misunderstanding. Candace got what she deserved, though."

She began to turn away from the other girl, but halted.

"How are you?"

It was Agatha's turn to blink.

"I—you've never asked me that before!" She stared at Camellia. "I'm okay. I… still haven't heard from my family back East."

"Oh, right," said Camellia vaguely. *Atlanta.* "Well, hope you hear soon." She shifted back and forth in her boots, her skirt whipping in the wind. She felt uncomfortable. The rain was picking up again, so the two girls dashed back under the awning near the entrance of the school. They had company, as other students waited for their rides. It wasn't effective shelter, however, as the rain began to whip sideways. There was some jostling, some scrambling, and occasional shrieking as everyone grew soaked.

"Just wanted to thank you again," Agatha continued. "My sisters met their fundraising goal." She beamed, her large, dark eyes shining.

Camellia drew herself up. "You're so welcome!"

"Do you—" and Camellia could tell Agatha was perhaps regretting the conversation as much as Camellia dreaded her questioning. "Do you need a ride? My mom's going to be here soon. She's just running a few minutes late. Oh! She's here now. We can drop you off—"

Camellia raised her hands. "No thank you."

"You sure you're okay? You don't seem like... well, like yourself."

"And what is that like from your perspective?" Camellia asked briskly, her green eyes hardening.

Agatha sighed. "Normally you're insulting people every other second."

"Do you *want* me to insult you?" Camellia looked at her fingernails. Her manicure was chipping at the tips.

Agatha shook her head. "Forget I said anything," she muttered.

She dashed off, hood up and pulled tightly, and jumped into the passenger side of a silver car. The rain was too heavy for Camellia to see what make it was. She thought she did see, however, two smaller shapes in the backseat: Agatha's sisters. She let out her own sigh, very small. One of relief: they were all together.

She glanced at her watch, again clustered with warnings, and she cleared them. By the time she looked up again, most of the other students were gone. The winds shifted again, the rain surged, and more thunder shook the slopes.

I've got to call a ride.

But she felt numb.

He's okay.

A quiet little thought bubbled up from where she'd pushed everything down. An uncertain one.

She realized she was hungry. That was far more certain. She was tempted to get a ride to the mall and park herself at the food court. She felt like eating a wedge of greasy mall pizza, the kind that curled under one's hand and dripped when you picked it up. Suddenly she wanted that more than anything in the world.

That was the last thing she'd eaten with her mother and father together.

She was six. It was a mall; she wasn't sure if it was Westgate or where it was. *Was it the Grove? No, it was inside…*

A movie, a wedge of gooey pizza, an ice cream: a very special time for Camellia. Her father had been irritable though, she remembered. Cranky. Fussing over whether they should have dinner downtown, maybe at the Six Seven rooftop restaurant. Her mother had laughed and won the discussion. That was all Camellia really remembered, aside from how everything tasted. Her father had thawed, and she sat between them, kicking her little legs in pleasure.

She could almost taste the pizza…

"Didn't you get detention, Camouflage?" someone asked.

She jostled herself from the memory and turned swiftly. It was Wray.

A complex and rapid-fire set of emotions spun in Camellia like firefly signals on a sultry night. She felt as though the world slid sideways, and she might stumble.

"What's it to you, Wraith?"

Better they don't know. Then: *There isn't anything to know anyway.*

131

"I don't care why you're choosing to hang out at school in a rainstorm when everyone else is gone." Wray swept their damp hair back under a cap. Their umbrella was wrapped; given the inside-out umbrellas Camellia had seen earlier, it didn't surprise her that Wray would find their own useless, ultimately opting for a trucker cap.

You really don't give a shit about anything, do you?

She didn't realize she was grinning...

"What's so funny?" frowned Wray.

"Your face right now."

Wray crinkled up their nose. "Weak!"

Camellia set out an exasperated sigh and said, "What are you doing, hanging out here in the rain? You don't even need to hail a ride. Don't you have that piece of shit truck?"

Wray snorted. "I don't want to be hanging out here. I'm not exactly in a hurry to go home, though."

They pulled their hair over the now yellowing, healing bruise. It was fairly well hidden, but Camellia, of course, knew it was there.

"No, I guess not," she reasoned. "Me neither."

"Pops still hanging you out to dry?"

Camellia's throat tightened; she instinctively placed her hand on it.

Wray watched her, eyes darting all over her face, and also below, taking her in.

"What is it?" Camellia asked.

"Nothing, I... Nothing."

Wray stepped closer to her. The wind whipped against the lid of their cap (almost seizing it as it had Camellia's umbrella earlier), so they took it off, and held it in their hands.

"No, it's something." Wray stared at her. "You're not acting like yourself."

"What is with you and Agatha?" Camellia complained. "She said the same thing."

"She's way smarter than I am," confessed Wray. "But I know the face you've got on right now."

"Oh, do you?" Camellia huffed, feeling hot and cranky. "And just what kind of face is that?"

"That's shutdown face."

Camellia's breath caught in her throat.

"What do you mean?"

As Wray studied her, she felt even hotter and pulled at the collar of her sweater. She did know what Wray meant. And she almost didn't want to hear it spelled out. But it was too hard to resist. She needed to hear... something. Some sort of validation, maybe.

"It's the face when you stomp down the bullshit so nobody can see it. I know. Because I wear it all the time."

"You don't know me at all," Camellia murmured.

"I see the mask. It's more obvious than the one at the party."

Jesus fuck, who else sees it?

Camellia felt exposed. She controlled her breathing, though.

"I saw it the first time I laid eyes on you," Wray continued, never taking their stormy eyes from hers.

Camellia laughed. "What a bullshit line."

"Whatever works."

Camellia gasped before she could stop herself.

"Wait, are you...?"

"Do you need a ride?" interrupted Wray. There was a knowing look in their eyes that appalled Camellia.

No, no, no. I'm not. I'm NOT.

She could not bring herself to finish the thought.

"I..." she began.

"I mean, I can drop you off, but I'm starving... so I could stop and get food. Delay the inevitable shitfest."

"Would it?" she found herself blurting out.

"Are you hungry?"

"Yes."

"What do you want?"

She tried to stop it from coming out, but "Pizza" burst forth, and she was breathless.

The corner of Wray's mouth twitched.

"Then pizza it is."

Blinking furiously, the rain whipping her, Camellia held her hands over her hair and ran with Wray to the parking lot, to the dodgy old pickup truck sitting forlornly and empty. Facing the thing up close, Camellia felt like she was losing her mind.

"This thing is garbage!" she cried, eyeing the pockmarks of rust.

"You could keep standing in the rain, with no pizza!" shouted Wray over the wind and rain. "Or you could deal!"

Camellia opened the door and climbed awkwardly in, taking in a deep gulp of metallic-smelling air and the odor of a dangling pine tree air freshener. She turned, ostensibly to look out the window, but really, she was stifling laughter.

This is bugfuck crazy.

Wray slammed the driver door shut with an unsettling creak and bang before starting the ancient truck. Buckling herself in, Camellia considered.

"Okay, the mall is too far, but I want mall-type pizza."

Wray nodded. "I know a place."

They drove to a strip mall and found a small, old-school pizza and pasta restaurant called Dino's West. The door was painted with a surfer holding a pizza. This was the kind of pizza joint with cracking red pleather seats and archaic, dark wood paneling. Camellia swept forth to order, but Wray jumped ahead quickly.

"I've got this one," they said.

"Absolutely the fuck not!" hissed Camellia.

"Too late!" laughed Wray, slamming a twenty-dollar bill on the counter, and winking devilishly at the cashier.

"Well played," she murmured.

Wray gave a nonchalant but confident shrug.

Within ten minutes, Camellia found herself facing Wray in a booth, holding a large, floppy cheese slice, and making eye contact.

"Officially," she said in a voice primed for scorn but faltering, "this is not how I wanted my day to go. And your truck stinks."

Wray didn't flinch.

"Unofficially," Camellia continued, lifting the floppy part of the pizza up, "thank you."

Wray laughed, a rich, rolling laugh.

"Don't thank me until you've tried it!"

Camellia dipped her head and took a bite. Her auburn eyebrows shot up, and her eyes rolled back.

Between chews, she sighed, "Oh my fucking God."

Wray grinned, took a bite of their own pizza, which was pepperoni and green pepper, and said, "Right?"

"How'd you find this place?" Camellia asked, eyes glazing over as she ate the slice, feeling transported.

Wray shrugged. "I get around. And I'm broke. I like good, cheap food."

When they finished, Camellia's insides felt warm... not just from pizza, but from something deeper within. Like a lantern turning up slowly, illuminating its globe and, as result, everything around it.

Then came awkward silence.

"Welp," Wray finally said. "Home?"

"Yep," said Camellia. "I'll navigate."

Wray's jaw worked, and Camellia asked, "What is it?"

"Nothing."

"Okay, you don't get to psychoanalyze *my* face and then deny me the right to do the same for you."

"Don't worry about it."

"Fine."

It was a terse, quiet ride back. The last of the main outer band of the storm finally sundered itself furiously over the peaks of the mountains. Wray fishtailed occasionally on the sodden roads and had to wait to drive around a few flooded roadways, but Camellia guided them up to her neighborhood. And there, improbably, the junker parked right outside her home.

Camellia took a breath, quickly exhaled, and slapped her hands on the tops of her thighs.

"Well!" she chirped, as the sun broke through and struck Wray through the windshield. "Aren't you a *Wray* of sunshine after all. Thanks for the ride! And the pizza."

"Sure."

Wray's face betrayed them though, as their eyes scanned the immense home.

"Fuckin' royalty," they muttered.

"Nah, it's not that fancy," Camellia shrugged.

"Um, you live in a goddamn *mansion*."

"It's just a big-ass, gaudy, empty house. Come see for yourself."

She blushed.

Wray stared at her.

"What, go *in there*?"

"No, wallow on the front lawn or something," Camellia said irritably. "Of course I want you to come in."

And she blushed deeper when she said it.

"I mean, risky, though, right? I could be a vampire. You invite me in, who knows?" Wray laughed nervously.

"If you were a vampire," Camellia noted, "I'm pretty sure you'd never survive Malibu on a sunny day. Come on before I change my mind."

Wray didn't have to be told again.

They stared at the columns of the house and stopped midway up the walk.

"Do you hear that?" Camellia asked. There was the popping again...

"Hear what?"

Wray looked dumfounded by the grounds.

"That popping sound."

"Huh, yeah, I guess so. Sounds kind of like bubble wrap being popped."

"I heard it at school too," muttered Camellia.

"Weird."

"Very."

She opened the door, let Wray in, and doffed her shoes.

Wray did the same, and blushed when revealing mismatched socks under their soaked jeans.

Fridge then called out, "Your groceries will be here within the hour. Will you be needing assistance with your guest?"

"Nah, thanks, Fridge," Camellia called through the kitchen door. Then she turned to Wray. "Unless you need something? Do you want anything from the store? And I do mean anything."

Wray shook their head, eyes wide. "I'm good. Wow. Thanks though."

"Want a tour?" she asked uncertainly.

What the fuck am I doing, letting this person into my house...

Then:

Can't be worse than Syd. I hope.

That thought spiraled into another, and Camellia decided she needed to drink some cold water, soon.

"So, do you, uh... have conversations with your fridge?"

"Yeah, sometimes. Like I said, empty house."

"Do you have like... a maid or a butler?"

Camellia grinned. "We have staff. They work when I'm at school, and they're usually gone by the time I'm home."

"It's like a fairy tale," muttered Wray. "Everything's just all done for you. You really are like a queen."

"Hardly," Camellia sniffed. "Come on, I'll show you

upstairs. I'd show you the pools, but it's too cold, not much to see."

"Pools, plural?" Wray whistled.

Once she ascended, she was relieved to see the carpets were pristine, vacuumed smooth of any footprints. She felt the stress ache in her neck fade and rubbed it unconsciously.

"I didn't know you had a tattoo," Wray said softly.

Camellia yanked her hair back over her neck. "Mmhmm."

"What's it of?"

"A camellia."

"You're shitting me."

"Nope."

"Can I see it again?"

Camellia considered, then pulled her hair aside. "Why not?"

Wray was very close to her as they stood outside her bedroom. She held the hair aside a bit longer than made sense, and Wray studied the tattoo.

"It's lovely. I like the tiny heart in the center."

"There's no heart there," said Camellia.

"Yeah, there is."

Camellia turned, brushing against Wray by doing so. "I don't think so."

"Do you have a hand mirror? You can see that way."

She walked into her bedroom and said casually, "Oh, this is my room."

"Jesus Christ, it's like an apartment! It's bigger than my home!"

"Can you come in here and help me with a mirror so I can see the heart?" she called.

"Sure."

Wray obliged. With some awkward angling, Camellia tried to see it.

"Show me where," she urged.

Wray pointed, and Camellia backed into their finger, so that it pressed gently into her neck.

"Sorry," Wray stammered.

Camellia found nothing to dislike in their touch.

"I can't see it this way," she complained. "Here, take a picture of it, I guess."

Wray took out their phone and took a picture.

Camellia instantly regretted the notion, and dithered. But she was at least able to zoom in and confirm: there was a tiny heart in the center of the tattoo.

"I had no idea!" she breathed. "What's it doing there?"

"Someone loves you, I guess," answered Wray.

"Loved," Camellia said. "Mom's dead now."

"I'm sorry, I didn't mean…"

"It's okay. I'm just… I didn't know. Thank you so much for telling me."

"Hey, you're welcome."

They stared at each other.

"It's just…" Camellia's voice trembled, low and halting. "It's just that it's so… very… fucking… empty here."

"Do you like it like that?" Wray asked. "Honest question. I… sometimes I like to be by myself. Just to… relax." *And to be safe*, Camellia thought. "But… it's lonely."

"Do *you* like it?" Camellia asked, watching the pulse in Wray's neck. It was speeding up. Just like her own.

"I… I don't want things to be… empty," Wray said slowly.

"Neither do I," said Camellia.

Their fingers touched, and then intertwined. Camellia's heart thundered more than the storm had in the mountains. It felt like gravity, magnetism, an event horizon maybe. Whatever it was, they pulled together, fingers and lips and tongues. And it was delicious.

Stumbling out of her bathroom, Camellia guided Wray to her bed. They collapsed upon it, Wray tracing her cheek with their fingers, Camellia pressing her lips on Wray's.

JENDIA GAMMON

"This is crazy," Wray gasped.

"Yes. It is."

More kissing, furious and gentle at the same time.

"What's next?" Wray asked softly.

"Not being empty," answered Camellia, cradling Wray's head against her beating heart.

"The heart," breathed Wray, kissing her neck. "It's not small at all. Maybe in ink, but not in you."

"Do you want to…"

"…yes."

"So do I."

140

CHAPTER 18

KILLER VIEW

Everything that had been pent up in Camellia, the hurt, fear, frustration, and powerful surge of longing—all of it swirled around that night and into the next morning. She and Wray tasted each other's tears, listened to each other's hearts, and twisted themselves together into a befuddled tangle. It terrified Camellia on many levels, but awed her more, so she dove into the latter sensation. She had been so vacant of any real joy for so long that even risking the fire meant she felt alive. Wray's rapt face, taking in Camellia and her powerful spirit at close range, touched her soul deeply, and she kissed gently all around the healing wound on Wray's cheek. She gazed into Wray's stormy eyes, mesmerized. She kissed their eyelids, nose, neck, chest, and everywhere else countless times. Wray did the same for her, and caressed her, held her firmly in their arms. She could not speak, and for once she found she didn't want to. Camellia had no idea what to do next, and while that frightened her, she also felt a deep satisfaction. She wanted more of that, and more *than* that. She wanted Wray to be safe.

She gently lifted her watch from her bedside table and found no new messages. She put the watch back and slid next to Wray, marveling at the warmth and comfort of having them next to her. The previous day washed over her again. She thought about messaging her dad but rolled her eyes.

He's totally fine. Kern County bullshit: he's just been on some bender, like always.

A slight tingling of doubt crept in, but she pushed it down swiftly.

She was very good at doing that.

She dozed again.

She blinked as the sunrise filtered through her bedroom curtains in creamy, gentle light. Wray had curled around her... much as she had curled around her sword before. This felt safer, somehow. Not being alone. She shifted Wray's hands and turned around to face them, their sandy and blue-tipped hair rumpled, the dark circles under their eyes and stress marks on their forehead belying a stressful life. The bruise was diminished a bit more today. Wray blinked awake and smiled; they pulled Camellia forward into a kiss. That led to several heightened minutes that left them both giddy. Camellia began to laugh and could not stop.

"What's so funny?" Wray asked with a grin, winding the fiery arc of Camellia's hair around their hands and drawing their fingers through it.

"Nothing funny, exactly." Camellia grinned back. "I don't know. I just feel like laughing. And... kind of dizzy."

"Well," Wray considered, "I feel pretty starved. We worked up an appetite."

Camellia laughed at that, a sound that rang true in the large house, and then her watch chimed. The intercom rang out.

"Good morning, Camellia!" came the chipper house voice through her room's speakers.

Wray gaped at her, and they both burst out laughing.

"Your house wakes you up?" they asked, astounded.

"Sometimes," she answered, smirking.

The house chimed again and said, "Fridge is ordering your breakfast smoothie. Shall they order two?"

Camellia blushed deep crimson; the cackling fits of the teen lovers echoed out into the hall and down the stairs.

"Well, aren't you a nosy shit!" cried Camellia. "Fucking Fridge. Sure, order two."

"Is that what you have for breakfast?" Wray looked shocked. "Just a smoothie?"

"What's wrong with that?" She was genuinely curious. "It's just a liquid bunch of fruit, vitamins, and protein. Lots of people drinks smoothies. It's not a new thing."

Wray blew a raspberry. "That's not a proper breakfast."

"Okay, so what's your idea of a good breakfast, then, my fine nutritionist?" Camellia kissed Wray's nose.

"Hmm." Wray touched her cheek. "Well, I mean, obviously anything with you on the other side of it. Or... maybe just you."

Wray worked downward and Camellia shrieked with laughter and delight.

"But seriously," she gasped, "We could eat out. It's Saturday."

"Dining in is fine too." Wray grinned up at her devilishly.

"You're incorrigible," she murmured back. "But I was thinking... how about the Pier? There's a great café at the end of it. Killer view."

"I've got a killer view right here," Wray told her, climbing back up and staring up at her.

She blushed. She felt uneasy, too, and tried to push that feeling aside. This was all new for her, and she could feel her old self bubbling up like an oil slick from a deep, dark pit within. The joyless abyss she was more familiar with. She fought it, for the moment, but was unsure she could win against her own hardened nature.

She kissed Wray and swung her legs over the bed.

"Let's shower, and then we can get a ride out there."

"I've got my truck," Wray reminded her.

She gave a short laugh. "Oh right, I forgot!"

And that feeling crept in again, something like dread. She hated it.

"Right," she said crisply. "Shower. Food."

Wray nodded, following her into the shower.

"Holy fuck, that tub is like a pool!" cried Wray.

Camellia bit her lip. "Maybe I'll show you the actual pools one day."

Dez had contracted more several pools... there, and at different properties (but she never ventured to those properties, and she never even used her own).

"Oh, let's swim later!"

Wray looked excited.

"Fuck no! It's cold!"

Wray shook their head, laughing. She enjoyed Wray's laugh more than anything she had ever heard before.

"Camellia, it's September."

"But we just had that storm! And also, the pool cleaners haven't been in yet. They're probably full of all kinds of shit."

"Okay, that might be true..." conceded Wray. They looked longingly at the tub while Camellia commanded the shower to pulse at certain speeds and angles.

She smiled to herself.

"We can use the tub later," she said.

"Really!" Wray's eyes lit up.

Camellia pulled them into the shower.

"Later," she said softly. The two kissed, water streaming over them. They drank each other in, along with some of the streaming water. They soaped each other up.

"This is fancy soap," Wray marveled. "High end shit... French?"

"Well, no, it's one of Kate Switch's things."

"Oh. The chick on the billboards?"

"Yeah, we're fri... we know each other." Camellia thought

for a second. Were she and Kate truly friends? And also... the memory of meeting Syd gave her relationship with Kate a different shadow now. Kate was bubble-headed and insipid, but upon reflection, not overtly harmful. Maybe negligent sometimes.

But aren't all trust fund Hollywood gals?

"You seem distracted," Wray pointed out. "Let me help with that."

Wray pressed their body against Camellia, held her face, and smoothed back her dark red hair from the shower soaking. Finally, after several minutes more than necessary in the shower, they both stepped and toweled off. Camellia then began to dress, and Wray watched in awe as she selected things from different closets and cabinets. Wray glanced down at the pile of clothes on the floor and grimaced.

"I... didn't think to pack," they confessed.

Camellia giggled. "Well, we didn't exactly *plan* this."

"True. Dreamed it, maybe. Not planned."

Camellia paused, wearing thigh-high stockings and her underwear. Wray whistled appreciatively as they pulled on their jeans and t-shirt and hoodie.

"Did you really?" she asked.

"Did I really what?"

"Dream about this. About... about us."

Her cheeks burned but she had no reason to explain why.

"You know," enthused Wray, straightening the bedcovers, "I'm pretty good at math."

Camellia laughed. "What's that got to do with anything?"

"Just... you know, considering the odds. The odds that I'd get the school lotto to go to Killian. The odds I'd actually *fuckin' go*, rather than bailing—because I almost did. The odds of then seeing you, gleaming in the sun like a fire goddess, and getting burned by you instantly."

Camellia felt uncertain and blinked while breathing quickly. She remembered that moment. A moment of something. Recognition. She'd not understood it then, and she wasn't sure she understood it now.

"I wasn't exactly… welcoming," she admitted.

"I could handle you."

Camellia winked. "You handle me *very* well."

"We're never going to breakfast, are we?" Wray grinned as Camellia kissed them.

"Yes, yes we are," she insisted. "I just need my lipstick."

She opened her lipstick cabinet in the bathroom.

"Holy hell," muttered Wray, observing the kaleidoscope of tubes at the ready. "You do love your makeup!"

"Yes, I do," she said simply, plucking one of them out: *Enchante No. 1: Enchantment.* She'd never worn this one before. As a former brand influencer, she'd tried some of the *Enchante* lip colors and been given every hue; a subscription arrived monthly with more of their products. But this one… she didn't think about it, despite its being the original, first color of the brand. It was deep raspberry with a hint of golden sparkle, a unique shade that changed subtly according to its wearer, responding to temperature and body chemistry. She smacked her lips together and glanced over her shoulder at Wray.

"Gorgeous," whispered Wray.

Camellia grinned back, tossing back her fresh, still-damp hair. She pulled on designer jeans with embroidered leaves all along their seams, and a dark green sweater with a cowl neck. She retrieved dark brown booties from her shoe closet.

"God, even in just jeans and a sweater, you're the hottest thing there is," sighed Wray.

"Speak for yourself," she murmured back, realizing she had been attracted to Wray immediately: their sharp features, the angle of their jaw, the intensity of their storm-shadowed gaze, the way their hair flickered between shadow and sunlit warmth. But especially that worldly, wise expression… the expression of someone who had grown up too fast, yet still clung to a sense of fun. That was what she'd been denying herself. Fun. And Wray was already the most fun she'd ever had. And more than that... But she was not ready to open that door to herself fully. It stood ajar.

That reminded her, momentarily, of the disturbing doors ajar in the house, the night Syd had been snooping. She didn't want to think of him just then, with Wray there.

They both climbed down the stairs to the kitchen. Camellia was about to get water for them, when a shadow in the hall startled her. She halted her steps, Wray close behind, and could see a silhouette in the glass doorway of the garden. She gasped.

"Who the fuck is that?" whispered Wray.

"I don't know," she confessed, heart racing. "House?" she asked quietly.

But before the house could answer, the door opened, and in stepped the gardener, Clifton, ruddy-cheeked and cheerful, in a straw hat and overalls. He beamed at Camellia.

"Well, hello, Miss Camellia!" he called in a warm voice. "I see you have a friend."

He stepped forward to shake Wray's hand. He glanced back and forth between the teens, and his soft, crinkled eyes rested on Camellia's face for a second. He smiled.

"Good to see you having fun," he said. "Sorry I didn't make it over sooner. We had a real mess to deal with at the nursery... a bunch of the plants wilted, and we couldn't figure out why. Then the storms came, washed a bunch of the gravel of the lot away..." He sighed. "Have you been out back lately?"

"No," admitted Camellia. "Not in several days."

"Something funny going on back there," he mused, rubbing his chin and glancing back. "Noisy... can't figure out what it is!"

"Is it..." Camellia cringed, almost not wanting to say it, "is it like a popping sound?"

"It is!" he exclaimed. "Weirdest thing. I know some plants make noises when they don't get much water, but Lord knows we've had plenty. I mean... maybe it isn't the plants, but..."

"No, I think it is," said Camellia. "I heard it at school too."

"At *school*?" echoed the gardener. "Well, that's weird, ain't it?" Then he shuffled back and forth on his worn work shoes. "You seen the news?"

"I... well, I've not been keeping up," admitted Camellia. She and Wray grinned at each other. "I heard about some sort of attack. Or a virus, or something?"

Gardener shook his head. "It's just some kind of overreaction, I think. And absolutely no popping! Not that I've heard of anyway. Still... weird. Well, I'm off for now for more supplies. The fertilizer bags were drained. Looks like an animal got into them, maybe. I'll be back later. You two have fun!"

"Thanks!" chirped Camellia.

Fridge then called out, "Miss Camellia, the smoothies are at the door. Also, I continue to experience glitches. Your father is not receiving my messages, so I rerouted, without success."

Camellia felt as though cold water spilled down her back.

"Well, he's like that," she said quietly.

"This is a different scenario than in the past. Ordinarily I can trace his whereabouts, which I am programmed to do for your protection. I cannot locate Mr. Dume."

Camellia felt her throat constrict.

"I'm sure he'll be back soon. He was just in Vegas, he'll be fine."

"I will continue reaching out."

"Okay, bye, Fridge—"

"An additional alert, begging your pardon," Fridge interrupted. "It could be part of the glitch, but I am missing data from the other evening, and I am concerned that my subroutines have been disrupted remotely somehow."

"Hmm." She immediately thought of Syd. What was it he did for the Navy? And the house hadn't detected his presence, either. "Fridge, try to repair the network and make sure the house is armed while I'm away."

"I will do my best. Enjoy your smoothies."

"Thanks, Fridge. We're actually going out to breakfast, so I'm giving them to you for now."

"Very well. I will keep them safe and cold until you return."

Wray stared as Camellia nonchalantly shouldered her purse and headed for the front door.

When they reached Wray's truck, Wray turned to her and said, "You just had a whole-ass conversation with your *fridge*. What the fuck is that all about? I know AI is getting good, but... that's pretty sophisticated."

"It's nothing new, actually," she remarked. "Apparently Mom had it set up a long time ago, once Dad got his first millions."

Wray shook their head. "Different world," they murmured. The look on their face troubled Camellia.

The truck snorted and snarled to a start; Wray turned around in the street, almost striking a Bentley.

"Whew, shit," Wray gasped. "That would... not have been good."

"It's fine, you'd be fine," said Camellia off-handedly.

"No, I'd probably lose my license because I couldn't pay for that!"

"I'd take care of it," Camellia shrugged.

Silence as they drove to the end of the lane.

"You shouldn't," Wray said quietly.

Camellia sighed irritably. "What's the big deal?"

"I think you're getting hangry," noted Wray.

"I am not *getting* hangry," she snapped. "I *am* hangry."

"Let's get you that brekkie STAT, then."

Wray raised her hand to kiss it, and she stroked their cheek.

Neither spoke, as Camellia stared out at the moody sea, not at all in keeping with its name at the moment. The remnant storm swells dashed waves upon the shore in fury and froth. The air smelled fresh yet putrid, almost as if the air were battling with itself. And still, a fine, strange shimmer morphed in and out of the horizon in all directions.

Just what the hell is *that?*

Wray parked across from the Malibu Pier despite Camellia's warning they could get a ticket.

"Didn't you *just* say it would be bad if something happened to your car?"

"Fuck it, nobody's gonna ticket me for parking in a fast-food lot. People will just assume I eat there. You on the other hand…" their voice trailed off.

"What's that supposed to mean?"

"Nothing, Jesus! Let's go to that café."

Camellia was feeling on edge, low on blood sugar, and heightened on anxiety. They were finally seated, with the chef himself taking them to a special corner overlooking the big, blue, not-so-Pacific Ocean. The wind whipped Camellia's hair and stung her eyes, so the chef personally brought out a folding room separator to cut the worst of it back. A heat lamp cast warmth over them, offsetting the stiff ocean breeze.

The mood of the café was subdued, and not as busy as usual… odd for a Saturday at the most popular café along the Malibu coastline. That meant, however, that their coffees and fresh-squeezed juices arrived quickly. And, shortly after, their meals: French toast with berries for Camellia, chilaquiles for Wray. They tried each other's food and chatted amiably about school, when a sharp cry rang out below. A few people rose from their seats, and sat down, not seeing anything.

The cry became a gurgling scream.

"Oh God! Oh God!" someone gibbered.

Everyone stood; Camellia and Wray pushed back their chairs and rushed to the side of the pier and looked down…

At bodies.

Warped, broken, twisted bodies; a dozen, maybe more, bobbing face down, bloated, against the pier… weirdly shaped, lacerated, and a sickly green. Something vaguely purple floated around their necks.

Camellia realized what she'd smelled in the air.

Death.

Chapter 19

The Point

The pier quickly swarmed with onlookers, most bearing phones, some piloting drones to hover over the bodies, the restaurant staff shouting at 911 operators, some folks vomiting over the pier, and general chaos. Camellia and Wray recoiled, looking at each other with wide eyes.

"One—one body," stammered Wray, "and you think, maybe someone drowned and floated down. But that many? Coming in on the tide, too."

"Where'd they come from?" murmured Camellia. The two of them gazed out to sea. As a Coast Guard vessel raced toward them, they could see another interception of a boat closer to the horizon. It was not a sailboat, or at least it had no sails aloft. "Tour boat, maybe?"

"Let's go," urged Wray.

"Yeah. I think so," agreed Camellia.

They shoved their way back through the increasing throngs, stopping just long enough for Wray to shove some cash into the hands of their unsettled server.

"I was going to get that!" objected Camellia.

But Wray took her hand and pulled gently, and they dashed across the Pacific Coast Highway to the truck.

Camellia heard sirens. She tilted her head left and right.

"Coming from the east I think."

Wray nodded, and they pulled out quickly headed west, pausing momentarily as police cars and paramedics came from both directions. Camellia felt sick... not just because they hadn't finished their meals, but because they were in shock.

And still no word from her dad.

She pressed her hands onto her knees, skin on skin through the decorative rips in the denim. She stared straight ahead while Wray drove.

"Can we... can we drive a bit, before we go home?" she asked suddenly.

"Sure." Wray glanced at her. "Where?"

"Point Dume."

"Ah, your place! Named after your family, right?"

She grimaced. She didn't want to go down *that* particular line of thinking.

She closed her eyes, and remembered her dad vehemently urging her not to drive with Syd out toward Zuma Beach. She wondered why. He hadn't known who she was with.

So, he couldn't have known anything else... right?

It didn't make sense.

The death beneath Malibu Pier was contrasted by the bright, glorious morning light sparkling on the choppy sea, glimpsed from PCH through neighborhoods full of green leaves and bright September flowers. The farther from the dead bodies they drove, the better she felt. She rolled her window down, and so did Wray. The stiff ocean breeze funneled in and, thankfully, smelled fresher, full of salt-tang. Wray took the turns off the highway to access Point Dume, past the residential hodgepodge of houses. Some of them were mansions, others old and comparatively quaint—but still expensive, because of their prime real estate. Camellia secretly liked those old houses better. She wondered what life must have been like along the shore, in the old beach cottages, before glittering glass-walled Hollywood mogul mansions snapped up the best views.

The morning road was empty for a weekend, with fewer tourists than there would be later in the day. The Point itself had a small pullout area, usually jammed with cars. A few were parked there, but it was mercifully calm. As soon as Wray set the parking brake, Camellia pushed the stiff, creaking pickup door open, jumped out onto gravel, and slammed it behind her. She set her feet upon the dirt path, coursing its way up a headland, and down along the edge of the sea cliffs. From there, one could see the crescent shape of the shore curving southeast, out toward the haze of Santa Monica. All along the path, shrubs, wildflowers and grasses grew.

And popped.

It was subtle… not to the level of the vigorous popping of the lush garden of her home, or that of the plants outside Killian High. It was more like faint popcorn. The wind buffeted the headland and set the grasses undulating the scrubby plants bobbing. It was familiar to her, although it had been a long time since she had stood there. Years. She was quite sure, however, that there had never been popping before.

Wray stepped up to her and nudged her. She stared out at the vibrant blue Pacific, past golden flowers contrasting the cobalt hue.

"Do you hear that?" she whispered.

She was mesmerized by the sound.

Two morning hikers walked past them; their faces pinched.

Wray blurted out, "What's it like out there? Everything okay?"

"Don't know," a gray-bearded man in a taupe, wide-brimmed hat with a mountain emblem on it replied. His companion, a woman, trudged on and opened their car's trunk. "Something weird. Starting to think maybe we're about to have an earthquake."

"Why?" Camellia refocused and asked quickly.

"Look at the birds. Like they know," the man murmured.

He paused.

"What's that sound?"

Camellia and Wray looked at each other.

"It's... popping. I think. Maybe." She stared at the man.

"Did you hear it out there?" asked Wray suddenly.

He shook his head. "No, too distracted by the birds and the wind. Could've been... I don't think so. Almost sounds like a fire crackling. Hope there *isn't* one starting with this wind like this..."

He muttered to himself before barking to his companion, "I'll be there in a minute."

Camellia hadn't noticed the birds until then: crows and gulls and other birds wheeling above them, some caught in the updrafts of the sea cliffs, none of them landing.

She shivered and folded her arms around herself.

Wray reached out to rub her arms.

"Cold?"

She pulled away from them and surged forward.

"I need to see."

"What do you need to see?"

"I just do. I—I'm trying to remember."

She tried to ignore the pops and clicks emanating from the plants all around her and took long strides on the path to the edge of the cliff. Wray, however, hung back. She did not notice until she made it to the cliff.

She looked back and squinted at them.

"You coming?" she called.

Wray nodded and joined her. The two stood facing the

wind in full, sending Camellia's hair skyward like flames. She tried unsuccessfully to tame it.

The popping continued.

"Camellia," Wray said softly.

She turned to look at them. Their face looked troubled, lips downturned, brow crinkled.

"What is it?"

"The—the sound. I waited until you were out here, away from me."

She stared at Wray.

"Yes?"

"It... it stopped."

"No it didn't, I can still hear it. You can hear that, right?"

The snaps and pops and crackles continued.

Wray touched her shoulder.

"It stopped when you went away."

She swiveled around, twisting her hair into a knot at the nape of her neck, so she could see Wray better.

"But it's here now, it's—"

"It's *you*."

"What do you mean, it's *me*?" She felt a flare of temper leap within her. "I'm not making these goddamn popping sounds!"

Wray threw their hands out. "I'm telling you—look. Let's test it again. This time, *you* go to the truck. I'll stay here."

"This is ridiculous," she sneered.

"Humor me. Please." Wray swept their hands around her cheeks and kissed her as the wind swirled, the birds dipping and screeching above, the sea thundering and moaning below.

Drawing away from Wray, Camellia nodded and sighed. "Okay, fine. Then I'll come back, though. I still want to see—I still need to see—"

She didn't finish the sentence but sighed again.

She walked back toward the truck, hearing the chorus of

pops and clicks. The man had been correct in describing the sound. It sounded like logs burning in a fireplace. Crackling and snapping. She reached the truck, and threw her arms out. She turned around, bent over, and swished from side to side before mooning Wray. She laughed out loud, turned, and saw more hikers coming down the path. She blushed but blew them a kiss. They shot her funny looks.

Rolling her eyes, she almost skipped back to Wray.

Wray was not smiling.

"Well?" she asked.

"First of all, nice ass..." Wray leaned in to place their hands firmly behind her to squeeze, pressing her against them. "Which I already know, having seen it up close."

She giggled and kissed Wray on the nose, returning the favor with her hands slipping into their back pockets.

"Second," and now Wray turned serious again, "I was right. It's you. You're making the plants pop."

Camellia rolled her eyes and shook her head. "That's stupid. I am not!"

"You *are*."

She continued shaking her head and loosened herself from Wray. She felt dizzy, but not in the pleasant way she had with Wray in her room. She stared at the sea and briefly closed her eyes, listening to the surf and the calling of sea birds.

She opened her eyes halfway and took a deep breath through her nose, exhaling through her mouth. She did this ten times. She felt a sense of calm. The sounds continued, but she could think more clearly.

This was where her mother liked to take her when she was little, before they would head down toward Zuma Beach. Her mother was a botanist, but also loved to paint plein air acrylics. And this view, with the crescent beach, the blooms, the ocean sapphire blending to aquamarine close to shore... this was one of her mother's favorite places on earth. She'd said so. It was an ancient memory, but powerful. The wind made her eyes stream with tears, or so she told herself. Wray came up behind her, briefly startling her, and held her close.

"It's okay. You're okay. Maybe you're a plant whisperer."

She laughed out loud at that, and turned in their arms to be face to face.

"What the fuck is going on, Wray? A goddamn hurricane, my dad goes missing, we end up fucking, plants are popping, dead bodies..."

"Wait, your dad's not really missing, though. He's just in Vegas."

"Actually..."

She had to face reality. It stared into her green eyes with gray ones.

"That's why I was staying late. I—was pulled from class. I met a sheriff."

Her voice began to shake, and she blushed from rage, balling her fists to still the trembling. She ignored the tears.

"What the fuck, Camellia!" breathed Wray, holding her carefully, pushing the wind-blown red-gold stray hairs from her face. "Why didn't you tell me?"

She shook the tears off, as Wray dabbed the corners of her eyes with their sleeve.

"I assumed it was bullshit. I thought, 'Oh, he's just late again, he's been on a gambling fit, got trash-drunk, fucked some whores, maybe did Molly or coke or something,' and that was that. But... but the house computer can't find him either."

She choked out the words while Wray stroked her face.

"They found his car. In the desert. In a flash flood. Mud flow. Whatever. I don't know! Some fucking thing like that, because of the storm."

"Jesus!"

"He wasn't in it. They—they couldn't locate him."

"Camellia..." Wray's voice channeled every bit of emotion

Camellia had denied herself from feeling, and she sobbed, falling to her knees, heaving.

The snapping and popping from the plants around her reached a crescendo.

Wray placed their hands under her arms and pulled her up.

"Let's get out of here. I'm taking you home. Then we're figuring out what happened to your dad."

Facing them, sniffling, she blinked. Her hand hovered over Wray's bruise.

"Don't go back to that place," she said in a low voice. "Stay with me."

"I'm not leaving you." They swiftly walked back to the truck, climbed in, and Wray peeled it out onto the road.

"Do you want to go down to Zuma first, or back the way we came?"

Camellia's father's words echoed in her mind. Warning her to stay away from Zuma Beach.

"I—"

What was so important about that conversation?

"No. Back the way we came; to the highway, then home."

Wray kept glancing at her, as she dully stared out the window.

What's happening to me?

What's happening everywhere?

She would get no answers by looking at the sea. But she felt some sense of peace, even so... having visited a place her mother loved.

Peace, on one hand, but on another... her father's words haunted her.

Why didn't he want her going to a place the love of his life adored?

Are you gone too, Dad?

She held fast to her watch, scrolling to the last communication with him. She read it over and over, and feeling queasy from looking down, leaned back to breathe the fresh air. She heard helicopters buzzing, more sirens. She wanted to get away from all of that, from everyone. But when she looked at Wray, she felt anchored.

Not everyone.

Don't you take Wray too, Universe.

You fucker.

CHAPTER 20

QUITE CONTRARY

The moment Wray pulled their pickup truck next to the Dume house, Camellia felt something was wrong. Then her watch chimed, flashing red.

"System offline," it chirped. *"Request reauthorization. Dume, Camellia."*

"What the fuck?" whispered Camellia, shooting a look of alarm at Wray. "The house alarm is off or something."

"Can you still get in?" Wray asked. "Or will it call the cops, or..."

Wray glanced in their rearview mirror and looked cagey. "I don't need any close attention."

Camellia stared at them. "Why not? What did you *do*?"

Wray flinched. "It's not what *I've* done. It's what my *dad's* done."

Camellia opened her mouth to say something, but shut it. She thought for a moment.

"Pull around the back, where the gardener parks. If he's back, I'll tell him to move. There's a gate—it should recognize me, at least. If not, we'll fucking push it open by hand," she said forcefully. "Let's just get you off the main road, out of sight."

Wray's shoulders slumped from relief.

"Thank you."

Camellia nodded, pointing ahead to the driveway, concealed behind swaying, tall cypress and a hedge of fuchsia bougainvillea. Through the partially opened window of Wray's truck, she could hear the same popping and crackling, albeit somewhat louder with the swaying and occasionally cracking of branches above.

"Jesus," she murmured, feeling sick. "It really *is* me, isn't it?"

Wray reached over and squeezed her left hand, and she squeezed theirs.

She was glad to be home, after the day's events. But still, the sounds set her on edge, and the knowledge that she was the cause of them sent her tripping along the edge of a full meltdown... because most of all, she wondered where her father was.

The gardener's pickup was still parked in its usual spot.

"So, he's back, at least," she said.

"Then if there's any problems, he could let us in, right?" Wray asked, looking over their shoulder at the lane. Camellia glanced back as well, and could not see the road from where the truck sat. The driveway curved back just enough among the plants. They pulled up to the gate, a simple affair with sensors on both sides for recognition entry. She motioned for Wray to roll the windows down.

"House," she spoke to a sensor embedded in an ostentatious marble lion (her father's idea, of course). "Let us in, House!"

Her watch flashed yellow. The gate did not move, and the sensor did not respond. She scowled.

The yellow is different from red... but I've never seen this before.

Wray sighed. "So, it's not working?"

She held her palm up at Wray.

"I don't know." She shouted at the sensor again, "Let me in, goddammit!"

A buzz and a click sounded as her watch face turned solid green. The gate rolled open as she sat back and sighed in relief. She covered her face.

"I just want to get inside."

Wray deftly pulled to the parking spot alongside Gardener's truck, at the edge of the upper garage. The lower garage, one of several, was around the back, accessed from the parallel alley behind the main house. It was far more secure, given its contents of McLarens, Lamborghinis, and the like. No one but Desmond had access to it, not even Camellia; her father's presence was required. That was how he preferred it, in case, as he'd said casually once, "Someone comes looking for them."

That never occurred to Camellia as ominous until now, thinking back to Syd's intrusion. Could he have accessed the garage without her knowing? She shuddered.

"What is it?" Wray asked, watching her attentively.

She wished Wray didn't see everything that she did. It felt too personal. She liked operating from a distance so no one *could* see her reactions. Yet she also liked Wray's company. It was a strange and confusing thing she did not understand, and she was too drained to figure it out just then.

"Where's Gardener?" she wondered aloud.

"His truck's here," Wray said. "I'm assuming he is too, somewhere. Maybe he went in the house?"

"If he did," Camellia mused, "then I hope he's not stuck inside or something."

"Is he usually this messy?" Wray asked, pointing to the end of the truck.

Camellia stepped around to look and could see bags of fertilizer spilling out of the truck, trailing off into the garden. She frowned.

"I—I don't really know," she confessed. "I've not really, ever... you know, watched him do the dirty stuff."

"The dirty stuff?" Wray snorted. "It's fertilizer, nothing to be afraid of. Just need gloves. It helps the plants grow. You know *that*, right?"

She shot Wray a savage look. "Do I look like a bubblehead to you? My mother was a *scientist*."

Wray raised their hands up. "Fine! You don't exactly advertise how smart you are."

Camellia's mouth fell open and she quickly rearranged her lips to spew an insult, her natural instinct. "Wraith— Wray." They huffed out a breath at her. "Just because I don't show off everywhere doesn't mean I'm stupid."

"Jesus, forget I said anything!" Wray said bitterly. "Anyway, maybe that's this guy's method, I don't know. It's not how *I'd* do it."

"Oh, are *you* a gardener?"

"Me?" scoffed Wray. "No. I admire their work, but I suck with plants. I *like* plants, and I know what some of them are; I know their roles in the environment. But I can't *grow* them for shit."

"My mother sure could," Camellia murmured. "That was kind of her thing." She let out a tiny, quiet, wistful sigh, and hoped Wray didn't hear it.

She led Wray on a winding path through the popping and crackling trees and shrubs, trying not to panic at the sound *she* was apparently causing them to make. She headed toward one of the pools, glinting in the distance. Several camellias were planted around it in honor of her, by her mother. So Gardener Clifton liked to tell her.

He'd said, "She loved those best, which is why she named you Camellia."

It was a more cogent statement than she could get from her father, who was checked out most of the time after her mother died. In many ways, Gardener provided more of a paternal figure than her own father, or perhaps he was more like a grandfather, given his age. She used to fantasize about him marrying her Appalachian Mammaw, if only they'd had a chance to meet.

She halted for a moment, considering the trail. It was strewn with fertilizer, and even though she was no gardener, she knew that made no sense. Stepping forward, she beheld a weird pattern in it, as if something had swished it from side to side. The hairs on the back of her neck rose.

CHAPTER 21

COMPROMISE

"Gardener?" she called out.

Wray moved closer to her.

"What is it?" they murmured. Then Wray leaned down to look through the brush. "Do you have a dog or something?"

"No," said Camellia. "Not since Mom died. Dad gave away the corgis. Said they reminded him too much of Mom."

Wray stared at her. "Okay, I'm *really* not liking your dad. He gave away your dogs? Seriously?"

Camellia sighed. She didn't want to think about it, didn't want to relive how she had run for the door on her little legs, screaming for Taffy and Corky, crying bitter tears. She'd pushed all that down inside too, until she'd deadened herself to the pain. Cauterized by her own anger and hurt.

"Why do you care?" she asked bluntly, feeling pops of rage within her, matching the sounds around them.

"It looks—" Wray knelt again and pointed, so she joined them. "It looks like something big went through the bushes there. Like... a dog, maybe. Something low. Almost tunneling..."

Wray's voice trailed off, and they stood quickly, looking in all directions.

"Can we go inside now?" Wray's voice shook.

"We're about to. What's the hurry? Did you want to see the pools?"

Wray turned to her, eyes wide.

"No. I—I think we should go inside. Now."

Camellia seized their arms.

"What is it?"

"Please, just go inside."

Heart racing, she stepped quickly to one of the back French doors, glancing at the swaying trees and shrubs, hearing loud *cracks* above, like in the nights previous.

"What was that?" Wray hissed, as Camellia tried the door.

It was locked, as she expected. She held her hand to the access panel and said, "House, let me in."

The panel flashed green, along with her watch, and she exhaled in relief. She opened the door, and urged Wray to enter first, before shutting and locking it behind them.

"House," she called, taking her booties off. "I'm in, can you arm everything?"

This time, Fridge's voice rang through the intercom. "Camellia, welcome home. I have overridden the glitch and the house is armed. There were several minutes offline prior to your arrival. All seems to be in working order now."

Well, another thing that's weird as shit.

She walked to the kitchen, where Fridge greeted her with a panel display of brilliant white and pink-striped camellias. That relieved her, at least. Something was working right. Fridge always greeted her warmly.

"Would you like your smoothies now?" the fridge asked her.

She gasped in relief. "Oh, holy shit, yes!" she cried. "I'd forgotten about them. Yes. Thank you, Fridge. Breakfast was... interrupted."

She grimaced and watched Fridge's special smoothie panel open; two smoothies sat just above freezing. She took one for herself and handed the other to Wray. First, she eyed the thing. It was brown and streaked with fuchsia.

"Which one is this?" she asked. She took a sip from the metal straw in the cup.

"This is Chocolate Passion," answered Fridge cheerfully. "A mixture of cacao nibs, sunflower seed butter, raspberry and hibiscus swirl. And adaptogens to enhance romantic feelings."

Camellia spat explosively as she and Wray howled with laughter.

"Fridge!" she gasped between spasms. "Are you... did you... how much do you know about..."

"What she means to say, O Fridge," Wray said wryly, a hand on one hip before the display showing a laughing red panda face, "is that she wants to know if you're a voyeur. Have you been naughty, Fridge?"

Camellia cackled.

The red panda face blushed, to their amusement, and Wray bent over laughing. "I am here to protect you, Camellia," said Fridge, "and anyone you deem also worthy of protection. This includes your companion. You are safe."

"Are we?" she wondered aloud.

"You are safe in my protection."

"What about outside? What about Dad?"

The red panda face lowered and blinked. "I am unable to access Desmond's location. I assume he is without his tracking watch or phone."

"*Was* it really his car, then?" she asked softly. "They found in the mud?"

"I have accessed the Kern County records, and yes, it is one of your father's cars. There is no record of his whereabouts after he left Las Vegas."

"That's odd, don't you think?" she asked, trying to act casually, without panicking.

She finished her smoothie, and felt energized by it. She

laced her fingers with Wray's across the breakfast nook table. Wray picked up the camellia-shaped container she'd brought out of her mother's room, and turned it over and over in their hand, opening it to see the empty slots.

Fridge finally answered, "It is not Desmond's typical behavior pattern, I agree. Because of this aberration, and current national events, I have ordered drone delivery emergency supplies as a backup."

Camellia's head flew up at that.

"What for?"

"As always, Camellia, for your protection."

She blinked and furrowed her brow.

"Aw," said Wray with a grin. "I think Fridge likes you. It's like your mo—"

Wray froze.

"I'm sorry."

Camellia shook her head. She sighed.

"Well, I wouldn't know, would I? Not anymore."

She glanced at Wray's fading bruise, as they blinked and pulled their hair down.

"Good smoothie," they said. A downcast expression seeped over their face.

"What's wrong?" asked Camellia, heart pounding.

Don't leave. Don't leave. Don't leave.

She couldn't help but think it.

"I just—I don't have any clothes other than these. Can I do my laundry here? Do you have a robe?"

"I've got more than that. I've got Dad's clothes, and some guest clothes too."

"Okay, I guess…"

Camellia beamed.

"What is this?" Wray asked, examining the flower-shaped case.

She shrugged. "I don't know. It was in my mother's office, in her desk. I found all sorts of things in there!"

Wray examined the lid, opened and shut it again. "It looks like it's missing something. Earbuds, maybe?" Wray touched the design on the front, the engraved camellia pattern with a bumpy center. A little frown formed and Wray's tongue partially stuck out in concentration.

"Yeah, maybe. No idea."

She felt suddenly eager. Ever a fan of makeovers, she considered the possibilities of what might fit Wray. She pulled them up from their seat, as Wray dropped the empty container on the table. The two hurried excitedly up the stairs to her father's room and threw the doors open. She crinkled her nose once inside.

"Ew," she said reflexively. "Lights," she called out, and they began to turn on, illuminating slowly. She never liked that; she liked immediate lights. But her father was often hungover in some fashion or other, and preferred a gentler approach for a pounding head. Once the room was as bright as it would ever be (still dimmed), she could see a green bottle of something had been splashed across his dresser.

Wray made a gagging sound.

"Is that his *cologne*?"

"Ugh, God," Camellia held her nose. "One of them, yes, my least favorite. Smells like Jägermeister."

"Are you sure it *isn't*?"

"Fair," she responded, walking over and holding her nose. She put the stopper back in.

She didn't want to touch the spill, lest she stink of the stuff as well. It was a high-end bottle of cut glass, Italian, and just the sort of ostentatious thing he preferred.

"Weird," she muttered. "I can't imagine one of the cleaning staff turning that thing over."

Her skin prickled. *Was it Syd?*

That thought made her breathe quickly. *Did he go in here too? Did he come* back?

But no; she and Wray had been there, and House would have alerted her to any presence.

Or would it?

"Are you okay?" Wray nudged her elbow.

She shook herself back to her surroundings.

"Just... you know, I'm really tired."

"Me too."

They leaned into each other for a moment.

"Let me find you some clothes," she said briskly. She rummaged through her father's drawers, curling her lips in disgust at his gaudy taste... sometimes downright offensive.

Once again, she wondered what anyone saw in him, particularly her mother. Now, he was rich; she supposed that was the draw. But what had her *mother* seen? She was a scientist. She hadn't been rich, but wouldn't have needed wealth either. Camellia couldn't fathom a time when her father could have appealed to anyone not wanting money.

In some ways, she understood that.

Finally, she found a drawer full of sweatpants, most of them gray, some navy blue. She found a set of t-shirts for various marathons he'd helped sponsor, years before. She gestured to Wray.

"Not the finest, not the worst," she said, looking up at them uncertainly.

Wray grinned and picked out a white Malibu Fall Marathon T-shirt with a red and orange sunset design and gray sweats.

"They're clean, they're solid; they work." Wray said.

"You'll need to take the old ones off to get them cleaned," noted Camellia. She flashed a bright smile at Wray, and bolted for the door.

Wray chased after her, into her bedroom, and she shut the door and locked it. She said wickedly, "Let me help you out of those."

She kissed Wray on the mouth, their neck, chest, and beyond. Wray nuzzled her neck. Their lips met, their fingers interwove, and they blended together; curves and angles and everything in between. Then they spent a long time exploring each other. Camellia felt more at ease with Wray. The initial newness had shifted. She knew Wray fully now, down to every hair, every pore... and every scar. She was pierced by those markings of violence, and spent time gently kissing each one.

"I'm sorry," Wray said finally, swallowing back tears. "I'm not—I'm not perfect like—like your kind of people."

Camellia propped herself on her elbows, tracing Wray's shoulders with her fingers.

"What kind of people?" she asked, grinning.

Wray twisted their face a bit before answering, "Rich."

Camellia threw herself onto her back and laughed.

"My kind of people, we 'rich' people," she cried out, "are not perfect at all! We—well, not me, not yet—get work done because we're miserable. We're fucking *miserable*! I see so many people with old duck lips from old, failed fillers and liposuction and all that shit."

"So... you've never had work done?" Wray asked.

"Just braces. Oh, and the tattoo..." She rubbed the back of her neck. "That's not the same thing though."

"Good," said Wray, watching her.

She squinted up at them. "Why?"

"Because you don't need it, and you never will. You're *perfect*."

"Oh *you*," she grinned, and she embraced Wray. "You're perfect."

The day slipped away with the two of them only venturing to the bathroom, the kitchen, or to watch TV in the den, blissfully unaware of anything else—and also in denial.

Inside the house, Camellia could not hear the popping of the plants outside, and pretended it wasn't really happening. Being distracted by Wray was the most fun she had ever had.

They worked their way through old movies and ate popcorn, curling into each other like cats and kissing at every opportunity. Finally, in the evening, they climbed back up the stairs and, to Wray's delight, Camellia turned on the huge bathtub tap, pouring bubble bath into its basin.

She grinned, looking at Wray's expression. It was a far cry from the other night, when she was alone with a bottle of rum, feeling bruised by Syd's behavior. It may as well have been years ago, Camellia felt so changed by Wray. She held out her hands and pulled them into the foaming bowl with her. She turned the jacuzzi jets on, and they kissed among the bubbles, washing each other's hair, swirling together at every opportunity like otters at sea (and this time, singing together).

The lights flickered.

Fridge's voice came through the intercom, "Camellia, I am having trouble connecting again, and am trying to reroute. There was a momentary lapse in the security. I fear it mayyyyyy beeeeeeee…"

The power went out, and this time, the backup generator did not come on. Camellia and Wray sat in darkness, their sloshing gone silent.

"What the fuck?" she whispered.

"This ever happen before?" asked Wray quietly.

"No, I—"

A strange, high-pitched sound echoed throughout the house.

The lights returned.

"Cameeeeeeeliaaaaaa," whined Fridge. "The house is compromised. I have called securrrrrriiiiiiityyyyyy."

"What does it mean," Wray gasped, "the house is compromised?"

Camellia sloshed out of the tub and pressed a towel into Wray's hands while quickly drying herself off. "Someone's in here."

CHAPTER 22

ALL RELATIVE

She dressed quickly and grabbed her sword, still next to her bed.

"You just casually have a sword next to your bed?" hissed Wray, owl-eyed.

"It's a movie prop. There's another one under there. Get it!"

"Do you have any working gun props under there too?"

She rolled her eyes.

"Not in this room. There's a vault..."

"Of course there is."

"Shhh!"

Wray rolled under the bed and retrieved another wrapped sword, a short one; they also pulled a folding knife from their back jeans pocket, winking at Camellia.

"Ya never know."

The two held their swords up and grinned nervously at each other. Camellia carefully unlocked her bedroom door and opened it just enough to look up and down the upper hallway. It was dim, lit only by a skylight and a window opposite the stairwell above the front entry. Streetlights from across the road shone in ghostly blue-white. No other power was on, no backup emergency lighting. Only some automatic, battery powered LED lights, small, glowed softly along the stairwell. She listened.

The air conditioning had stopped, along with all the electrically powered devices.

Fucking Dad, not converting everything to solar.

She raged inwardly as she quaked from fear.

She looked at her watch: 9:37 PM. She opened the door fully and stepped out. Staring down the set of stairs, she saw a shape move, and pulled away quickly out of sight. She covered her mouth to stop from screaming, then quickly recovered and held to her sword.

There was a loud crash of pottery. The vase downstairs.

A shriek.

Then—

"CAMELLIA!"

A crackling woman's voice bellowed through the empty house.

Breathing quickly, Camellia stepped forward then. She leaned over the banister and stared. A phone flashlight shone up at her.

"Who the fuck are you!" she yelled.

"Camellia Dume! Is that anyway to treat family?"

Camellia hesitated, then dropped the sword.

"*Darla?*" she called softly.

The woman below tutted.

"Can you turn on the lights, please?" she grumbled. "I had one helluva time getting in here. What's going on with the security system? Took four tries. I finally hit it with my purse, and it let me in. What do you have to do around here? Give away your bank account info? Look at this mess."

Camellia's face, even in the dim light, reflected a deep scowl. Wray watched as she lifted her sword back up to her shoulder for a moment, then lowered it with a long, bitter sigh.

"Cousin Darla," she called down in her smarmiest Dream Teen Queen voice. "So good of you to drop by! What brings you here at"—she looked down—"9:45 PM on a Saturday night?"

Darla kept her piercing phone light on as Camellia descended. Camellia gestured for Wray to follow.

"Just doing a little check-up is all." Darla's voice was unctuous and did not sound sympathetic whatsoever. "My Lord, what's that you're carrying?"

Camellia's sword dragged behind her, thunk-thunk-thunk down each step; she brought it forth to use like a cane.

"Protection," she answered simply. "Hi, Cousin Darla," she sighed irritably, giving her cousin, who was really more like an aunt, a perfunctory and very quick hug. The woman reeked of some mainstream perfume and too much of it. She was a solid, tank-like woman with huge breasts, who was fond of polyester florals, a lot of hair product, clumpy mascara, and badly drawn lipliner and eyebrows. These things assailed Camellia, even in the darkness. In fact, in the dim light, Darla looked ghoulish.

Maybe an improvement, actually, she thought.

"A sword!" Darla cackled loudly. "Where's your gun, honey? Dez needs to train you better. You Hollywood types. It's a wonder you've lived this long." She tsked and then jerked, noticing Wray for the first time. "Who the hell are you?"

Camellia's temper, already skittering on the surface like oil in a hot frying pan, flamed up, channeled right through her mouth, and inflected every syllable with fury.

"This is my *lover*, Wray, *Cousin Darla*. Wray, meet our darling and not at all manipulative and gaslighting Cousin Darla."

Wray extended a hand. "Nice to meet you."

Darla harrumphed and did not return the gesture.

"Young lady," Darla began, and with that opening, Camellia knew where the conversation would lead.

She walked right past the older woman straight for the kitchen. Wray followed.

"Why are the lights off? What's going on with the power? I thought you Hollywood types had all that newfangled shit. What do they call it, *sustainable energy*? I always told Dez you can't go wrong with good, old-fashioned electricity and a gas generator. These homeless and illegal-loving degenerates want to control every aspect of our lives."

Camellia clenched the hilt of her sword and stared at the dark panel of Fridge with longing, while Wray touched her shoulder. She flinched and relaxed.

"Sorry," she said under her breath.

"What was your name?" Darla crowed, swishing her polyester pants as she followed them into the dim kitchen.

"Wray," they answered.

"Who's your family? Or are you one of those extras from a set or something?"

Silence. Camellia gripped the sword tighter, never in her life more tempted than that moment to slap someone in the face with the flat of its blade.

"It's me and my dad," said Wray simply, and evenly. "He's in construction."

Camellia was amazed at their calm. She realized that, of course, Wray was probably well-practiced in diversion.

Darla sniffed, but it wasn't a derisive sniff, for once. "Good solid work then. He'll have raised you right."

Camellia didn't even have to see Wray to sense their immediate tension from such a statement.

Darla turned to Camellia. "For once you've got good taste, honey."

Camellia stared at her.

"What's that supposed to mean?" she demanded, breathing hard. Wray caressed her shoulder.

"Not as good as mine," Wray said, in a smooth voice. They leaned forward and kissed Camellia, whose blood surged to her cheeks... not that anyone could see well in the low light.

Darla hooted. "Oh, I like you!"

Testily, Camellia snapped, "Darla, can you please turn that fucking light off?"

"Language! Then again, Dez always had a way with words. I'll go off in search of something to drink. One thing I can count on in this home: good booze!"

"Darla," said Camellia as carefully as she could manage, finding it hard to still the quavering of disgust in her voice, "couldn't you have called?"

"What's the matter, honey? Did I interrupt something?"

Darla bayed with laughter and nudged Wray with such force they bounced a bit.

She went on, "I don't trust these devices y'all have. Thought I'd just show up."

"Don't you get in because those very devices *let* you in because they *recognize* you?" Camellia bored her eyes into the woman's face.

Darla shrugged.

"Well, they don't work, do they? Not tonight, anyway. Look at all this." She swept her arms around grandly. "All this money gone to waste. If I had that, I'd have a bugout bunker. I mean, a good one."

Camellia thought briefly about a cabin her father owned at Big Bear Lake.

Come to think of it, a mountain cabin sounds pretty good right now.

She'd never actually been up there. But it was the *idea* of it that appealed to her. Crunching through leaves and pine needles, sitting in front of a log fire...

I'm thinking like one of those Christian autumn girls, she thought bitterly.

Only in this image, Wray was with her too, bringing her a cup of cocoa...

Can't we just get away from everything?

"Why so late, then?" she asked with a frustrated sigh.

Darla clinked and fussed in the cabinets, retrieving a glass. She set it on the dark counter, illuminated only by her phone's light, and brought out two more.

"Y'all want some too?" She laughed. "I'm gonna see what top shelf shit Dez has in his private bar." She deliberately stepped over to Wray to nudge them again and cackled.

Camellia's stomach churned.

"Seriously, Cousin Darla, why are you here?"

Darla swept her voluminous, frosted, faux-bronze, shellacked hair back grandly and said, "Well, your dad wasn't responding and then someone dropped by the house in a cop car. I didn't answer, of course. I saw the news about the desert floods. See, that's what happens when liberals are in charge!"

"Excuse me, what?" Camellia interjected, mouth agape.

"Shoulda built dams in the desert to catch all that rain!" Darla clucked, without a drop of irony in her body.

Wray turned away from both of them, and Camellia's lips twitched when she noticed their shoulders shaking from suppressed laughter. Wray coughed to cover it up.

"What's the matter, Wray, baby?" crowed Darla. "Let me go get that whiskey! Camellia, got any honey, honey?" She laughed at her joke. "Nothing better for a cough than whiskey and honey. These people talking about *pandemics* like the last three weren't government ops made by illegals—"

"I'm sorry, what does a pandemic have to do with—never mind," sighed Camellia, frowning. "Get back to Dad, please. Did you hear from him?"

"No, and I'm a little ticked off at ol' Dez. I had placed some bets and he was supposed to collect winnings for me," Darla put on an injured air. "Not like him not to get back. So I thought I'd come on over and see what's up. Sometimes he doesn't get back to me right away. I don't know why that is! But it's been a little longer than usual."

Well, I know why that is...

Camellia rolled her eyes.

"Well, you didn't have to wreck our security system to get in," she said acidly.

Darla laughed. "Honey, you are too wound up. Starting to sound like your mother."

Camellia froze.

"And what would you know about that?" she asked, eyebrows arched.

"Too protective. She was tight as a guitar string, that one."

Camellia flushed with anger.

"She was a good mom," she said, voice shaking. Wray moved closer to her.

"Not a good driver, though, honey," said Darla, with a syrupy inflection of sadness. She tsked. "Sad business."

Camellia's blood drained from her face.

"What about it?"

"Hang on, honey, I'm gonna get that whiskey. Guessing your Dez has got some fine Kentucky bourbon in there. I hope so. I don't drink a thing bottled out here by those illegals..." and she trailed off, swishing to the living room, toward Desmond's office.

"Camellia," said Wray softly. "Don't let her get to you. I know her type. I'm *related* to her type." They said that last part with an edge. "She's manipulating you. Don't let her."

Camellia felt exhausted by the whole interchange, though, and sat at the breakfast nook bench, hooking her right arm around the sword and leaning on it.

"Can't she just go the fuck away?" she whispered.

Wray shrugged, sitting across from her. "She's trying to look after you."

"You're kidding, right?" hissed Camellia. "She offered you booze. She wrecked the security system, she—"

And with a bright flash from the Fridge, the power came back on.

Camellia leaned back and sighed with relief.

Fridge came online with a bright, full-moon face. "Good evening, Camellia! Your cousin Darla is on the premises."

"Well, *no fucking shit*," Camellia spat.

Said cousin sashayed back with a bottle of dark, amber liquid and a fine crystal rocks glass.

"Yahoo!" she cried out, holding the bottle high. "Now we can have a proper party."

She hefted herself toward the fridge and bounced her breasts upon the panel.

"Hey, Fridge, baby, I need some proper ice for my glass. Did it all melt?"

"Greetings, Darla Most Exalted," chirped Fridge. Camellia snorted and Wray laughed out loud. "I do still have solid ice in the freezer. How many pieces would you like? And would you like them square or round today?"

"That's my Fridge, baby, I love you so!"

"I thought you hated our technology," muttered Camellia in a low voice.

Darla ignored her.

"So yes, I'm glad you're not driving yet, Camellia," she went on. "Even though you *should* have your license by now. Back in my day, we were driving by 15! It's this government, trying to make kittens out of you all."

"I'm sorry, what does the government have to do with my driver's license?"

Darla deflected by asking, "Wray, honey, do you drive?"

"Yes, I do."

JENDIA GAMMON

"What do you drive? I hope you have a proper gas car. They keep trying to outlaw those here! I swear, I miss Texas."

"It's still there," Camellia snapped. "I think."

"Well, the border is like Swiss cheese," sighed Darla.

Camellia cleared her throat as Wray answered, "I drive an old Ford pickup truck. Real piece of shit. Gas."

Darla clapped vigorously.

"You've done well, Camellia. Just don't go driving out to Zuma Beach or anything. Dez will be at his wits' end."

Camellia stifled a gasp.

"Why?"

Darla tilted her head and stared at her through vividly goopy mascara-laden eyes.

"Honey, you know she ran off the road out there one night, don't you? Just right off the cliff." Darla shook her head and sighed. "Your dad's never been the same since."

She threw back the bourbon and then poured another, swirling its ice around.

"I—I still don't understand how she could have... didn't she have guidance in her car, or a warning, or anything?" Camellia stammered. Wray clasped her left hand in their right hand.

Darla sighed. "See, all the brains, beauty, money and technology in the world, and all those Ph.Ds. or whatever she had, and yet... not a good driver!"

She shook her head.

Camellia leapt to her feet.

"I think you can go now," she said coldly.

"Yep," grinned Darla. She got up and patted Wray on the shoulder with so much force that it flung them to the side. "I can see you're in good hands, Mimi, honey."

Wray mouthed, "Mimi?" to Camellia, who shot back a murderous look.

"Listen, you get into that vault. I know there is one! Get in there and get some guns and ammo. At least your mom set up the vault. You're gonna need all that. World's gone to hell in a handbasket. I'm thinkin' I'll bug out soon. You let me know if you want to come along."

I'd rather die, thought Camellia viciously.

Darla gathered up her purse and smoothed her shirt like the sail of a strong vessel, before kissing Camellia on the temple. She did the same for Wray and laughed indulgently.

She picked up the bourbon glass, refilled it, raised it to Fridge (who winked back at her from its moon avatar), and swished right out of the house, glass twinkling in her left hand.

"Fridge," commanded Camellia, "arm the property. Nobody's getting in or out after she leaves."

Fridge hummed. "There is one problem, however."

"What?"

"The gardener's truck is here, but he is no longer on the premises."

Camellia felt a cold tingle creep up her spine.

"Can you contact him?"

"I have made several attempts since coming back online. It would appear his phone is in the garden, but he is not."

"Do you have any video?"

"Unfortunately, the system glitches disrupted the feed. Accessing what I do have."

Camellia and Wray jumped up and rushed to stand in front of Fridge.

"Oh dear," Fridge said in dismayed tones.

Camellia's heart raced.

"What is it?"

"I am not entirely sure. I hesitate to show you such content."

"Show. Me." She bit the words out.

A softly smudged set of jerky video emerged from the screen. At first, Camellia could not comprehend what she was seeing. It was as if all the plants in the yard—save the camellias, which stuck in her mind as even odder—bent down toward something. That something was a man. Something suddenly shot out from under the trees and wrapped around that man, toppling him, and dragging him away.

"Gardener!" cried Camellia.

"Holy fuck!" gasped Wray. "The—the plants. They grabbed him!"

CHAPTER 23

ETCHED

Camellia held her hands to her chest as tears sprang into her eyes.

"Maybe—maybe he just got tripped on the hose and he fell," she said faintly. "Fridge, where is he?"

Fridge said nothing for a moment. Then: "Gardener Clifton is no longer on the premises. Without his phone on his person, I cannot locate him. I am sorry, Camellia. I have failed the home security. I still believe you are safe here."

"Really?" shouted Wray. "A worker on the grounds gets attacked, and you think she's safe?"

"It is my duty to provide protection for Camellia and those dear to her."

"Gardener was dear to me," choked Camellia, weeping openly.

The avatar of Fridge turned into a sad-faced red panda.

"I was not programmed to protect staff. Only you and those closely associated with you."

Camellia sank to the floor and pulled her knees up, shaking from sobs.

"Not Gardener. Not Gardener."

Wray sat next to her, pulled her tightly against them, and

said, "I'm so sorry. We have to get out of here *now*. It isn't safe."

"*You* are safe," Fridge said suddenly. "You are in Camellia's care. If you leave the premises, I cannot guarantee the safety of either of you."

"We could—we could go to Big Bear, to the cabin, to one of the other houses—" Camellia began.

"All roads to Big Bear Lake are closed due to multiple aberrant events," Fridge announced.

Camellia lifted her head. "What… aberrant events?"

"The tropical storm destroyed several mountain roads, and the resultant proliferation of macromolecule infestation has transformed several trees, throttled the remaining roads, and siphoned up part of the lake."

Camellia jumped to her feet.

"*What?* What is happening?"

She thought back to several things at once: the disaster back East, her Mammaw's hometown swallowed, the bodies under Malibu pier.

"The President is going to speak momentarily about the several crises unfolding nationwide," Fridge said in its red panda visage with calming tones. "I have detected National Guard activity in the Los Angeles area. The governor is speaking now."

Camellia and Wray looked at each other.

"Show us," Camellia urged.

Fridge switched its panel to a|live feed of the governor, who was just finishing the speech and answering questions from chosen media representatives. In the throng around them, flashbulbs flickering nonstop like the 4th of July.

"As I said, we are awaiting the President's response. Due to the nature of the storm and the damage in the mountains and deserts, my disaster declaration request was already approved. I do not have an update for the events unfolding in isolated areas of the state."

"Is it true that it's a virus?"

"What are these *Flortids*, Governor?"

"Is it going to mutate our plants to the level of the kudzu in the East?"

"Are we safe because of our dry weather?"

Someone barbed loudly, "In case you hadn't noticed, we had fucking flash floods in the desert. Everything's wet, dumbass!"

Voices rose and fell, smearing into one. The governor did not answer anything substantial, just addressed storm damage. There was no official acknowledgment that anything strange was going on with the plants of California. But Camellia and Wray, of course, knew otherwise.

"It's my fault!" wailed Camellia.

"What? Get the fuck out of here," Wray objected. "How is a freak mutant plant pandemic *your* fault?"

"You've seen it! You've heard it!" she cried. "I'm causing the plants to pop. Gardener is dead. It's me!"

Wray rolled their eyes. "You weren't even *here* when that happened. Right? Am I right, Fridge?"

"Correct," came the simple answer. "You cannot be implicated in the disappearance of Gardener."

"H-how? Why not?" asked Camellia, clinging to the doors of the fridge and staring at the red panda avatar, almost touching her forehead to it.

"You are protected."

"How?" she pressed.

"You are protected."

She smacked the fridge's doors.

"That's a bullshit answer!"

Wray took a deep breath and exhaled, hands on hips. "Fridge," they said, "what is the manner of Camellia's protection from these plants?"

"That is classified information. You do not have authority to access it."

Camellia stepped back and stared at the fridge.

"Tell *me*, then, Fridge. That's an order!"

The red panda blinked.

"That is classified information. You do not have authority to access it."

"How fucking dare you?" she shouted. "You're supposed to protect me!"

"I am protecting you."

Camellia threw her hands in the air.

Wray held their hands up and squinted.

"Fridge, how far does Camellia's protection extend?"

"That is classified information. You do not have authority to access it."

Wray sighed and furrowed their brow.

"How am I safe?" Wray then asked.

"You are under Camellia's care."

Wray nodded at Camellia, who stared back.

This is all such bullshit, she thought miserably. She wished her dad was there; he could set things right. Maybe. But she also wished for her mother.

"Okay," Wray said. "I think I'm getting it. I'm safe because I'm with Camellia. The plants pop when she's around them, but not when she isn't. She wasn't here when Gardener was grabbed by the plants."

Camellia threw her hair back.

"What does this mean, that I'm—I'm controlling *the plants*?"

Fridge said nothing.

"Wait, you must be on to something, Camellia," Wray said. "Holy shit, are you like a mutant superhero with plant controlling powers? You are, aren't you?"

Camellia laughed loudly. "That's dumb. If I were, I'd be better at growing them, and I'm terrible at that." She sighed. "I'm terrible at a lot of things."

"The hell you are," Wray protested. "You're very good at

most things." Wray rubbed her arms and kissed her softly on the mouth. "In more ways than one."

She snickered and kissed Wray back.

"So..." she mused. "The plants pop when I'm around. Wray is safe with me. Good. That means you can stay with me. But are we safe here?"

"That's why I wanted to know how far this... protection extends," Wray pointed out. "We know it's not just here... you said you heard popping at school, we heard it at Point Dume... so wherever *you* are, you're safe. And so is anyone with you."

Camellia bit her lip. "Fridge," she said slowly, "has school been canceled for Monday?"

Fridge's face smiled. "I am happy to report that Killian High is back to regular operating hours on Monday. There is no change from the school district either, if you are curious."

Camellia nodded.

"Can you still get those emergency supplies delivered?"

"They should all arrive tomorrow morning. I recommend you stay."

"Fridge, cancel all staff work, send them double pay, tell them they have vacations, and we'll call when... when..." She flailed. "Just make sure they're well paid. Straight from my account. And... and I guess we should file a missing persons account for Gardener Clifton."

A lump formed in her throat and her eyes stung.

Fridge made a "ding" epiphany sound. "Would you like for me to access other networks and see if any other bots have seen Gardener's whereabouts, before filing?"

Camellia nodded vigorously. "Yes! Excellent idea, Fridge." She sighed. "Now what?"

Fridge beamed at her and shifted into a bouquet of camellias. "You are safe. I recommend resting. I will alert you if any additional aberrations occur."

Camellia nodded and felt drained.

"I'm starving," Wray said, "and you must be too. Got any frozen meals?"

Camellia staggered over to the breakfast nook and sat looking numbly at her watch. She couldn't remember where her phone was at the moment, for she was too tired to concentrate. She didn't understand anything happening, and for once was oddly reassured that no one else seemed to, either. She was frustrated with Fridge, but begrudgingly understood that, maybe, she didn't have the skill or knowledge to answer questions about her situation with the plants.

She accepted the plastic container, steaming, from Wray's hands, and blew on the curry meal inside it.

"Thank you," she murmured. Wray set a tall glass of cool water before her.

She set her fork down.

"I'm glad you're here," she said, glancing up shyly at Wray.

Why do I feel shy? It's not like they've not already got to know every single bit of me. I don't know what I'm feeling.

The look Wray gave her sent her soul trembling.

"There is nowhere I'd rather be," Wray said.

"You're in danger, but... I guess for now, you're safe with me, and that's what I want," she stammered.

"You're safe with me too," Wray assured her. "Ride or die, I'm with you now. Finish the food. We'll need our strength."

Camellia laughed and quickened her pace.

Upstairs, after lighting candles, Camellia turned to Wray and embraced them. They swept her hair away from her neck and she shivered from their hot breath, tingling all over. Wray pulled the long coil of dark ginger hair away from her back and kissed up and down her back, lingering at the nape of her neck. In the warm, flickering light, they stroked the tattoo.

Wray abruptly stopped.

"I've seen this before," Wray murmured.

"Seen what before?" she asked, turning her head.

"This picture," answered Wray.

"I mean, of course you have. It's a camellia!" She snorted.

"No, I mean... obviously, yes. But. The actual design. I—" Wray jumped up, wearing only boxers, and said, "Hold on. I'll be right back."

Camellia made a funny face.

"Should I come with you?"

"No," Wray called, bounding down the stairs, "I'll be right back."

She sat, absently turning the loose waves of her hair over in her hands, listening to Wray jumping up the stairs two and three at a time.

Breathless, Wray leapt onto the bed, and held an object out to Camellia.

"What?" she asked.

It was the plastic case from her mother's desk. The one with empty slots inside it.

The etched cover design was exactly the same as the tattoo on her neck, down to the tiny heart in the center.

CHAPTER 24

SHAME

Camellia rubbed the tattoo.

"It's just ink."

"Is it, though?" Wray wondered. "What was in this case?"

"I don't know, it's empty."

Wray's eyebrows lifted.

"Was it always empty?"

"I don't know, it was in Mom's office and…"

She froze.

She remembered the footsteps in the carpet, the door slightly ajar.

She felt as if icy hands squeezed her neck.

Syd was in there.

"He saw," she whispered. "He saw the tattoo."

Wray sat up straight.

"Who?"

"Syd."

"Syd?"

"The… the Navy guy," she stammered.

Wray looked as if the wind had been knocked out of them.

"Oh. Okay. Um…" They ran their fingers through their hair. "What—what else did he, um… see?"

She blushed, thinking back to the drive, and the message from her father, warning against driving out the coast highway. She felt nauseous, after what Darla had said about her mother and the crash. She also remembered Syd noticing the tattoo, the painful evening with him in her house, and seeing those footsteps later.

"This house," she whispered.

Wray blinked several times.

"I—" and they took a deep breath and let it out, shakily, slowly. "It's none of my business what happened before— before we—"

Camellia looked deep into Wray's eyes and took their face in her hands.

"He's garbage," she said to Wray. "I used to think he was this amazing, stunning person, but he's trash."

"Is that—is that what you used to think of me?"

Camellia's mouth opened and shut. She felt deep shame.

"I—I didn't mean those things I said."

"You did at the time though."

Oh please, oh please no…

"No… Wray. Wray, I'm sorry. I was—I *am*—a bitch. It's kind of my brand. And it's nothing… personal."

Wray squirmed and moved away from her.

"Is *this* personal?"

Wray gestured back and forth between them.

She gaped.

"What? What do you mean?"

"Whatever we're doing, are we… are you going to go to school Monday and—and pretend this didn't happen?"

Camellia stared at Wray. She was silent a little too long.

Wray stood.

"I—I should go."

"No!" she cried. "Please, no. I'm sorry, I didn't mean it."

"Will you, though?" Wray's eyes were red, and their fists were balled. "Will you pretend, on Monday? Is this an act, one of your ploys? Am I a notch in one of those lipsticks of yours?"

Camellia stood too and tried to approach Wray, but they held their hands up to halt her steps.

"I'm leaving."

"No! Wray, I'll do anything, I'll say anything," she cried breathlessly.

"Who is this Syd, Camellia?" Wray demanded. "Do you love him?"

Camellia stopped cold.

Did she? Had she?

And again, she waited too long to reply.

Wray nodded.

"It's okay. It's okay. I'm going. I should've known. Why would you want to be seen with me, anyway? I'm nobody. I'm poor. I'm not this hunky military dude."

"Wray, I don't—"

"Stop," Wray said, eyes streaming. "You need to figure this out. Figure out if you want that guy, or you want me. I can't get involved in whatever's going on with you two."

They charged out of the room and down the stairs, Camellia running after.

"Wray, no! You can't leave! You'll be hurt, something will happen to you!" she screamed.

Wray stopped at the door and turned to face her.

"What could be any worse than how you've made me feel?"

Camellia felt as though she'd been kicked in the chest.

"You're ashamed of me. I could see it in your face when your cousin talked about me."

"Wray, you're imagining things, I totally am *not* ashamed of you!" she cried, desperate. She reached for Wray, but they backed away from her.

"Fridge," Wray called coldly. "Open the gate, please."

"May I make a suggestion that you stay, Wray?" Fridge called.

Camellia felt a surge of warmth toward the AI.

"No, thank you," Wray said, voice flat.

They turned back to Camellia, and the look in their eyes crushed her.

"See you at school."

Wray closed the door and left.

CHAPTER 25

ROOTS

She thought that crying oneself to sleep was an urban legend, but after the day Gardener had apparently been snatched by something inhuman and Wray had suddenly left her, she found herself so exhausted that she could barely make it to her bed. She sobbed into her pillow for a long time, not understanding anything, frightened of it all, and too tired to feel angry. She fell asleep with tears on her cheeks, her fingernails digging into her hands, her jaw tight and teeth grinding.

She woke up to the cracks and crackles of the trees outside, and it depressed her. She was changing their behavior somehow, but apparently by *not* being there, she couldn't protect Gardener.

Things were bigger than Camellia could grasp. She wished she could talk to her dad. Yes, even her shyster dad, who was a glorified charlatan. She knew it deep down. She resented it, but she'd used it. It was, after all, the only thing she had left to cling to: the phony persona of Desmond Dume. She wondered what kind of person her mother was to have gone along with it. Then again, she reasoned, she didn't have proof of that, either. Her mother was dead; she couldn't ask her. Her mother's *mother* was dead, and her community destroyed. It was as if the world wanted to erase everything related to her.

"I can't protect Wray anyway," she whispered to herself miserably. And no one could protect her.

The world as she knew it was ending, and, again, she was alone. Only one thing seemed to give a damn about her: her fridge. The AI that she'd known since she was a little girl.

Groaning at the time, 3:47 AM, she wrapped herself in a robe and descended the stairs. She was grateful the power was on, and so was Fridge.

"Hello, Camellia," Fridge greeted her in softer tones than usual. "You are up rather early. Is there something I can assist you with?"

She pulled a cup from the cabinet, filled it with water, and took a sip. Sinking down to the floor, back against the refrigerator, she stared up the microwave lights on the opposite wall. Next to that was a window with sheer curtains; the streetlamp glowed through it a bit, set away from the house. Lights among the shrubs (that she assumed were snapping like bubble wrap, since she was home) shone up on the house, diminishing that of the street lamps. Still, she could see one of them, like a little brilliantly lit orb, across the street. She focused on it for a few minutes, zoning in and out, and took another drink.

Considering her cup of water, she said, "I don't remember Mom so well. What was she like?"

"Dr. Tracey Madeline Edgars, later Edgars-Dume but not in publication," intoned Fridge, "was a brilliant botanist, who used her skills in planetary astrobiology at NASA's Jet Propulsion Labs in Pasadena, California."

Camellia sat up straighter.

"She worked at JPL? I thought she taught."

"Dr. Edgars did teach, at JPL, Caltech, and as a guest lecturer at UCLA and other universities."

Camellia frowned. "I wonder why Dad never talked about the JPL stuff?"

"That was a source of contention between your parents."

She turned to stare up at Fridge. It bore the red panda face again, with downcast eyes.

"What do you mean? Did they argue over it?"

"Your mother was most curious, always discovering, and known for questioning. Your father felt that she was asking too much, and worried for her."

Camellia felt chilled.

"She sounded driven."

"Dr. Edgars was famed for her tenacity as much as her research. Also for her generous giving, which she urged your father to continue."

"Did he?" Camellia asked.

"Yes and no. Some charitable donations continued after her death, but your father suspended most of them."

Camellia's cheeks burned.

"Why? Why would he do that?"

"He insisted that the moneys were not appropriated in the way your mother wished."

"But she'd have set that up, I'm sure. So… he just didn't want to honor her anymore. Backed out, like he always does," she said acidly.

She thought, with a heavy sigh, about some of the questions Wray had tried to ask Fridge. That set her on a spiral into remorse.

"I fucked up, Fridge," she choked. Her tears flowed again. "I don't know how to fix this."

Fridge let out a calming coo. "What is it you think you need to fix, Camellia?"

Camellia swept tears from her eyes and rubbed her hands on her pajamas, covered with little Kate Switch brand bombshell cartoons. Free pajamas, of course. One of the perks for being associated with the influencer, but well-made. She wore a tank top with a shelf bra, and its straps irritated her. She missed the touch of Wray's hands on hers, and that made her more wretched.

"I want to fix things with Wray," she said, voice quavering. "How do I deal with a breakup? This is different from what happened with Sy—with other people. Why? Why does this hurt so much?"

For a few moments, Fridge emitted soft, calming music. "Perhaps it is because you felt so deeply for Wray, unlike others you associated with in the past. You had a special bond."

"I was so mean to them at school. I—I'm always mean. I'm the Mean Teen Queen. But I was savage with Wray!"

"Why, then, do you think it was different with Wray? Compared to others you insulted."

Camellia flinched. She felt judged. And considering it was her mother who set up the AI of the house, she felt that some extension of her mother also judged her.

That's ridiculous, she chided herself. But she couldn't shake the feeling.

"I—I think because I didn't expect Wray," she murmured slowly. "They showed up out of nowhere. Just—improbable, right? They said so themselves, how, of all places, they moved here, got into the school, met me… and I felt this strong reaction to Wray from the first."

"Then your story of meeting Wray is not unlike that of Tracey and Desmond."

She wheeled around and stared up at the screen.

"Really?" she gasped. "Tell me, tell me! How did they meet?"

"The first time was at Trader Joe's, where they got into an argument over plants."

Camellia giggled despite her tears. "They met at a grocery store? I wonder what their argument was."

"Your father wanted to get an orchid for a girlfriend at the time, and your mother cautioned him against it. She said that if the person didn't know how to take care of orchids, the plant would likely die. Your father was persistent, and the argument grew heated enough that the store removed them both."

Camellia laughed out loud. "Then what?"

"There was a tea shop in the same shopping center. Your father thought he might one-up your mother with his knowledge of tea, for he had traveled to Asia a number of times on business. He did not realize she was a brilliant botanist."

Camellia grinned until her face hurt. "I'll bet she showed him!"

"She was patient with him, for he wanted to prove himself, and she had already agitated him. But in the end, she proved to know more about the varietals. They fell into discussing their favorites, each getting a cup of tea. And they went their separate ways. They met again the following week, at Trader Joe's. Your mother claimed that she had a feeling he would be there again, and he was. This time he asked her what the perfect flowers for a date would be."

Camellia bowed her head and smiled.

"I wonder what she answered?"

"She answered, 'No matter which one you pick, she's lucky.' And he said, 'They're for you. If you'd like to go to tea again.'"

Camellia hugged herself.

"Thank you, thank you!" she gasped. "I'm guessing Mom told you this story for me."

"She did use me to record certain parts of her life, although not all."

Camellia could swear there was a note of sadness in the AI's voice. She felt a surge of emotion, and thought of her father.

"I have to believe he's okay," she murmured.

Fridge did not have to guess. "Your father is nothing if not resourceful."

"Guess so, since he tricked a genius into falling in love with him." She grinned and then sighed. "I miss them."

"I know."

"I miss Wray. Tell me how to deal with a breakup."

"Time."

She snorted. "That's something you didn't take much of in your response!"

"It is the most common method for coping: the passage of time. But not being a passive participant. Actively moving forward. Engaging in positive pursuits. Helping others."

Something took root in Camellia's mind with that statement. She rolled it over in her thoughts.

But she still needed… something. Something more to help her understand.

"What do you know about Wray?"

Silence for a moment. The eyes on the red panda's face were closed, and it looked meditative.

"What is it you wish to know?"

"Where they're from, their family history… hell, I don't know. Just… more. All the things I can't ask."

"Why is it that you did not ask Wray yourself?"

Camellia went hot.

"I—I was too nervous. I was also, well… I was swept up in the moment."

Her eyes glazed over, remembering the intensity of making eye contact with Wray. She had heard about this kind of thing in movies, but was blown away by the reality of it. She missed Wray terribly, felt as if she had been cut down the center of her being. That surprised her too.

Fridge said, "Wray was born in La Connor, Washington State. Their mother was a cashier, their father a construction worker."

"And?"

Fridge said nothing at first.

"What happened to their mother?"

"I do not think that information is relevant at this time," Fridge said, with surprising curtness.

"Why?"

"I think you should ask Wray about their own family history. It is not my place to do that."

"Wray doesn't want to talk to me!"

"Not now, perhaps. Given time, maybe."

Her shoulders slumped. She took a swig of water.

"Can you make me a breakup playlist?"

"I can. What would you like on it?"

"Something to capture... all this mess."

"Very well."

The speakers of the house reverberated to Prince's song, "The Beautiful Ones."

Camellia sat on the floor, back against the fridge, eyes closed, listening to the lyrics. She felt immersed in them. And toward the end of the song, her heart began to pound.

"Do you want him, or do you want me?"

She remembered what Wray had said about Syd. She stood and said, "Fridge, how did you know?"

Fridge did not respond. The additional tracks, by different musicians, were all fine, she thought, but none as on the nose. Camellia lay on the couch in the living room, covered in the same blanket that, just the night before, had covered them both. She breathed in the hints of Wray's scent, and she slept.

CHAPTER 26

INFLUENCER

Camellia woke to a young woman's voice: "Wake up, sleepyhead!" and Fridge saying, "Miss Switch has been trying to reach you for thirty minutes."

Groaning, she stretched, took another deep sniff of the blanket that had held her all night, and rubbed her eyes. She looked at her watch. Kate Switch's sunny head bobbed and she waved. Camellia had to think for a few seconds. The time was 9:22, so she'd slept much later than usual. She felt weak with hunger. And here was Kate, calling her out of the blue, for the first time in ages.

Fumbling in the kitchen, she made herself a cup of coffee and pulled one of Kate's special breakfast bars from their dedicated shelf in the fridge.

"Nothing before coffee with her," she muttered.

Then, once ensconced in the breakfast nook, staring down at the camellia-etched case with her mug of coffee on one knee, she called Kate.

"Heeeyyyy!" cried Kate, as if there were no natural disasters and plant monsters roaming the earth. She looked suspiciously chipper, and she could have been anywhere. Ibiza, Tulum, Rarotonga. She wore her wide-brimmed white hat and huge tortoise shell sunglasses. Her toned, tanned arms waved. "Girl, how *are* you? I haven't seen you in *ages*."

"Hmm, yes," and Camellia tried rearranging her voice into Miss Bitch mode. It was not as easy without the proper lipstick. But she made the effort. "I've been busy whipping the youths in line."

Kate cackled at that.

"Hey, listen!" she said breathlessly. "I wondered if you could do me a little, *teeny-tiny favor.* Just, like two minutes, max."

"What's that?" Camellia didn't even try to hide her bitter tone. She was in no mood for the performative sunshine of Kate Switch on this of all days. She heard, in the background, "Sunday Morning" by No Doubt, and found she was paying more attention to its lyrics than Kate's words.

"Cah-MEEEEL-ya!" cried Kate. "Wake up, girl! What's gotten into you? Are you stoned? Did someone slip you Molly last night at the party?"

"I wasn't *at* a party last night," she answered through gritted teeth. Her head was pounding, grated by Kate's lilting, breezy voice.

"Oh!" Kate giggled. "Right, that was someone else. Thought I saw your guy though!"

Camellia felt like a spike of ice had entered her skull.

"Yeah?" she said, keeping her voice controlled and even.

"Blonde hunk, right? Sam? Seth?"

Camellia coughed. She remembered all too well who Kate was talking about. And the amount of time she'd wasted thinking about Syd. *So much wasted itme. If I'd met Wray sooner…*

"What did you want, again?" She heaved a great sigh.

"Okay, you know I really don't ask you for much—" Kate began.

Just the grip on my sanity, thought Camellia.

"But yeah, a *teeny-tiny ask!*"

"Fine, what is it?"

"I need you to get on the socials and, you know, smooth things *over*. We're getting hit on the plant-based protein bars and smoothie powders, also the algae creams. People are, you know, kind of freaking out about all things plant right now, with everything going on!"

"You're shitting me bigger than hell!" blurted Camellia, quoting her grandmother.

"Yeah, no. *Dead* serious. I mean, I stopped using them too, of course!"

Camellia turned aside to whisper out of earshot, "For fuck's fucking sake, you absolute balloon brain!" and then composed herself.

"Let me get this straight," she said harshly. "You want me to get some of your shi—I mean some products out of my fridge and get on the socials and talk about how they're—safe, right now, in a killer plant pandemic or whatever-the-fuck. That's what you want me to do? Reassure the public when I have no idea what I'm talking about?"

Kate beamed.

"Perfect."

Camellia just stared at her image.

"To be honest," she said testily, "I'm not in the mood to be anyone's public face right now."

Kate waved her hands on the screen. "You *do* look a little washed out. Where's the lippy, girl? What's going on?"

With as much inner strength as she could muster, Camellia said, "I've just had a breakup."

Kate Switch did a switch then. She was all ears, quite suddenly, attention rapt. And Camellia could see, at least, that her reaction was somewhat genuine.

"Oh! My *God*. Oh, girl. I'm sorry. Was it that guy? Sal? Sonny? The military guy? Well, he *did* kind of have that vibe, you know, like he was a player."

"Oh, you're telling me this *now*?" Camellia could've spat

knives. She shook her brilliant hair. "No, not that piece of shit," she said firmly.

"Oh! Oh, girl. Oh! I'm so *sorry*. You know what? Use it in the posts! Say something *snappy*, like you always do. They eat your words up! They're always the posts with the most impressions."

Camellia bit her tongue to keep from shrieking.

She blinked three times and said, "Fine. Consider it done."

"Oh! Girl, thank you *so* much," crooned Kate.

"Kate, where the fuck are you, anyway? Are you in L.A.? You were last night, I take it?"

"Oh, yeah, no. I flew out later, after the party got boring. I'm on an island. Shh! My handlers don't want me to say *where*."

"So is that what everyone's doing?" Camellia murmured. "The rich people are flying off in their private jets to islands?"

"I'm sorry, it's kind of getting *windy* here, didn't catch that!" Kate cried, holding her hat down. "Look girl, the best way to get over someone is to get *under* someone." She laughed in a high staccato. "Get out there and do something! Don't wallow! The right person will come to *you*. Mmkay, you stay safe and all that! When this little thing blows over, let's go to *Corfu* or something."

"Sure," droned Camellia. "That would be spectac."

Kate gurgled some reply that Camellia couldn't understand, so she ended the call.

She sighed, stalked over to the Fridge, gathered some of Kate's refrigerated products, and said, "Fridge, I'm supposed to extol the safety of these plant-based items. Do you think they're safe? I'm assuming they are. But I don't trust myself not to say something to scare the shit out of these imbeciles who want to buy Kate's garbage."

"The products in Kate Switch's lines are not living, aside from active cultures in yogurt. Those are not plants."

Camellia nodded. "I mean, I knew *that*."'

She practiced lines for each product, smoothed her hair, put on lipstick, but could not be bothered to use special lighting or filters. *Fuck it.*

She slumped with fatigue and said, "I sure as shit wish I knew as much about botany as Mom did in her pinky finger."

"You can get an education in botany."

"Through direct neural link with you?" she snapped.

"No, from her friend. Mr. Levin, your teacher."

She flung her chin up. She remembered the picture in her mother's office.

"They were friends, yes?"

"They shared employment."

"But were they actual friends? Mr. Levin said—"

"Perhaps it would be better if you contacted Mr. Levin. Perhaps before school begins tomorrow."

Camellia nodded. "He's the only plant person I know now," she thought drearily. "Everyone else is dead."

CHAPTER 27

SUNDAY SCARIES

It had taken her a long time to fall asleep that Saturday night. She kept hoping that, somehow, Wray would show up, wanting to spend another night with her. Now she faced a one-night stand situation, and it made her feel physically ill.

She dreamed, just prior to waking, of Wray, with storm clouds behind them, just matching their mercurial eyes. The sun shone on their face as they simply looked at her. She tried reaching out to Wray but could not touch them. This made her sob, within the dream and out of it. But the dream shifted; Wray was with her, making her gasp in joy...

She woke sweaty and excited and bereft. There was nothing worse, she realized, than being alone and filled with longing. She felt explosive from wanting Wray. She'd never known such a powerful attraction. And she'd had the hots for Syd for a long time. With Wray, it was completely different, and unbearable. She made sure the shower was a bit colder than usual before heading down to get her breakfast smoothie. It didn't help much.

She didn't just want Wray for their extraordinary fit with her passion, she wanted Wray just... there. Across from her at the breakfast nook. Holding her hand. Eating popcorn on the couch. She wanted to know more about Wray. She sensed it wasn't just Wray's eyes that were stormy, but their soul as well… a person deeply marked by life, yet still able to be optimistic, still able to read poetry like no one else she had ever heard.

She read *"Ode to the West Wing"* over and over while skimming through horrific news. If anything, the mayhem and destruction spreading east to west across the country made her miss Wray even more. She felt like a tsunami was hovering above them all. It had inundated many already, but had not quite consumed the West Coast… or at least, not the Southwest. There were reports of chaos spreading from the Pacific Northwest. It was all funneling toward Camellia, she felt… She also mourned Gardener.

She pressed her fingertips to her temples, and took a sip of smoothie. It wasn't her usual. Her usual smoothie shop was closed on Sundays… and she wondered if they would ever open again. She wondered if this might be the last smoothie she ever had. As it was, the replacement was decent, but too thin.

"Fridge," she called hoarsely, realizing how hard she had cried, and her throat hurt from it. "Any updates on Gardener?"

The sad red panda face replaced a sunshine face. "I am sorry, Camellia. There has been no sign of Gardener Clifton. Would you like me to keep looking?"

"Of course. You probably have better and faster access to cameras and things than police."

"This is an accurate assessment."

Her shoulders sagged. "I don't get it. Where could he be? Where could a plant *take* him?"

"You assume a plant did take him."

"I saw it with my own eyes! So did Wray—" and she let out something between a hiccup and a sob. She lowered her head to the table and felt its cool, flat surface against her cheek.

"Perhaps it is time to make that call to Mr. Levin."

She lifted her head.

"Fridge, who gave me the tattoo?"

"That is classified information. You do not have authority to access it." Then, surprising her, "The person is, however, deceased."

Well, that rules out Mr. Levin, and she snorted in spite of herself, trying to imagine her tweedy botany teacher inking tats.

Then she sat upright.

"Who were Mom's best friends?"

The red panda avatar looked happy. "Desmond Dume and Austin Levin."

Her eyes bulged. "Austin Levin as in Mr. Levin, my botany teacher?"

"Yes, although certainly you must have known Mr. Levin's name from your class curriculum."

"I always delete those." She tapped her chin with her forefinger. "He was one of Mom's best friends! I wonder how long they knew each other. Did she meet him or Dad first?"

"She met Austin Levin first."

Her thoughts spun.

"Do you have his phone number?" she asked Fridge.

"It should be part of your curriculum... but then, you did say you deleted it."

She sighed irritably. "*You* get it for me."

"Are you ready?"

She stood. "Yes."

"Sending to your phone."

"Thank you!" she said happily.

Fridge burst into a bouquet of camellias in several hues.

"You are most welcome! You seem to have cheered up."

"I'm still pissed and worried and—"

She did not add *"Horny, missing Wray, wanting Wray every second, in agony, going crazy, panicking about life, worried about Dad, sad about Gardener, wondering where the fuck Selah is, hoping Syd has food poisoning..."*

But she came close.

She sat on the couch, covered herself with the blanket she'd shared with Wray two days prior (she hated that time hadn't stopped, that it moved ever forward, as if it would push her over into an abyss), and dialed Mr. Levin's number.

She felt nervous; absurdly so. She'd never called a teacher at home before. She hated calling anyone. Even though she desperately wanted to call Wray.

On the third ring, he answered.

"Hello?"

Her voice broke high. "Mr. Levin?"

"Yes? Who is this?"

She cleared her throat and swallowed. "It's Camellia."

A pause.

"Oh!" he responded in surprised voice. "Is everything okay? Are you safe?"

This alarmed her. She stammered, "Y-yes, I'm okay. Are—are you?"

"Yes. For now, at least."

That disturbed her even more.

"Why, what's going on?"

"You do follow *some* news, right?" he asked, with an edge to his voice.

"I—well. There's a lot going on."

"Yes. There is. I suggest you start paying attention, Miss Dume."

She sighed. "Look, I... there are some... things I'd like to know. Can we meet?" She felt small and terribly young and didn't know what she was doing.

But I'm trying, goddammit.

"Ah, well, if it's that important..." Mr. Levin began, sounding confused.

"It's... it's about Mom."

Silence for a moment.

"Ah. Okay." She could visualize him nodding. "Then why don't I drive to the school, and we can meet in my office?"

"Okay, yes. Good." She exhaled in relief. "Thank you."

"You're... welcome. See you in a few minutes?"

"Yes. Good."

Before heading out, Camellia ran up to her mother's office and searched for the picture with the lab coworkers. She seized it, changed into jeans and a sweatshirt, pulled her hair into a ponytail, and ran back down to put her trainers on.

Her ride dropped her off at school and she felt self-conscious exiting the car, clinging to the photo. The Killian High campus was empty, shuttered of activity and life, and she found it ominous. The plants around her snapped and popped as she sighed and walked along the empty courtyard path.

Will it look like this forever, soon? she wondered.

She'd purposely avoided thinking too much about the trouble evolving around her. The plants' popping reminded her, and she felt more disquieted by the sound than ever.

"Miss Dume."

She jumped and turned to see Mr. Levin. He was not wearing his customary tweed, just a navy-blue sweater and brown corduroy jeans. His dark eyes shone over the rims of his round glasses.

She realized her fists were clenched, and loosened them.

"Shall we?" he asked, pointing at his classroom.

"Is the classroom your office?" she asked, without her usual snark.

He smirked. "Most of the time. I figured it's a good place to breathe, so to speak."

He tilted his head.

"Do you hear that?" he asked.

"Popping, right?" she asked.

He nodded, with an odd expression on his face. She blinked.

He knows it's me.

Her palms began to sweat. She had a feeling she would soon know more than she bargained for about her mother—and about everything else. She was not sure she was ready. But, as she had felt pulled powerfully to Wray, she was similarly driven into that classroom, to stand or sit or fall before Mr. Levin, and hear the truth.

It scared the hell out of her.

He seemed to sense it. He closed the door, locked it, turned on the lights, and, strangely, the projector as well. He powered up the system for his notes, and stood, feet crossed, hands intertwined, nodding for to her to sit. She did so. In the front row, where she would never sit in any other classroom.

"You've got questions," he said simply.

"Yes."

"I don't know if I've got all the answers. But I'll answer what I can."

Is he sad?

She could not read his face.

"Should I insult you before or after?" she asked.

He chuckled, breaking the ice. "Dealer's choice," he said, eyes twinkling.

"Okay," she breathed, "I'm just gonna say it: you *need* someone to clothes shop for you."

He laughed loud and long, slapping his hands together.

"Noted!" he cried. "Now that you've exorcised that particular demon out of yourself, ask me some questions."

She gave him a large-eyed look then that visibly unnerved

him, and he closed his eyes for a moment. She'd seen that expression on her father's face from time to time.

"What's wrong?" she asked, genuinely curious.

"That's your first of three!" he teased.

She stared, then laughed. "So you're a djinn now? Makes much more sense."

He shook his head. His grin slowly faded. "You looked like your mother just then. That curious face."

Something in the way he said it made her marvel.

She couldn't help it; she blurted it out: "Did you date her?"

His eyes popped wide and he guffawed.

"No! No. She was my bestie. Camellia, I'm *gay*."

She rolled her eyes.

"How did I miss that?"

He grinned at her indulgently.

"She was my bestie… aside from Jim."

Then his smile died.

"Who's Jim?"

"He was my fiancé."

She blinked. *Was.*

"And… and what happened?"

"He died."

The way he said it made Camellia think going down this road of questioning would shut Mr. Levin down.

"I'm so sorry," she said, barely audible.

He nodded. "I am too."

They both sighed.

He gestured for her to continue.

"So, I have this picture," she said slowly, uncurling it from her purse. "You're in it, Mom's in it. So, I knew you knew each other. I just found it."

"Wait a minute!" he exclaimed. "Let me see, if you don't mind."

She gladly handed it to him, and watched his face flicker with surprise and momentary joy, before fading into something off... something unpleasant. He handed it carefully back to her.

"That was a long time ago," he said simply.

"Before I was born?"

"Yes, before she even met Dez."

"Did you know Dad?"

"Not before then, but I met him after." Mr. Levin looked at her slyly.

"What—what did you think of him?"

Mr. Levin looked skyward for a moment. "He was... gregarious. Funny. Charming. Wild about your mother."

She smiled.

"You have a lot of her expressions. When you're not scowling, that is," Mr. Levin said.

That felt like a slight barb into her soul.

"But you have your dad's coloring. And you absolutely have a striking combo of their force-of-nature personalities, blended into one person. I only wish—"

He sighed again.

"I'm sorry."

He didn't have to say what about. She knew it was about her mother.

"Tracey and I worked together for years on some projects. She was *just brilliant*. My God. And so under-appreciated! She could've won the Nobel."

"But?"

"But not everyone appreciated her," he said darkly, glimpsing the picture Camellia held. "She... was involved in some projects I'm not fully aware of. She warned about... potential disaster. With climate change, with... exterior influences too. She warned against... this."

He spread his arms out.

"Nobody listened to her?" Camellia asked, mouth agape.

He lowered his eyelids and his voice. "It's worse than that, I think. I think... I think it was deliberate."

She felt stabbed by ice.

"What—like, it *is* bioterrorism?"

He grimaced at the term. "I think it was a perfect storm, but I don't think it was completely natural. That's all I'll say on that."

She trembled. "Is—is the popping thing—I'm causing it, I know."

She could see his pulse bouncing in his throat.

"What is it?"

"There's a lot Tracey didn't tell me, Camellia," said Mr. Levin. "So I don't know everything... and I don't want to. What I *do* know is that she wanted to keep you safe. She felt that she... wasn't safe."

Camellia's heart pounded. She could feel the blood leaving her face.

"She thought that if her worst nightmare came true, there might be a way to save you. She didn't tell me everything. She just said she had... insurance. I... I think I see what it is, now."

"So what is it?" she asked breathlessly.

"You're putting off a signal, disrupting plants around you."

She stood abruptly.

"What? How?"

"Well, that part I'm not sure about, but if it's a signal, then logically... you're transmitting it."

"But—but—" her voice shook. He watched her carefully, with wide eyes. "If—if I'm sending a signal, then—I wasn't always, which means—"

"Something triggered you to send it. I'm guessing... all this mess."

"How?"

"Another signal, logically."

"What the fuck?"

"It means… you're a transponder."

"I'm a fucking *transponder*? What do you mean? Like an airplane?"

"A transponder is something that receives a signal and then transmits a different signal."

"How, where from?"

"It would have to be on your person."

"I don't have anything—"

She froze.

She touched the back of her neck. Her thoughts sprang to the camellia container and Wray touching the tiny heart in the center of the tattoo.

Mr. Levin sprang forward.

"What is it?" he asked.

"It's this, isn't it?" she gasped, lifting her ponytail to reveal the tattoo.

He gasped.

"Where did you get this? Do you remember?"

He was shaking all over, and it frightened Camellia.

"I—was very little. It was a—a man, I think. No idea who he was."

She was stunned to see tears in Mr. Levin's eyes.

"I know who he was," his voice trembled. "He was Jim. My fiancé, Jim."

And Jim was dead.

CHAPTER 28

AGENDA

Mr. Levin paced back and forth, swearing.

"Ah fuck! I'm sorry, Camellia."

She rolled her eyes and grew impatient.

"So what do we do?"

"Ah, shit!" muttered Mr. Levin.

"Goddammit, you'd better have some ideas," fumed Camellia.

Mr. Levin steepled his fingers under his chin, put his hands together and exhaled loudly. He rubbed his hands together and walked up to his projector.

"Okay. Okay. Let's think about this. Camellia," he said, making sketches on the projection pad. "Do you have any idea what the range is for—for the popping?"

She bit her lip. "Well, when Wr—when I went to Point Dume, I… tested it."

Mr. Levin's eyes flashed upward to hers for a moment and then down again. He sighed.

"Yeah?"

"I—was able to move a distance away and it had no effect on the plants anymore."

"What kind of distance?" Mr. Levin's face was all concentration.

"I don't know. Fifty yards? Less? Not more though," she pondered.

"Fuck," he hissed. "Shit, sorry. Dammit! Ugh. Sorry." He sighed. "So much for being a good influence on my students!"

She laughed. "You're talking to *me*, remember? I've made sailors blush."

And then *she* blushed, thinking of Syd. She wondered where he was. She had half a mind to send a plant chasing after him, if only her signal worked in reverse. *It wasn't fair, what had happened to Gardener Clifton*, she thought sadly.

"That's not enough to cover the school," Mr. Levin said slowly. "Not entirely. Okay. So we have range info. Now... signal info. Is the source being sent to you from your house, by chance? Because *that* signal isn't coming from you. It's coming from somewhere else."

"I don't... think so," she muttered. She thought of Fridge. "I lost power a few times, and there were some... routing disruptions or something with the AI. It didn't pick up on—"

She stopped, and rubbed her temples, blushing furiously.

"Didn't pick up on what?" pressed Mr. Levin, watching her.

"I had... a guest one night," and she wanted a cavern to open in the floor to swallow her whole. "He... didn't stay. But. The AI didn't pick up that he was even there."

Mr. Levin's face twisted. "What? There's no way. I know she made that AI great..."

"But there were power outages."

"Surely with backups!"

"Well, they weren't great, but even so, it doesn't explain the missing info."

She went cold.

"He... I discovered he'd been snooping, while I was in the shower."

"Wait, who is this guy?" Mr. Levin's eyes were wide. "And what do you mean, snooping? Did he find... something? I want to know more."

"He's called Syd," Camellia said, and felt dread creeping through her. "He's in the Navy."

Mr. Levin dropped his stylus; it rolled off the tablet onto the floor.

The two of them stared at each other.

"What is it?" she whispered. "What the fuck is going on?"

"Did he find anything?" he asked again.

"I—I don't know—" and then she clapped her hand over her mouth. "The container. The container with the etching shaped just like my tattoo."

Mr. Levin's hands flew to his forehead, and he groaned loudly.

"Oh *fuck fuck FUCK!*" He approached Camellia and looked at her with pleading eyes. "Please tell me there was nothing in it."

"Well, there wasn't after he was gone, but no idea about before."

He shook his head, and then paced again. "No, no... if he got the other piece... you'd maybe not be able to do this."

"Other piece?"

"Your transponder. You have a piece, implanted somewhere in your neck, that's sending and receiving. But what we *don't* know is, where is that transmission coming from? The one that you're receiving, I'm assuming, tripped the switch so that you began transmitting some kind of... disruption signal, so plants... acquiesce, for a better word. Camellia."

"Yes?" she asked in a shaking voice, afraid of what might happen next.

"You have the key to stopping this fucking invasion. It's *in your neck.*"

She blinked at him. *No pressure there!*

"But where's the other signal coming from?" she wondered.

He shook his head. "I don't know. But we'd better hope to fuck—sorry! —that it doesn't stop. Because we're about to go through some things."

"What can we do? I only have so much range!"

She almost hyperventilated, but she recovered. She wagged her dark copper ponytail as she shook her head. "I can't save everyone."

"You can protect some. And you can buy time."

"How?"

"Get people in the same place as you."

"But it won't work here. You said it's too big."

Mr. Levin shrugged.

"The auditorium?"

"Is it safe?"

"Hm… good point. Where's a safe place, with some kind of protection?"

Camellia raised and lowered herself on her heels. "Well. I know a place."

She hoped she was not crazy for suggesting it…

"Where?"

"My house. Party at Camellia's," she said, with a rueful smile.

Mr. Levin gasped with relief. "Brilliant idea! But that's not all we need. We need… okay. We need to figure out the frequency of the transponder, the signal you're sending out. If we can figure that out, then we can tell others what to use, and control the plants. Maybe. But the other signal, the one you're receiving…"

"Does it matter? Do we need *that* signal?"

"We need it to work long enough to figure out your transmitting signal. If we knew where it was coming from, we could maybe protect it. Because I have a feeling we're running out of time on that one. The man that was in your house—and I don't want to know the details, only that you're safe—"

"Nothing really... happened," said Camellia, feeling nauseous, remembering Syd's cold eyes and questions, among other things.

Mr. Levin covered his face with his hands, and then drew them away gasping, "Thank God." Shaking his head, he went on, "He's working for someone."

"Yeah, the Navy."

"Well, maybe he *was*. But I suspect this is for someone else. Camellia, you're not safe. Neither am I. And... I'd call on JPL folks. But given who I think it is, I don't trust them either. Not their fault. I just... we can't be too careful. Who do we know that's good with signals? I'd ask Mr. Welsh, but he's probably stoned out of his mind right now."

Camellia snorted. The physics teacher, Mr. Welsh, spent a fair amount of his class bopping to music in his head that no one else could hear. More remarkably, he still wore Grateful Dead t-shirts.

"The Glitches. The Bandages," she answered quickly, thinking through the cliques. "Aka the techies and band kids... and maybe the Cadre."

"Gather these folks up. Invite them over for a party. We'll figure this out. But we'd better act fast."

"On it," she said quickly. "I'll invite the whole school, even the shitheads. I've got a place where the nerds can work. Mom's vault."

Mr. Levin stared. "She had a *vault*?"

"Yes."

He laughed. "Oh, Tracey! Well. I would like to see the vault."

"Definitely."

"Hey," Mr. Levin said. "You're doing brave things. I just

wish your dad were in town. I hope you're right, that he's just on a bender. That sounds bad, I know." He grimaced. Camellia shrugged. "I know it's been a hard ten years... but he should be with you."

Camellia nodded, not wanting to tell Mr. Levin her worst fears. "One day. Maybe."

"Everything else okay?" Mr. Levin asked, seeing her expression change.

She thought of her dad and she thought of Wray. She chewed her lower lip.

"Did they... did Mom and Dad have a tough start?" She felt embarrassed asking, but she didn't know many people who knew both her parents. She closed her eyes, and could see Wray staring back at her, smiling, in her home. She missed Wray with a physical pain.

Mr. Levin's smile broke like sunshine after a storm.

"Yep," he grinned. "But you could see that love from space! They figured it out. Then, later, they had you. And hoo-boy, did Tracey and Dez adore you!"

"Did Mom make sure you were here?" she asked softly.

Mr. Levin lowered his head, his smile softening. His dark eyes looked kind; his expression lost to the memories of time.

"She did. She urged Dez to keep funding my post, too, if anyone objected." He sighed. "But the school kept me on, thankfully, for other reasons."

"Because you're a damn good teacher."

She wasn't sugar-coating it: he was the best teacher at Killian High.

Mr. Levin dipped his head.

They parted ways.

Camellia thought quickly, texting commands to Fridge to order snacks and beverages for delivery en masse. But the moment she requested a ride, she saw a massive delay. Traffic was clogged everywhere. She texted Mickey, her reliable ride, but he didn't answer at first.

Eventually, he wrote back and said, "Shit's going down. I'll try to get you. If I don't make it, it's been a pleasure."

Her mouth fell open.

Then the alerts came.

The plant assault on Southern California had begun.

CHAPTER 29

ENTANGLEMENTS

Mickey looked ten years older than he had a few days prior, and was possibly on speed, when he careened to the school.

"You're lucky you caught me," he coughed, puffing on a cigar. She gagged at its reek. "Sorry. Figured it was time to bust out the good stuff. End of the world shit, ya know? I'm bugging out. Got my boat ready. Hope to fuck the kelp doesn't do this too. Shit. Now I wish I hadn't said that."

"Kelp isn't a plant," Camellia pointed out.

"Okay, but do we know for sure it's not gonna happen to the kelp? The algae? The lettuce on my burger?"

In truth, she *didn't* know. So, for once, she kept her mouth shut.

She watched the hillsides of Malibu shiver like a great wind blew upon them, and could see emergency vehicles everywhere, glittering like lights on a monstrous Christmas tree.

Mickey pulled alongside her house and she jumped out. No sooner had she shut the passenger door than he fled, his tires screeching on the pavement.

At home, she heard raucous popping, snapping, and creaking among every plant on the property. It unnerved her.

She looked across the street and saw no aberrant activity at first… just a dog barking nonstop. Overhead, she heard helicopters. In the distance, sirens.

The living tsunami wasn't everywhere, but it was coming. It was close. It had apparently happened in her own back yard, snatching poor Clifton. But it wasn't universal.

She noticed, for the first time in a few days, the haze toward the foothills. She blinked.

Ah. It wasn't smog.

Whatever it was, she felt it must have something to do with the calamity.

She looked about as the grass and the shrubs clacked like teeth and she shuddered. She froze. Someone stood at the end of the driveway, next to the stone fence. Watching her.

"Camellia," they called.

For a second, she wondered if it was Wray, but the voice was a bit lower. And the person was a bit taller.

Oh fuck.

It was Syd.

His Corvette was nowhere to be seen.

As he walked toward her, she felt the impulse to run. But run *where*?

She stood firm. This was *her* home. She slid out of her fears like a cheap dress and slipped into the mode she was most familiar with: mega bitch.

As he approached, she tapped her phone, surreptitiously dialing the Fridge. She hoped there was no signal disruption this time. It picked up. She smirked to herself.

"Well, well, well," she said in a low voice. "What brings you, slithering Syd? Did your fiancée give you permission to come? Did you grow a spine?"

Syd's GQ-handsome face creased into a wincing smile; his hands stretched out, placating.

"Hey, I'm sorry. I fucked up."

She gaped for a second, then quickly recovered.

"O-ho!" she sneered. "Did you ever, you fuckboy pimple on Satan's asshole."

"We broke up."

She scrunched her forehead and shook her head. "So? Are you for real? Why should I give a shit? You blew it with me. I've moved on."

"You and I, we… had something," he murmured now, and she held her purse in front of her as a feeble shield—and also so Fridge could listen via her phone. "I just wanted to let you know, it was wrong. I should have broken up with her ages ago. It was you I really cared about."

Camellia threw back her coppery mane and laughed richly.

"You must be drinking your own piss," she said through gritted teeth.

Syd sighed. She could see he was trembling. It was strange. He held his hands up again.

"I really *did* fuck up, blowing it with you. Can we… can we at least be friends?"

As the plants around her made chattering noises, she noticed something even stranger. He said nothing about the sounds. And he surely would have noticed. The hairs on her neck rose.

"Why?" she asked him coldly and simply.

"Everything's going to hell. I could help you. You could make it out of this. Let me do this for you."

She squinted. "How the hell could *you* help *me*?"

"It's the least I could do."

He was locked onto her, his eyes unflinching, his physicality sincere. His tremble was odd, but she wasn't sure what it meant. He meant *something* of what he was saying, maybe, but she could not tell how much. And she didn't trust him now. There was nothing he could do to fix that part.

"No," she said quietly.

"Think about it. Just, please... please think about it, Camellia," he pleaded. "If you need *anything*, text me, okay?"

"Get fucked," she snapped. She turned away, and walked toward the entry to the front walk.

But she was shaking too. The time she had spent thinking about this man was not insignificant. If she severed that connection, she'd maybe never see him again. She had valued his attention, his listening, his silly jokes, his just being there sometimes when she had no one else. With every step away from him, she was letting all that go, and it hurt far more than she thought it would. But she did not look back. She hefted up the several packages of supplies Fridge had ordered as the door opened for her. She stepped in, watched it close, and made damn sure it was locked and armed. She scooted the growing tower of packages around and put her hands on her hips for a moment. Then, she fell to her knees and wept.

"Wray," she said softly.

She heard her phone hang up. She lifted her head.

"Fridge? Did you get everything?"

Fridge played soft music for her as she walked in to look at the display; it showed the sea, with sun glinting on the waves.

"I did," Fridge answered. "And now I cannot detect him."

"Is he gone, then?" she wondered aloud, walking to the living room and peeking through the window.

"It would seem he is no longer on the property, nor within range."

Good luck without my protective field, she thought bitterly, but felt bad for thinking it.

What's wrong with me? I used to be tougher. Colder.

"Wray," she said aloud, biting her lip. "I'm going to message Wray. Maybe they'll ignore it. Maybe I'm blocked. But I want them to know they always have a safe space with me. Even at the end of everything."

The screen avatar of Fridge changed to a red panda smiling.

She texted with trembling fingers, "Wray. I'm sorry to bother you. I guess you hate me. I just want you to know I'm still here for you, no matter what. And whatever happens, I will keep you safe."

Tears streamed down her face. She waited several minutes, but no message came back. She nodded and began unpacking the party supplies and snacks. After setting everything up in the empty, hollow house, she went to her computer and began donating money to every cause she could think of. She maxed out school lunch plans, donated to 4-H for Agatha's sisters, fulfilled emergency funds, everything she could find, all over the country and the world.

Maybe it's too late. But I'm still here. So maybe it's never too late.

She entered her mother's old office, and she sat at her desk. She ignored the cacophonous crackling of plants outside. She ignored the yipping dogs in the neighborhood, though she did hope the range of her transponder was at least *helping* them and not hurting them. She thought of Kate, off on some island. She wondered if that island had plants... She thought of Mickey, about to launch out to sea. She supposed several people were trying that route. But she remembered the bodies at Malibu pier and suspected that not everything would go as people assumed, if they ran away.

She had no desire to run away. She wanted people to run to *her*.

She stared at a picture of her as a child with her parents, studied her mother's smile, and muttered, "What good is all this, if I can't share it? I know you'd want me to. Wherever you are, Dad, you're just going to have to get over it. This is how it's going to be. If we get a chance."

Camellia set the picture down and messaged Selah's dad.

"I've been thinking of you and hoping all is well."

She never heard back.

She went through all her associates' messages and reached out to them, but no one wrote back.

"It's not like I expected anyone to," she murmured. "It's not like that many people like me, either. One more day of class, and I'm guessing that's it. It was fun, being the Mean Teen Queen. But not fun enough, and not worth it, in the end."

She went through the motions of party prep, even inflating several balloons, gagging at their smell, and listening to music. Tomorrow she would walk into Killian High, and nothing would ever be the same again. But she hoped she could have one last party, give them all a place to be safe, for just a little while longer. She owed them all that much, and then some.

CHAPTER 30

BLOSSOMING

It was Monday, exactly seven days since the start of the craziest week Camellia had ever known. She did not know what the coming week held, but she was determined to get what she wanted: to throw the most epic house party ever.

She woke with a jolt and threw off her bedsheets. Then she remembered she'd ordered all the staff to stay on vacation, so she made the bed herself. She tidied up the bathroom, shoving dirty laundry down the chute.

She muttered aloud, "Gonna be able to ski down that laundry pile."

She felt a pang, realizing Wray's clothes were down there too. She descended, flipping on lights, and realized that the downstairs, outfitted with a small bar and deep, soft couches, TVs, and a fireplace, smelled musty and unused. She turned on a dehumidifier that sat in one corner.

She entered the laundry room, beautifully appointed with a teal and pewter chandelier, soft, gray carpets, and two sets of washers and dryers. The laundry chute's contents did sit in a reasonable pile. It was mostly towels, Camellia's clothes... and Wray's. She picked up Wray's shirt, pressed it against her face, and breathed. She felt a visceral tug in her body as she remembered Wray's scent, their breath, the taste of their tongue in her mouth, the firm and gentle grip of Wray's hands and arms. She clung to all these things for several minutes before sighing and starting the washers. She placed Wray's clothes and hers in one, and towels in the other.

She shook her head.

It doesn't matter.

The world was being torn to shreds. Everyone blamed America for the strange miasma-cloud making its way around the earth, its macromolecules spread by air travel, boat travel... no place was immune, save perhaps parts of Antarctica, up on the ice-covered land. Many people fled to boats, causing mass chaos along the shorelines of the country. There were reports of firebombing and otherwise attacking the plants, even discussions about using nukes. Clouds of pesticides were being dropped by drones. But nothing quite worked for long.

Everywhere, plants behaved abnormally... and more like kudzu on steroids. They grew with extreme rapidity and voracity, siphoning fresh water, growing at immense speed, surging, strangling everything in their path. An invasive agent morphed from an already invasive plant. Perhaps the strangest part of all: many of them had blooms that looked and smelled like the purple clusters of kudzu blossoms.

The miasma in the air was a mixture of kudzu isoprenes and macromolecules and scientists worldwide were racing to stop it. It made Los Angeles look like the smoggy hellscape it had been in the 1980s, before Camellia was even born. Over the course of a few days, the economy began to falter. Some communities seemed spared from the devastation while others were completely consumed by it. Anyone could become a victim of mutated plants at any time.

The news became ever more surreal, and some people just checked out completely. Denial, horror, rage... many couldn't cope. People turned on each other. Desperation brought many to the brink quickly, while others remained in shock.

Not Camellia. She was going to give it one more go. She figured she had nothing to lose, now.

She set out bowls and water bottles. She put out colas and juices. She took a long look at the various liquor cabinets and hid all the booze bottles behind lock and key. When she was finally satisfied, she dressed for school.

Killian High students were given the option of attending, as the neighborhood was relatively unscathed. Rumor got out that Camellia would be announcing something major because of the situation. That was unprecedented.

Given the end-of-the-world vibe, she decided to wear a royal purple dress she'd worn to the PGA Awards ceremony a year prior; she also wore a white lace halter beneath it. All of it was a homage to Prince. It wasn't 1999, but the mood was. For real, this time.

Mr. Levin picked her up. He arrived in an old Volvo, and she clucked at it.

"Really?" she asked, rolling her eyes.

"I'm guessing you dislike my taste in cars as much as my clothes," he said sheepishly.

"Don't get me started."

He gave a short laugh as they continued on.

Pulling into the teacher's lot at Killian High, Mr. Levin parked, as Camellia stepped out. She looked her grandest, her hair partly up at the sides, and down at the back, the rich, purple velvet dress swaying, her combat boots gleaming. She wore *Enchante 99: Amethyst Dusk*, a vibrant, deep raspberry lip color with purple undertones. Her eyes glowed ethereal green, and she walked the courtyard of Killian High like it was a runway, and she was its supermodel. The sparse plants made all the requisite popping noises thanks to the transponder in her neck. She smirked darkly, thinking it resembled applause.

But she didn't want any that day.

Not every student came, and many parents parked their cars close by, just in case. She did not see Wray's old, Ford pickup. She felt her resolve wobble but kept her chin high. Private traffic cops were hired, paid for by Camellia via her dad's money, since most of the public force was otherwise occupied. If anything went sideways, at least everyone would have a fighting chance to leave safely. Mr. Levin briefed the principal, and an assembly was called. The students clustered into the gym, as Camellia sighed wistfully, thinking how it had only been a few since they all danced there, before hell broke loose.

She tapped the mic and looked out at the sea of faces. Several phones were out, recording her. The mood was disturbingly off compared to pep rallies and other events. There was a low murmur, like the audience of a symphony, she thought.

Well. The conductor is here.

As she cleared her throat and opened her mouth, Wray entered the back of the gymnasium, the door shutting heavily behind them. Camellia faltered and puffed an exhalation. Wray sat near the doorway, as though ready to evacuate quickly. Camellia blinked, fighting the stinging in her eyes.

"We are gathered here today…" began Camellia, blushing deeply, realizing how she sounded and how she was dressed. A few cackles rippled throughout the crowd. She managed to laugh at herself too.

The Cadre sat rapt, close to her; Dewayne shouted, "Quiet! Mother is speaking!"

She beamed down at him as he looked at her adoringly, mouthing "You look fab!"

"I'll keep this brief. I am… providing you all protection from the invasion. It's a long story. But the range is short." When she caught Wray's eye, the swarm of faces disappeared and she could only see them. They held her gaze and looked down. She shook, swallowed, and briefly touched the back of her neck, before continuing. "So we're going to find a... a way to stop this thing for everyone. I'll need some of you to help; anyone with radio experience, tech stuff. I need loudspeakers, band people... I want you all to come to my house tonight. Bring your families. I'll feed you, give you a place to stay, and as long as we're all together, I'll keep you safe. Party at Camellia's tonight, 6 o'clock. Check yourself before you wreck yourself."

Dewayne, Mel, and Michel looked at her expectantly.

She took a deep breath and shouted, "I adore you all, you bunch of fucking troglodytes!"

The Cadre howled, and most of the crowd cheered. Landon and Candace did not; Ava did not, and she saw many cold stares.

Wray did not cheer.

She swallowed. "One more thing."

"Quiet please!" called Mr. Levin He looked at Camellia, her eyes holding unshed tears, and mouthed to her, "It's all right."

She turned back to the crowd, her gaze sweeping into the far corner of the room, and lingering there.

"I've never thanked you all for being the best high school there ever was or ever will be." Lusty cheers. "My repayment was... insults. Control. Judgment. I'll never stop those, probably." Laughs and boos. "But," she looked straight at Wray, "there is... one of you who stands out. Who—who changed my—my life." She was shaking from head to foot; her purple velvet dress trembled. Wray's head shot up, and they looked at her with wide eyes. "I've had an empty life. I filled it with money, and fashion, and anger. There was only one thing I ever wanted, and I didn't know how badly I did. Until they walked into me, into my life."

Wray stood and began walking toward her.

"I love you, Wray Blythe," Camellia said to them.

She dropped the mic, and ran.

And Wray ran.

They collapsed into each other, Wray lifting her up. They kissed, oblivious to the rest of the world, to the crowd's cheers and amazement.

"Camellia," breathed Wray, trembling, holding her face, "I love you too. I'm sorry... I was such a shit bag. You're my Dume... my doom."

"Shut up, Wraith," she whispered. As they clung to each other, many of the students spilled down and around her. But she had eyes only for Wray, and Wray only had eyes for her.

CHAPTER 31

BASH

Hand in hand, grinning like fools, the couple walked slowly toward Wray's pickup truck, pausing every couple of minutes to kiss. The turbulent, disintegrating world faded into background noise and Camellia felt buoyed at every step. Whatever happened next, she wouldn't be alone.

At the truck, Camellia embraced Wray again, pushing back their hair, and kissing the nearly faded bruise on their face.

"What will you do?" she asked Wray. "I want you to come stay with me. But I don't know what the situation is at home."

Wray swept the hair away from her neck and kissed her softly, tasting her sweat, and nuzzling her neck below her ear. Camellia sighed happily.

Wray looked into her eyes, their gaze turbulent, the color as stormy as ever on this chaotic day. "He's my dad," Wray said simply. "I took you at your word, when you said families could come."

She nodded, though she felt uneasy. She did not think she could look at anyone who had ever hurt Wray, and welcome them into her home, much less her life... but this was their only parent, and the world was ending.

"It's up to you, then," she said, standing firm, looking lovingly at Wray. "Whatever you do, I'll support you."

Wray's eyes filled with tears. They squeezed Camellia's hands and choked, "I—I never knew what it was like. To be supported. I just—thank you. I'll call him."

The phone rang while Camellia rested her head on Wray's shoulder, but no one answered. Wray held the phone out, looked at the time, and finally hung up. They sighed.

"I tried." Wray lowered their head.

"Yes, you did," Camellia said, soothingly. "Let's go home."

"I'm already home. I'm with you."

She trembled all over.

"Oh my God, I love you," she whispered, as they kissed furiously.

The drive home was fast. They careened around backed up traffic on Pacific Coast Highway as everyone else headed to the water or the highlands. But they made it to her street where found a procession of cars lined up. She urged Wray to pull into the driveway, beyond the gate.

They entered the back yard, to the cacophonous sounds of the trees. They were behaving, but strangely bent, as if caught dancing in precarious positions. It was an uncanny sight, and Camellia could not let it go. The path to the back door was scattered with refuse, and she thought sadly of Gardener Clifton again while glaring mutinously at all the plants.

"We're gonna figure this out, and you'll stop your murderous fuckery," she hissed at them.

Wray blinked at her.

She cleared her throat.

"Okay, let's go in."

She opened the front door and commanded the house to

unlock the front gate. She and Wray stood on the front steps, hand in hand, and watched the throngs approach.

"Hope you hid the good silverware," quipped Wray.

Camellia giggled uncontrollably. They bumped elbows gently, eyes lingering on each other. After everyone poured into the house, the music thundered as the Cadre quickly overtook the kitchen, creating playlists on Fridge. General chaos ensued until some of the teachers showed up.

Camellia gasped with relief at the sight of Mr. Levin, who had coaxed Mr. Welsh to come along after all. She could smell the dank, acrid aura of weed on the physics teacher.

That won't be the only time we smell it tonight, I'll bet.

"That stuff can kill you," she called to Mr. Welsh with a royal wave.

"I had to dry all my plants so they wouldn't!" he crowed. "So I'm smokin' 'em now, before they smoke me!"

"Touché," she conceded.

She ran up to Mr. Levin.

"Can you keep an eye on things for a bit?" she pleaded.

He gave her a dolorous look. "What, I'm the babysitter now?"

"Just need a few minutes." She blinked impishly at Wray.

"Fine, but not many. We've got important stuff to do, and we need you."

She seized Wray's hand and whispered in their ear, "And I need *you.*"

They ran up the stairs, past the clambering looky-loos and exploring teens, some with parents. A few lingered outside her door as she stood with her hands on her hips facing them.

"You're gonna fuck off, right now," she demanded, "or I'm gonna fuck you up."

They all dispersed. She pulled Wray into the room, shut the door, and locked it securely. The house bumped with music, so no matter what happened in that room, no one would hear the lovers. They gripped each other tightly, in every direction, for several minutes, gasping and laughing and sometimes just silently staring into each other's eyes. Camellia rested on Wray's chest and swept their blonde and blue chin-length hair back, kissing them.

"I couldn't stand being without you," she murmured.

"I couldn't either." Wray kissed the freckles on her nose. "I'm an idiot, I never should have doubted. It's just... *look at you*. I didn't believe you really *would* be proud to be seen with me. I'm a nobody."

"You're not a nobody, Wray Blythe," Camellia murmured, kissing them in several choice areas as they grinned. "You're everything. And you're perfect."

She and Wray wobbled back down the stairs, flushed and silly and ecstatic. She turned the knob to what looked like a closet off from her father's office in the living room.

"Time to distribute some emergency supplies," she told Wray.

"What's in here?"

"The vault."

Behind the wooden door, there was a metal door with a keypad on its face. When Camellia placed her hand on it, it turned green. It opened with a *shloooock*, revealing all the emergency supplies her mother had stocked many years ago. Earthquake kits, pandemic supplies, potable water, air filters, the works; some things were in shelves embedded in the walls, some were in chests or durable plastic tubs. Several swords hung on one wall, as well as a shotgun and a few rifles.

The Cadre and Mr. Levin peered in curiously.

"*Ohmyfuckinggod*, you have whole-ass *swords*?" Dewayne gasped.

"Yes, Dedoofus," laughed Camellia. "There's a couple

more in my room. I had to learn longsword fighting for a bit part. I got to keep two, but these were the ones my parents picked out."

"Okay, impressive, I'll admit," said Mr. Levin. "I knew Tracey would set you up, but this is beyond what I imagined! Very on brand for Tracey, though."

"I would like a *whole-ass* sword," sniped Mel as Michel guffawed.

Dewayne rolled his eyes. "Seriously, though. How fucking warrior goddess are you? I wish I could swordfight."

"Yeah," Michel snickered. "The closest you'll ever get is one of those little saber swizzle sticks."

"Hey, I love those things!" exclaimed Dewayne. "I have a whole collection of vintage swizzle sticks."

Mel roared with laughter. "That's the queeniest thing you've ever said, Dewayne."

He shrugged. "Maybe I'll design my own one day."

"What, for your smoothie cantina empire?" snickered Mel.

"Play time's over," admonished Camellia. "I mean, if things go sideways—"

"You mean *when*," Wray pointed out.

"Babe, so dark!" Camellia cried, stroking Wray's arm. "Anyway, guess we can use them in a pinch. Mr. Levin?"

He was chatting at the breakfast nook table with Mr. Welsh, encircled by a cloud of marijuana smoke like an active cinder cone volcano in miniature. The two looked up.

"Hey!" Mr. Welsh said excitedly. "I think we've got it sorted. We can triangulate the source of your transmission, if we can make a receiver that mimics your device."

"Sounds… simple," Camellia said doubtfully.

"But meanwhile," Mr. Welsh said, eyes glazed over, "we can broadcast *your* signal."

"Can you?" she cried, eyes lighting up.

"Yep, let's go see how this all works around the plants. Back yard?" Mr. Welsh asked.

"You're not nervous?" she asked, hesitantly.

"Miss Dume," grinned Mr. Welsh, "I'm on the strongest bud I own. I'm impervious to fear."

"And possibly logic," Mr. Levin pointed out.

Mr. Welsh bopped in his seat and clapped his hands together. "AV club!" he called to the raucous crowd clustered in the living room and draped along the stairs. The air grew hazy from weed, and who knew what else.

Camellia whispered to Fridge, "Turn the air filters on high, please."

A few students clustered around Mr. Welsh.

"Let's get to it!"

Camellia led them to the back door and hesitantly opened it. What she saw displeased her. Someone had rolled the trees in toilet paper. The trees stood clacking and shivering, and the bushes danced, but not the camellias. They sat perfectly still, resistant to any changes.

Mr. Welsh looked up at the streamers of white tissue and the quavering trees, his mouth forming an O. "Maybe I should lay off that particular leaf." He swayed.

She glared at him.

"Right," he said, still watching the behavior of the trees. "You're radiating the signal in all directions. But I have a suspicion that the one you're *receiving* is direct, a beam; possibly—probably—encrypted and not scattered. We just have to figure out from where it's coming from." He squinted at the cotton candy sunset sky. "Not a satellite, or you'd lose the signal at different times of the day. Guessing that's not a good idea... so it's earthbound. But! We can figure that out later. For now, your broadcast. The Camellia channel. The plants are *tuned. In.* Dancing to the beat. So let's figure out the frequency."

"How will you repeat it?"

"Well, that's what the AV folks are for."

Camellia stared at the assemblage; one had pizza dripping

on the lawn, another chugged soda, and another played a virtual game on a headset.

"All right, Glitches, my bitches," she snapped loudly. "Record this fucking signal! Save the world or something."

They quickly determined the frequency and recorded the transmission.

Camellia's heart soared. *Mom, you'd be so happy right now, I'll bet!*

"How will you retransmit it?" she asked Mr. Welsh.

He nodded to Mr. Levin. "We've got to test it on some plants first. Let's try it away from these. You stay here, and we'll go across the stree—"

Camellia and Mr. Levin both complained at once.

"No, no, no!" he said.

"Way too fucking risky!" she cried. "Why don't I come with you, and I can maintain a distance. You can test it on plants farther away, and see what happens... but maybe, I don't know, be armed or something. I have swords."

"Casual," said Mr. Welsh, grinning. "I dig it."

As they made their way back to the front of the house and out the door, Camellia flew into a rage. Someone had rolled the front yard! And not just her yard, but the yards of every house on the block.

"What motherfucker did this!" she screamed.

She tilted her head and saw words on her lawn.

"Someone who doesn't like you, babe," Wray noted.

In giant letters, someone spelled "CUNTMELA" with toilet paper.

She snorted. "They can't even spell my part of the name right! Dumbass!" She heard laughter down the lane.

"Who is it?" Wray asked.

"I know that smarmy, cheap-sounding laugh anywhere," growled Camellia. "It's Landon and some of the Ballsacks. Hey, you flaming assholes!" she shrieked down the lane. "Come clean this shit up, or I'll—"

A loud yell broke out, followed by a slithering sound, a crack, and a scream.

Mr. Levin and Mr. Welsh ran out into the street.

"What are you doing!" screamed Camellia. "Get back here!"

"Help!" someone yelled.

It was chaos, and it was gruesome. The jocks and some hangers-on had indeed gone down the street to roll yards... but they went beyond the range of Camellia's transmission. And the plants noticed.

She watched in horror and pushed Wray gently. "Go get my swords," she urged.

"I'm coming!" she yelled.

"Camellia, you can't!" screamed Mr. Levin. "If you leave, *your* plants will attack all of us!"

CHAPTER 32

LIFE ON EARTH

Camellia pressed her hands to her temples. Wray bounded out with a sheathed sword. Dewayne goggled. Mr. Levin and Mr. Welsh yelled at the jocks to run for it, but two of them had already been seized by vines. Landon was dangling in the air by his foot, screaming; the other jock made terrible gurgling sounds. She could see whipping movements high in the air and recoiled.

"Jesus," she murmured.

Then: staccato.

"Gunfire!" she screamed. "Who's shooting, for fuck's sake!"

An SUV barreled around the corner onto her street, and she saw flashes of light and the resulting explosive bursts of machine gun fire.

"Get inside!" Mr. Levin screamed.

Shrieks erupted as everyone, except for Mr. Levin, Mr. Welsh, Camellia, and Wray, bolted back.

Mr. Welsh, joint still hanging from the corner of his mouth, held a transmitter and shouted, "Turn it up!" at one of the AV kids. He began to advance down the street.

"You idiot!" Camellia shrieked. "Get back here. Guard the house with that thing! I'll go!"

Before Wray could stop her, she seized the sword and ran down the lane.

"Camellia!" shouted Wray.

But Camellia was overcome with adrenaline and rage.

"Who the fuck is shooting!"

When she made it to Landon and his goons, the plants froze in place and shivered, halted by her presence.

"Get me down, you stupid bitch!" Yelled Landon, hanging from high up.

More machine gun fire. Camellia whirled and her mouth fell agape.

"Cousin Darla!"

Darla leaned out the window of her SUV as her wizened husband Bud drove.

"Move it, sugar!" she shouted. "I'll get that one. You cut the other one!"

"Holy fuck!" screamed Landon. "What's she gonna do, shoot it?"

Camellia backed away as a line of fire struck the great vine holding Landon in the air. The plant listed quickly and snapped, sending a shrieking Landon flying off into a light post. He slid to the ground, unconscious.

The other jock thrashed, tangled within a web of vines.

"Hold still, numb nuts!" Camellia yelled, slashing through the calmed vines. The other jocks limped along, some missing shoes. She pointed to Landon.

"Carry that radish-brained prick back to the house," she commanded.

She was of half a mind to run off and let the plants grab them again, out of spite.

As they dispersed, she watched Cousin Darla and Bud park illegally in someone's driveway.

Seeing her expression, Darla shrugged. "Well? What are

they gonna do in the apocalypse? Give me a parking ticket? Fuck 'em."

Camellia covered her smile with the hilt of her sword.

Darla helped Bud out of the SUV and gave him his walker.

"Hey, Mimi!" he waved.

Camellia groaned quietly.

"Cousin Darla... what are you doing here?"

Darla beamed at her.

"Fridge-baby called me," she said with a smile. She brushed back her frosted hair and blinked her goopy mascara-edged eyes. "Said you might need some help. So here I am!"

"Great," said Camellia, with her most plastic of fake smiles. She brightened. "Actually, you'll be perfect. We need to keep these shits in line."

"Now there's the spirit!" cried Darla. "Oh, and I brought more guns and ammo, too."

"Great," repeated Camellia, gritting her teeth, although she fervently hoped nobody would need them.

Darla proved to be a welcome addition, brusque yet friendly. Bud regaled what he called "you youngsters" and some of their parents with old war stories (many of them borrowed), and Darla ordering cocktails from the Cadre, who had somehow broken into Dez's bar. Camellia was suspicious about that, and glanced darkly at her cousin.

Mr. Welsh and Mr. Levin constructed a better broadcaster. Then, they made it redundant. They borrowed amplifiers from the Bandages, who brought various bits of equipment. They were ready to roll out.

And then Fridge rang.

"Camellia," it called loudly over the intercom, startling everyone momentarily. "You have a call in the kitchen."

She made a face and entered the kitchen. Her phone beamed, so she picked it up.

"Hello?" she answered.

A woman's voice on the other line asked, "Is this Camellia Dume?"

"Yes."

"Stand by, please."

She made a face. Wray watched her and raised their eyebrows. She shrugged.

"Miss Dume," a deeper voice spoke.

"Yes?"

"This is Commander Aldrin Morrell of the LAPD."

She gasped. "Look, we can turn the music down."

"Ma'am, nobody's cracking down on music tonight. We're in a disaster. We need to speak to a Mr. Welsh or a Mr. Levin."

"Can—can I ask why?"

"This is a matter of national security. Can you confirm their whereabouts?"

The two teachers stared at her. She tentatively held the phone out to Mr. Levin. He promptly handed it to Mr. Welsh.

Mr. Welsh listened and nodded. "Yep. Yep. Groovy. Gotcha. Yep. Yep. We'll be here. Over and out!"

He hung up and took a massive toke on his joint.

"What the fuck was that about?" Camellia demanded.

"We'll get our loudspeakers soon," grinned Mr. Welsh. "I'm giving them the signal."

"So we're saved?" gasped Camellia.

"Well…" Mr. Welsh took another drag, held it in his lungs, and let it back out slowly. Mr. Levin gagged and waved his hands to clear the air. "Guess we'll see. I think, tonight, L.A. can sleep easier."

The constant roar of helicopters buffeted the night skies. The police, fire and rescue, National Guard, and other government vehicles roamed the streets, transmitting the signal.

A fleet of donated drones made its way about, although it would take some time before everyone in Southern California would be safe. Roads had been destroyed, hampering aid, and hospitals were overwhelmed. But the drone network and the ingenuity of Killian High students and teachers went a long way toward giving people hope.

Partiers began making their way out of the house, while Mr. Levin and Mr. Welsh lingered a bit longer, chatting with some students. The Cadre basked in the open, large house as everyone else went home. Darla and Bud made them all cackle loudly with laughter, and it became an easygoing evening.

"Let's go for a walk," Camellia suggested, taking Wray's hand. "I could use some fresh air."

"Will everything be okay at the house?" Wray asked.

"With those nerds? And Cousin Darla? Definitely," Camellia said with a smile.

They walked out of the gate, and up the lane, which was mercifully quiet. The trees were clattering and whispering, but not attacking.

"So now we just find a way to reverse their behavior, right?" Wray asked.

"That's the idea." Camellia looked out at the horizon where various boats bobbed in the sea; some were coming in, others lingered. Their tiny lights flickered like fireflies. It was a beautiful sight, but not without suffering. *Life on Earth*, she mused.

"Wonder what we'll need to do for tha—UNFF!"

Wray collapsed. Camellia shrieked. Something grabbed her from behind.

She knew the smell and knew who it was before he opened his mouth.

"Sweet Caramel," murmured Syd. "Let's go for a ride."

CHAPTER 33

DETENTION

She awoke to the streaks of blurring taillights, briefly, before slipping away again, groggy, confused. Gradually, she could lift her head. She pressed her teeth against something. A gag, shoved in her mouth and tied around her head. She thrashed.

Her hands were tied behind her back; her ankles were also tied. She whipped her head around to see Syd driving. He stared at the road ahead, but managed to wink at her. She tried screaming through the rag. Then she bucked and strained to look behind her. Wray lay in the back seat, unconscious. As the lights flickered in through the dark, tinted windows of Syd's vehicle, she could see a large lump on Wray's face.

"Waaaaay!" she shouted through her rag.

"Out cold," Syd said.

She lunged at him, and he abruptly pulled over. He got out of the car, walked around to the passenger side, and opened the door. She tried to see where she was, and would have leapt it out, if she could have. She caught sight of a stop sign and the headlights glowing on "Arroyo Seco." She thought quickly. They were somewhere in the San Gabriel Valley.

Syd pulled something from the floorboard and held it up, snakelike. For a moment, she panicked. She then realized it was a set of bungee cords. He wrapped one around her in the passenger's seat and calmly shut her door before proceeding around to his seat.

He reached across, held a little cuplike object up to her nose, and squeezed. She felt herself drift away into a dream-like state as they drove onward.

She had the sensation of going down and down. A parking garage? She was unsure. The lights were strange. Something smelled like vinegar. She slid in and out of wake-fulness. But every other thought was of Wray.

At some point, they halted, and she heard the rear driver's side car door open and shut.

"Waaaaay," she said softly, unable to do much. She heard a thump and saw a long object on the hood of the car. She tensed up. It was Wray, splayed out. Syd drew back his hand and it cracked across Wray's face.

She shrieked through her gag and watched as Syd bound Wray's hands behind them. He stood Wray on their feet, stag-gering. Tears streamed down Camellia's face.

Syd opened her door, as if they were on a date, smiled at her, and unhooked the bungee cords. She was too groggy to fight, so he pulled her up and stood her next to Wray. He hooked the two of them together with one of the bungee cords and marched them through a dimly lit garage to a large freight elevator. Syd tapped his watch against the panel, and it opened. He marched the teens in and touched the watch to another panel inside. They were moving, but she could not tell if it was down or up; it was subtle, smooth, and eerily quiet.

The door opened, and a long, fluorescently lit hallway stretched far ahead. He took them to the end of it, stumbling occasionally, and through another door. They trudged down a dark well of a space to yet another door before he led them inside.

It was a large, square room with slate gray walls. A sink with a cabinet stood at one corner and a chair rested nearby. It looked like a fancy dental office chair to Camellia. As she was swiveled around, she saw the opposite wall held a ledge, where a man sagged, his arms tied up, his head drooping. His hair faded red and gray.

She screamed through her gag. "Daaaaaa!"

It was Dez. He jerked awake, swayed his head back and forth, and brought his eyes into focus. His face was runneled with blood stains, his eyes yellow from bruising.

He jerked, pulled at his shackles, and yelled, "Nooooo! Nooooo!"

Camellia fainted.

~

She awoke to a voice she knew. A voice she had once greatly admired. She realized that this voice was talking about *her*.

It was Syd. And he was leering at Wray, who was not gagged. She soon understood why.

"So you fucked her," Syd hissed in Wray's face. Camellia went ice cold. "How'd you manage that? You don't look like you have much to offer. Did you taste her too? What's she taste like?"

Wray thrashed, and Dez groaned weakly, eyes streaming over his crusty, blood-stained face. He tried to raise his arms to cover his ears.

Syd paced before Wray, who looked up through their swollen eye petulantly, blood and spittle dripping from their mouth. Camellia gnashed against her gag, trying to scream.

"I could protect her," Syd spat into Wray's ear. "What could YOU do for her? You've got nothing. No money, dead-beat dad. She's better than you."

"She's... better than me. And she's... way... out... of your league," panted Wray.

Sad strolled over to Camellia and lifted her chin; she tried to pull her face away. He ran his fingers over her brow, along her cheeks, along her gagged lips, and down her neck. His eyes were cold yet wild.

"What do you see in that little fish, there, Caramel?" he asked in a smooth, sultry voice. "Huh? What do you see, ginger girl? I'll do right by you. I'll give you... every-thing..." he ran his finger down her neck to just above her cleavage. "Everything you could ever want. I could teach you."

She shook all over, feeling defiled, sickened by his touch. She glared at him through rage tears, and growled in agony.

How could I have ever liked you?

"Caramel baby," Syd murmured, and he brought his lips to her temple and to her neck. Now she really loathed his pet name for her, and could not believe she'd ever liked it.

Dez bucked, groaned, and thrashed, weeping while watching his daughter.

"Leave her alone!" yelled Wray, twisting this way and that.

Syd leaned in to take Camellia's dangling form into his arms, when the door lock cracked. He jerked upright, stood ramrod straight, and stepped a bit away from her. She let her muscles relax a touch. The door opened.

In walked a man with tablet in one arm, and chin length, greasy gray hair, shot through with dark streaks, pushed back by glasses on the top of his head. He wore a white lab coat, simple but well-made denim jeans, and very high-end shoes. His eyebrows were black, and his eyes piercing hazel, rimmed with long, dark eyelashes. The effect made his eyes look almost golden, and predatory. His face bore few lines, and she knew he must have had cosmetic work done.

"Bring her over," the man said dismissively. He took the

cover off the sleek, white chair, revealing an instrument panel and straps hanging from its sides. "Buckle her in."

She fought and moaned but could do nothing to get herself out of the situation. She did not like the look of the chair. It was clinical yet it had straps.

The man opened the cabinet door against the wall. He pulled out a tray with several wrapped, sterilized items resting on it. Camellia's breath quickened, and her heart began to race.

He glanced over at her briefly, at Dez, and Wray. His strange eyes flickered while looking at Wray.

"Who's that?"

His tone did not seem overly curious or upset. Just flat and clinical.

"They were together," answered Syd, his voice a growl of disgust.

The man briefly raised his eyebrows, and glanced at Syd, but otherwise remained expressionless. He gave a light shrug. "We'll use them later."

He pointed to the chair and he brought a syringe out of his pocket. Camellia went frigid with fear.

"Strap her in," he said in a calm voice. He didn't sound at all aggressive, but the casual manner he made the command, and the immediate obedience by Syd, disturbed Camellia far more than if he had been full of bluster.

Syd loosened Camellia from where she hung. She thrashed, but he was too strong for her. He threw her over his shoulder like a bag of grain.

Wray yelled, "Put her down!"

Dez rocked back-and-forth, as though trying to break free.

Camellia could see them both struggling, and it destroyed her, being powerless to help them. It was a nightmare she wanted desperately to break free from but could not.

Syd eased her down onto the chair, reached into his pocket for a knife, and cut her wristbands free. She swung instantly, striking his neck and thrashing... but he was quick, and strapped her in before she could do much else. She jerked in the chair, until the lab coat man brought a little rubber cup up to her nose, like the one Syd had used in the vehicle. When she breathed, she instantly felt lightheaded, soft, and pliable.

No, oh no...

The other man set the syringe on the instrument tray and turned on the chair's panel. He sat down and observed the readings. The screen showed all her vital signs, as well as two bands along the bottom, in different wavelengths.

Oh, shit fuck.

The transponder signals.

She heard a soft clap and lolled her face around to look through slightly blurry green eyes into the man's dark-bordered gold ones.

Syd watched them both, arms crossed. He eyed the panel too. Camellia's heart rate had leapt, she knew, and she watched it bounce. Her O2 levels stayed stable.

"There we go, good signal," murmured the strange man, looking at the screen. He pulled a hand-length wand from a compartment on the chair panel. He turned to her and said, "I'm Dr. Grelling."

He smiled in the way an animal might bare its teeth, with cold eyes.

"Now, you won't remember me, but I do remember you. You were a small thing; Dr. Edgars and I were associates, prior to your birth, and for a little while after."

Mom! She realized that this was the strange man she'd seen in the group picture of scientists, and she remembered the flicker that hurried across Mr. Levin's face when he'd held it.

She tried to yell through the gag. Dr. Grelling glanced from her to Syd, and signaled for his assistant to remove her gag.

Syd stepped forward. "You sure about this?" he asked. "She's got a mouth on her."

"I need her to answer some questions, but thank you for the warning," answered Dr. Grelling coldly.

Syd removed the gag, and Camellia took great gulps of air until she hiccupped. She licked her lips. Dr. Grelling pointed to the sink in the corner, and Syd stepped over to get a disposable cup of water. He brought it to Camellia's lips; she slurped at it, and would have given anything to have wiped her mouth. But Syd did it for her, delicately, making her squirm. But she felt tired, oh so very tired, and weak... like a tottering new kitten.

"You *sick fucks*!" she shouted. "Let Dad and Wray go! Just deal with me, if you have to."

Dr. Grelling glanced over his shoulder at Wray and Dez, and turned back, blinking once. His emotionless gaze chilled her.

"I'll need them soon," he said, with the baring of teeth again.

She shuddered.

"Caramel," said Syd softly, "are you cold?"

Camellia turned to him with her eyes ablaze and yelled, "Stop calling me that! You're sympathetic *now*? I'm strapped in, you pus-brained psycho! Where are we? What's going on? You'd better fucking tell me. And people will know I'm gone. They'll search—"

Dr. Grelling ignored her, taking the wand and touching it to the screen.

"Lower your head, Camellia."

She glared at him. "Why?"

"This won't hurt," the scientist said. "I'm going to examine the implant area."

She sat stubbornly, not obeying.

Dr. Grelling looked to Syd and said, "Adjust her."

She didn't like the sound of that, as though she were a device.

Syd leaned over and pulled her hair up, placing one hand on her forehead and the other on the back of her head, and forced her head down.

"Ack!" she cried, but she could not move her head; Syd had her in his grip.

She flinched at the touch of the silicon-covered wand on her skin. It made a light humming sound, but the doctor was right; it didn't hurt. He held it there for a few seconds, and Camellia watched an image appear on the screen, something between an x-ray and an ultrasound. It showed a bright, tiny device burrowed into her neck. She was surprised by how deep it was. Syd released her head, and she reclined back in the chair, staring.

"What is it?" called Wray hoarsely.

"The implant," she said thickly.

Dr. Grelling leaned back, arms crossed, and stared at the image. He let out a small sigh.

"It's not subcutaneous like I thought," he muttered.

"So… what is it?" Syd asked, a strange highness in his voice. Camellia glanced up at him, feeling drunk, and his eyes had widened. He looked… frightened.

"She… that is, your mother, Camellia," Dr. Grelling said, "chose not to insert this device close to the surface of your skin. This means a couple of things: the signal going into it needed to be stronger than that going out. It's only made to protect you… but at a distance. How far a distance, I'm not quite sure. We'll figure that out soon enough. It's coming from somewhere. Not via satellite, I'm fairly sure. I have a feeling I know the general area, but we never could figure out where she'd been that night."

Dez let out a moan.

Camellia gasped, "What night?"

Dr. Grelling turned to her, and the lighting of the room

turned his eyes a ghoulish yellow. "Your mother had an unfortunate accident one evening. Such a waste." He made a quick shake of the head. "All she had to do was say where."

Camellia's eyes darted from Dr. Grelling's to Syd's. Syd would have been too young that night, the night her world really ended; when her mother's car flew off a cliff along the Pacific Coast Highway, killing her.

So it's you, she thought, staring at Dr. Grelling.

"You killed Mom," she said in a deathly quiet voice.

Dez thrashed and pulsed with red rage.

"You fucking killed my mom!" screamed Camellia.

"Tell me, Camellia," said Dr. Grelling smoothly, as if she were a student in a library, checking out a book, and he was a calm, quiet librarian, there to guide her. "Where's the transmitter?"

"I have no fucking idea, dickhead!" she spat.

"What about your AI?" mused Dr. Grelling calmly. "Why don't you ask it. I'll wait."

"It's not going to know that!" she cried.

"Well, there's one way to find out."

"I'm not asking it shit."

Dr. Grelling nodded slowly and glanced up at Syd, who watched Camellia's flushed, drugged face.

"Syd, let's open it up."

Her heart hammered.

Open what *up?*

"Sure you're ready?" asked Syd.

"Whenever you are. You're the one who has to do the work."

Camellia watched as Syd took a long look at Wray and Dez, his face twitching.

"What's he going to do?" Wray yelled.

Dr. Grelling ignored them and pointed to a lighted green button on the far wall. Syd stepped across the dark gray, concrete floor and pressed the button. The walls around them slid apart, as did the ceiling tiles. And all around them, above, and along the side of the walls, long, pulsating green tendrils and vines twisted and snapped, some of them as thick as logs, others spindly and whippy. They all crackled and popped... because Camellia sat there among them.

Camellia's breath came hard and fast.

"I'll need to cut into her spinal cord a bit to get it out," Dr. Grelling said casually.

"No!" yelled Wray. "You fucker! Don't you touch her!"

Camellia let out a wail of fear, and every vein in Dez's face popped as if he would go mad from horror and rage.

"Wait," said Syd, his voice cracking, "what do you mean, her spinal cord? I thought it was just an implant, and you could just cut it out easily."

"Hmm, yes," Dr. Grelling, "that's what I'd supposed it was. Tracey burrowed it in there... or maybe it adapted, since it was placed when the girl was fairly young, before she grew."

"What will it do to her?" Syd asked, voice hard.

"She'll sustain motor damage, but she should live," Dr. Grelling answered coldly.

"What do you mean, motor damage?" Camellia shouted. "I won't be able to move? I'll be paralyzed?"

"Well," huffed Dr. Grelling, "I'm no neurosurgeon, and we don't have time to get one. I need to figure out where the transmission is coming from and shut it down. So we need the device out. I'll take my chances."

Camellia let out a shriek. "The fuck you will, you putty-faced bitch!"

Syd's forearms bulged, and Camellia saw that he was clenching his fists.

"I thought this was straightforward. Can't we just shut this signal down somehow, disrupt it? Come on!"

Dr. Grelling squinted up at him from where he sat.

"If I shut the one signal down, the other one might go as

well. Then we have two problems: the protection she's beaming out goes away, and in case you hadn't noticed, we have a captive audience in here, as well as outside. We need that a little longer. I want it intact. But she'll be out of commission, I'm afraid. Is there a problem?"

Syd stared down at Camellia, who at first refused to meet his gaze.

When she did, it conveyed more hatred than she had ever felt or directed in her life, and he flinched. But he stared back at her just the same.

"No," said Syd quietly. He blinked and swallowed.

"Can't... can't we try something else," gasped Camellia. "What if—what if I called the AI, and it told you everything you need to know."

Dr. Grelling leaned back, arms behind his head.

"By all means, if you think you can get the info. Do you have her phone, Syd?"

Syd walked over to a duffle bag by the far door, as the plants swayed and snapped, their purple blooms shivering, emitting a softly mesmerizing scent. He brought back Camellia's bag.

Dr. Grelling pointed at the bag, and at her. "You'll call your AI, and no one else, or I shut the others behind the wall with the plants, away from your signal. Understood?"

Goddammit, she breathed.

"Understood, fuckface," she sneered.

Syd loosened her arms, but she knew better than to try and swing at him now; she had no weapons. She turned on her phone and dialed "Fridge."

Syd loomed over her, took the phone, put it on speaker, and held it out so that she could not touch it.

"Hello, Camellia, how are you?" the musical, calm voice of Fridge called out. It was the only thing that sounded safe here in this hellish chamber.

"Hi Fridge," and her voice broke high. "I wondered if you

could tell me... where the transmission's coming from. The one in my transponder. I know you know what I'm talking about."

Fridge chirped: "That is classified information. You do not have authority to access it."

Camellia looked miserably up at Syd and Dr. Grelling, who stared unblinking with those bizarre, gold eyes of his.

"Okay, I get that. I do, Fridge," she said nervously. "But I need to know. And I wondered if, as Tracey's daughter, you could override that authority. Or tell me who has access to it."

"That is classified information. You do not have authority to access it."

Camellia began to shake. Dr. Grelling slowly shook his head, pointed at the plants behind them, and over to her father and Wray. Syd mouthed to her, "Don't cry."

"Is—is there another way we can access the signal?" she asked, as calmly as she could manage, even though she was on the verge of panic.

"That is classified information. You do not have authority to access it."

She swallowed. "Okay. Okay. I'm—I'm sorry. I just— hoped you could help."

"Is there anything else I can help you with, Camellia?" the calm voice asked.

She blinked back tears, thinking of the cute red panda face on the fridge panel at her home. "I—I think that's it. I'd love a smoothie though."

Syd glared at her.

She gave him the stink eye.

"Would you like it from Dewayne's Smoothie Hut, or Cap'n James' Organics?"

She controlled her breathing. *Dewayne. James... Jim...*

"The Cap'n James' Organics one. With the little saber swizzle stick. I love that one!"

"I will get that ordered for you."

"Thank you," Camellia said carefully. "I'll—I'll be home soon."

Syd ended the call. The room sat ominously still, except for the whipping and crackling of the plants all around, chittering, chattering, and swaying like an audience held back from a wrestling ring.

"That was optimistic," said Dr. Grelling with the specter of a grin. "I'm assuming that meant more than you were saying, but it would seem the AI is not forthcoming for you anyway. So. We'll proceed. Syd, strap her back in."

"No!" screamed Wray.

"Mmmmm!" Dez tried to scream, and she understood that he meant "Meems." She closed her eyes.

"Let them go, they don't need to be here to see this," begged Camellia. "There's no reason."

"Well, see, I can't do that, Camellia Dume," said Dr. Grelling. "Now they know too much, and so do you."

"Why... why are you doing this? Why aren't you helping stop it?"

Dr. Grelling said softly, "Dr. Edgars—Tracey, your mother —was brilliant, but not forward-thinking enough. When we got the readings about the object entering the atmosphere, she detected the macromolecules... and found they contained gene-editing codes. I'm the one who translated the codes. They overexpress plant qualities; you can do anything you want, engineer enormous produce, mass-produce and express drugs, switch plants from senescent to mobile. But they worked best with kudzu, which already had some of those properties. It just needed a little nudge. I tried it at Oak Ridge Labs, not too far from your grandmother's home, as a matter of fact. Wasn't she in Cowl's Mountain?"

Camellia's entire body shuddered. *Cowl's Mountain. Overtaken completely.*

Dr. Grelling continued, "Tracey thought it should be used on something simpler: *Arabidopsis*, maybe. I disagreed. I saw the potential. But she didn't like that course, and she wanted to go public with the findings. There's no way the public would understand: an extrasolar object, entering the atmosphere, containing genetic coding. We had the potential to mass produce drugs without ever needing factories, or people. We had the capability to grow wood quickly. But I wanted to master it first. She felt otherwise."

He shrugged.

"She apparently thought it would be a good idea to prevent it from happening, and it looks like she tried to make a transmitter somewhere, to instruct how to stop it. She implanted a transponder in you; and it protects you and those around you. Or it did. It won't after we remove it."

"But won't the plants attack you too?" Camellia asked, her dizzy mind spinning. "And what if you're too late, and a helicopter comes over and…"

"Not if I tool the frequency. Then I can command it. I can will it to attack others, while protecting my investments."

Shit.

"You're insane," she murmured. She turned to Syd. "Do you not see how insane this is? Why would you want to kill everyone?"

Dr. Grelling blinked. "Better to be the ruler of hell than a follower in heaven. I get to do my research, unimpeded, and finally plants will have their domain returned to them."

He inserted the syringe into a vial and withdrew a liquid. He adjusted the plunger on the syringe until he was satisfied with its volume.

"Syd, hold her down."

Wray yelled, Dez groaned, and Camellia cried out.

She met Syd's eyes and he blinked as Dr. Grelling pointed from him to her neck.

"Now, Syd. If she's alerted someone in code, we don't have much time."

Syd again placed one hand on Camellia's forehead, and the other on the back of her head as she wept.

"Please," she whispered.

He bent her head down.

Dr. Grelling leaned in, to inject her at the base of her neck. She felt the needle graze her skin...

But Syd struck the syringe from Dr. Grelling's hand.

The scientist reached in his pocket for something, but Syd caught him by the throat with one hand, seizing the object, a small gun, with his other. He threw the gun aside.

"You're not cutting her," Syd said through gritted teeth. "She's *mine!*"

Flailing, Dr. Grelling slapped the instrument panel on the chair, and an alarm sounded. Syd squeezed him around the throat with both hands.

Camellia wrestled against her straps and managed to get one hand free; she undid her other strap and sat up while Syd was squeezing Dr. Grelling's neck. She quickly seized some of the packaged items on the surgery tray.

And she ran.

CHAPTER 34

THE WALL

She ran first to Wray. Unwrapping one of the scalpels with shaking hands, she cut their bindings, kissed them, and whispered, "Pretend you're still tied." She looked deep into Wray's eyes. "Please trust me."

Wray nodded.

Camellia heard a thud and turned to see Dr. Grelling slumped over in front of the cabinet by the door. She started to run for Dez, but he shook his head, eyes darting to Syd. Syd turned to Camellia.

She brought forth all the charm and fakery she'd honed her entire life, every coping mechanism she'd ever mined to survive, and approached him, smiling. He held his arms out, smiling back at her, eyes only for her. She pushed everything down into the little box in her mind and focused on him.

"It's over," he said, grinning. "Sweet Caramel," he murmured as he held her in his arms, lifted her up, and kissed her. Over his shoulder, she could see Wray. Wray watched her keenly and thrashed, pretending they were still bound.

"Let us go! You don't need us!" Wray screamed.

Syd ignored Wray. Softly kissing Camellia's neck, he said, "Tell me you're mine."

She took a deep breath, and locked eyes with Wray.

"I'm yours."

Dez thrashed and groaned, weeping.

Syd kissed the other side of her neck, and said, "Tell me you want me."

She looked straight at Wray.

"I want you."

"That's my girl," Syd smiled. "You're mine now; you're *safe*."

"Oh, Syd," she breathed, drawing forth her fakest smile.

Dez groaned in abject misery, then halted.

Syd leaned down to stroke the hair fallen back from her face She felt him lurch, and grunt "Uff!"

Releasing her, he whirled, holding his side, wheezing. He yanked the scalpel from his ribs and yelled in fury, his face hideously twisted in rage and shock, and rounded on Wray. Camellia reached in Syd's pocket and grabbed his knife, as he wheeled on her with eyes wide. She slashed down and tried to cut his face but missed, striking his wrist, severing both it and his watch band.

Wray yanked the instrument tray and bashed Syd's head from behind, as Camellia jumped to her feet and scrambled to her dad. She used the knife to cut him free, and released his gag.

"Camellia," he said hoarsely and urgently, "Meems. Give me the knife. Get the button. The button! I'll say when."

He staggered over as Syd lunged for Wray, and charged for Camellia. She froze for a second.

"Camellia!" Syd shouted. He seized her in his arms, and she shrieked.

"*GET YOUR FUCKING HANDS OFF MY DAUGHTER!*" roared Dez, and he stabbed Syd in the neck.

Syd dropped Camellia roughly, mouth frothing, eyes insane, and rounded on Dez.

"Now!" shouted Dez.

Camellia ran, seized Wray's hand, and slammed her fist on the green button.

Dez struggled with the flailing Syd, pummeling them both full-body toward the wall of plants. Syd, blood surging from his wrist, neck and ribs, seized Dez's left arm and snapped it. Dez yelled in agony but kept shoving. Then they both fell into the dense plants. Dez kicked and stabbed again. Syd went for his neck as the walls lowered, blocking Camellia's signal, and severing them from her.

"Dad!" Camellia screamed.

The plants responded quickly, thrusting, buckling, spinning ropes, entangling the two men.

"No, Dad!" Camellia went mad with grief. She hit the green button again.

"Camellia, no!" cried Wray. They had Syd's watch in their hands and opened the door with it. "We've got to get out of here. Syd's gonna kill us! Or at least me!

"I'm not leaving my dad!" she choked.

A horrible roar with gurgling and splitting sounds erupted from behind the now-paused wall. She could only see their legs and heard her father gasping. It was unbearable.

"Stop the wall!" Dez screamed, so Camellia hit the button again, halting it. Dez scrambled out, leaving Syd inside.

An unearthly shuddering and rushing sound, full of whispers and cracks and slithers, and the groans and moans of Syd, emitted from the other side of that wall. Dez lay panting on the ground, arm limp, and blood and shit fountained out, along with eyeballs and sinew and intestines, and the severed hands of Syd.

Camellia felt sick. She ran for Dez as Wray shouted, "Look out!"

A long tendril shot from under that wall, thrashing and

JENDIA GAMMON

whipping, and caught Dez at the knees where he lay. He screamed in agony as the plant severed one leg at the knee with horrific slurping and cracking noises.

Camellia screamed and ran forth.

Staccato gunfire.

Wray wheeled around.

"Holy fuck!" Wray screamed.

It was Darla, Mr. Levin, Mr. Welsh, Dewayne, and Mel. Dewayne ran to Camellia and held out something long.

"Your sword, Queen!" he gasped, looking with horror down at Dez; his face had gone gray, and he was convulsing.

Camellia seized the scabbard, drew out the sword, and chopped the attacking vine.

"Hit the green button!" she screamed.

As the wall rose again, she stood before it with sword in hand. The plants stilled. Syd's destroyed body hung suspended, ribs shattered outward as if he had exploded, his skull crushed open, with blood still spewing out.

Mr. Levin and Mr. Welsh held Dez. Mr. Levin used his belt to tie off Dez's thigh in an effort to stop the bleeding. Darla shrieked a deeply primal yowl and opened fire on the plants and Syd, shredding what remained of him with heavy artillery.

"Fuck!" yelled Mr. Levin, as he seized Camellia from harm's way.

Darla looked possessed, sweeping the machine gun back and forth like a thrasher.

Camellia fell to her knees beside her father.

"He's gonna bleed out," Mr. Welsh said grimly as he brought out a fat doobie, lighting it up then and there. "Stay with me, pal," he told Dez, whose eyes began to roll. He took a puff and placed it into Dez's mouth. "Take a big one off this, it'll help with the pain."

Camellia was stunned speechless, for once in her life. Then she whispered, "Dad, Dad!" over and over.

"Meems," he gasped weakly.

She saw movement by the door as Dr. Grelling staggered forth on hands and knees. Mel ran at the man, picked him up, threw him onto his back, and roared, throwing his hands into the air. "Para Cassandro!" he screamed.

Mr. Levin had 911 on the phone. There were several dark moments, with Camellia by Dez's side, Mr. Welsh looking sadly at her, and Wray holding her from behind.

Darla shot off another couple of volleys with the machine gun.

"Jesus Christ!" Mr. Levin yelled. "Enough!"

Darla winked at him. "Just want to be extra sure that motherfucker is dead. Nobody fucks with *my* family."

She rounded the gun on the suplexed Dr. Grelling, but Mr. Levin cried, "We need him alive! We need to know how he manipulated the plants, or we're never going to be rid of this thing. He can't be working alone. Someone else can keep doing this shit!"

Darla groaned. "Do we have to?"

"Well, this bitch isn't going anywhere," hissed Dewayne, as he and Mel sat on Dr. Grelling, keeping the man pinned down, unconscious.

Camellia breathed in and out, slowly, guided to calmness by Wray's loving arms. She held her father's head in her lap and stroked his brow.

"Daddy," she whispered, "I love you, Daddy. Please don't leave me."

CHAPTER 35

BEYOND THE SEA

The journey there had been a blur, and the trip to the hospital smeared Camellia's thoughts. The hospital was overwhelmed as it was, but Dez was rushed in and prepped; his blood pressure was low, and she feared he would code. She stayed by his side while Wray waited in the lobby. Darla found food for everyone, and, outside, Mr. Levin and Mr. Welsh fielded phone calls with NASA, the LAPD, and other government organizations. Dr. Grelling was under lock and key, receiving treatment for a concussion and damaged windpipe. Once treated, he would go to jail.

As Dez's next of kin, Camellia faced a difficult moment when asked for authorization to amputate his left leg above the knee. It was touch and go for his right leg, which had been flayed by the plants. His arm, broken, would need a cast as well. It was a long night, and she only left his side when it was time to operate. Darla made sure she was fed, and that she had a break so she could walk with Wray. The snapping noises of the trees continued, and not every pocket had been exposed to the broadcast of her frequency. She faced interviews from government officials as well, particularly over what happened in the underground plant laboratory of Dr. Grelling.

She greeted dawn with Wray by her side, and anxiety over her father.

When the sun broke, she found herself staring at a bloom, a vibrant, twilight purple blossom of morning glory. It shivered around her, ultimately falling still, as if it, too, had had a difficult night and needed rest. She dozed on Wray's lap until they woke her gently.

"Darla's here," Wray murmured, wiping Camellia's fiery hair away from her face.

"Mimi sugar," Darla said in a low voice.

Camellia jerked upright, heart pounding, searching her cousin's face. It was difficult to read, but it was streaked with tears.

"He's alive," Darla told her.

Camellia dissolved into tears. She convulsed and wailed, as both Wray and Darla held her.

"Baby," Darla said through tears. "I'm sorry. I shouldn't have said what I did about your mom. I want that fucker in the clink, maybe thrown in with some plants. I know, I know, your teacher says we *need* the little, yellow-eyed worm." She shook her head. "Bud and I will help with Dez, so it won't just be you. I know you can afford care..."

Camellia only heard half of the words, but clung to the ones that matter.

"We'll stay in the guest house until things settle out."

She sat up straight and scrunched up her face.

"Great."

~

The next day, Fridge announced, "There are two individuals approaching the door."

Camellia felt numb, but still allowed this to irritate her.

JENDIA GAMMON

"You can tell them to fuck off."

"They are Mr. Levin and Mr. Welsh."

She sighed. Wray nuzzled her neck and they kissed. Camellia nodded. "Fine."

She opened the door, Wray by her side, and saw Mr. Levin with his arms crossed. The look in his eyes troubled her.

"Sorry, kiddo," Mr. Welsh said, looking apologetic. "We've got some news."

She went ice cold.

"Dad?"

"No! Sorry," and Mr. Levin glared at Mr. Welsh. "It's something else."

"Fucking great. Well, come in, then."

She and Wray guided the two men out to the garden, now silent and peaceful... yet somehow mournful. Wray brought out bottles of sparkling water for the men. Mr. Welsh examined his and crinkled his eyebrows before shrugging, taking a swig, and grimacing.

Camellia's cheeks began to burn as she waited for them to speak.

"Would you get on with it?" she snapped. Wray shot her a look, and she rolled her eyes. "Please?"

"Well, kiddo—" and noting briefly her expression, Mr. Welsh added, "Camellia, our friendly little mad scientist escaped the hospital."

"You're shitting me!" she shouted, eyes wild, fists clenched. "How?"

Mr. Levin bit his lip. "Likely another goon of his."

"So now what?" Wray asked, their face anxious, their storm-hued eyes darting from Camellia to the teachers.

"Now we can expect our happy little murder plants to wake back up any minute," Mr. Welsh replied. He pulled out a joint, lit it, and drew in a huge drag before exhaling.

Mr. Levin cleared his throat. "I... hope not, but I think he'll use another signal, when he's recovered enough."

"But... but can my signal overcome it?" Camellia asked, her mouth gone dry.

Mr. Welsh shook his head. She didn't like that at all.

"No idea."

Mr. Levin looked into her green eyes and said, "My hope is that your mom allowed for that possibility. Maybe your transponder can adjust."

"Maybe *not*," puffed Mr. Welsh.

All three scowled at him.

"What do we do?" Camellia felt, quite suddenly, tiny and helpless, as she had in those first days and months after her mother's death.

"We need more info before we can know that," said Mr. Welsh. "I'm guessing the military might wonder the same thing."

They all sat in silence for several minutes.

"Where the hell is your signal coming from?" Mr. Levin sighed, frustrated.

It was now Wednesday. Dez was recuperating in the hospital, tired, in pain, but grateful. Camellia and Wray sat in her garden, the one her mother had so adored.

The section of dormant camellias in the center of the garden, would bloom in November, Camellia knew. She marveled that they were so stalwart, unfazed by everything that had happened.

"I think they are cream colored," she murmured. "There are pink ones out front, but not these. I wonder what kind they are?"

Mr. Levin considered them and stood to examine their buds. "Resilient things, aren't they? I *think* these are... they're named after a song. 'Beyond the Sea.'"

"Like Mom," said Camellia softly. Wray squeezed her hand.

She looked at Mr. Levin and he looked at her. They blinked through tears.

"Deep," interjected Mr. Welsh, eyes red, smile broad. "She's out there, somewhere. A sea of stars, maybe."

Mr. Levin's mouth opened just at the same time as Camellia's. He rubbed his face.

"Let's take a drive," he said suddenly.

"Yes," said Camellia quickly.

Wray sent her a questioning look.

"What is it?" they asked.

"We need to get to the Point," said Camellia.

They piled in, the four of them, with more exhaust flowing out of Mr. Levin's old Volvo than from Mr. Welsh smoking weed.

"Dad wouldn't like it," Camellia said softly. "But he's not able to argue with me this time."

"You're sure about this?" Mr. Levin asked her gently, as the Pacific Coast Highway twisted before them.

"Yes."

They drove to Point Dume, and down. They could see much damage from gnarled trees, but made it to Zuma Beach. She wanted to see it again, see where she had played as a young girl with her mother and father in the sand. Mr. Levin drove on until they found a spot near a rugged drop with a well-kept guardrail.

"That was where?" Camellia asked.

"Yes," Mr. Levin said, swallowing back tears.

"So… somewhere beyond here," she said, thoughtfully. Mr. Levin nodded, and they drove on.

Camellia suddenly felt dizzy and cried out, "Stop!"

They pulled over at a spot with a magnificent view, where sea rocks dotted the ocean. Clambering out, Camellia stood facing the Pacific, the west wind catching her hair. The rocks looked like teeth to her.

"*I fall upon the thorns of life, I bleed,*" she quoted Shelley. Wray wrapped their arm around her.

"Think this is it?" Mr. Welsh asked.

Camellia nodded, brushing back tears.

"Somewhere out there."

"I'm here for you," Wray said lovingly.

She turned and met Wray's stormy-sea eyes, and only found calm.

Mr. Levin said, "We're all here for you."

Mr. Welsh patted her on the back and exhaled a smoke ring. "We'll figure this out. She won't have died in vain."

Mr. Levin added, "My God, she'd be so proud of you, Camellia. I know I am."

Acknowledgments

This book came about during one my train rides to LA before the pandemic began. I tinkered with the idea of how to distill all the farcical 80s and 90s high school movies into something that I personally related to, as a former new kid in school and as someone who never felt like I belonged. Then I flipped it on its head, and imagined what it would be like to have almost everything, but with its meaning carved away by grief. I couldn't foresee how truly relevant that feeling would become in a short period of time. Camellia Dume and Wray Blythe dance around the gravity well that is high school, in all its hideousness, but also in its zeitgeist. This is their journey. Grief can make monsters, but it can also make us appreciate those who are still with us.

As for the rest of it, *Doomflower* is a love letter to Los Angeles, film, and pop culture. I used to think that everything said about LA was hyperbole, and that Malibu was an extension of that. But when you live here, things change. LA is a crown of a city and a region, and Malibu is a diadem in that crown. I love driving out to it and feeling the city slip away as the Pacific curls in cobalt sparkles into the thin strand of Highway 1. Beyond that, the nooks and crannies of LA invite you off the freeways, so if you're ever here, go exploring. You might find the perfect view, the perfect pizza place, the moment when you realize you finally belong…and you might be inspired to wrap up all the best and worst experiences of your youth you ever had—whether in reality or on the silver screen—into one book. So that's what I did.

Now, with great appreciation, I thank the dynamic duo at Encyclopocalypse Publications for believing in this book and giving it a home: Sean Duregger and Mark Alan Miller. Thank you to Joshua Millican for copyedits.

Thank you to my beta reader, Pam Magnus, who has read every novel I've written, bless her! And to Helen Glynn Jones for her constant and radiant support. Big thanks to my teens, who inspire me and make me laugh every single day. Thank you to my three older siblings, whose constant and snappy one-liners helped me hone my own. And of course thank you to my husband, Gareth L. Powell, whose constant belief in me lifts me up.

Once upon a time, I was the new kid at school. It wasn't fun, but I figured it out. Things do get better.

ABOUT THE AUTHOR

Jendia Gammon is a Nebula and BSFA Awards finalist author of fantasy, science fiction, and horror novels and short stories. She has also previously written as J. Dianne Dotson. Jendia was longlisted for the Lodestar Award and two British Fantasy Awards. She is CEO of Roaring Spring Productions, LLC and Editor-in-Chief of its publishing imprint, Stars and Sabers Publishing. Jendia is also a science writer and artist. Born in Southern Appalachia, Jendia lives in Los Angeles with her family.

Also by Jendia Gammon

As Jendia Gammon:

Atacama (2025)

Vale of Seven Dragons Saga:

The Vale of Seven Dragons (2026)

Coursers of Wings and Flame (2027)

The Vale of Fire Wrought (2028)

Godfestation (2026)

As J. Dianne Dotson:

The Inn at the Amethyst Lantern (Nebula and BSFA Award Finalist)

The Shadow Galaxy: A Collection of Short Stories and Poetry

The Questrison Saga:

Heliopause: The Questrison Saga, Book One

Ephemeris: The Questrison Saga, Book Two

Accretion: The Questrison Saga, Book Three

Luminiferous: The Questrison Saga, Book Four

Books Two and Three of the *Amethyst Lantern* Series:

The Secret of the Sapphire Sentinel (2025)

The Dawn of Dusk and Twilight (2026)